RUIN
VALUE

RUIN VALUE

A Mystery of the Third Reich

J. Sydney Jones

MYSTERIOUSPRESS.COM

INTEGRATED MEDIA

NEW YORK

Cover design by Mauricio Díaz

ISBN 978-1-4804-2691-7

Published in 2013 by MysteriousPress.com/Open Road Integrated Media
345 Hudson Street
New York, NY 10014
www.mysteriouspress.com
www.openroadmedia.com

To dear friends, George and Francoise Vance—
remembering good times in Vienna, Paris,
Champagne, and Brussels.

RUIN
VALUE

The Nazis called it ruin value: the construction of their Thousand-Year Reich so that in another thousand years, when tourists came to gape and scrawl graffiti, their buildings and monuments would be as ennobled in ruins as were those of the Greeks at the Acropolis, the Romans at the Colosseum.

PART I

November 8, 1945
Nuremberg, Germany

There are 1.5 gallons of blood in the human body. It comes out warm, if allowed an exit wound, around 89.6 degrees Fahrenheit. It's also red, though that is something of an illusion. Actually, plasma, the water of life, the real source of the blood liquid, is clear, like thick water. No color, only clarity.

Sasha Orlov, a corporal in Supply for the Seventh Army Corps in the Soviet military, had blood group type O.

Sasha was known to his comrades as "the Calculator." He counted everything. It was a compulsion. He could do nothing to stop the ceaseless, unrelenting tally of steps walked, buildings passed, glasses of water consumed, birds darting in a flock overhead. Because of it, he was the butt of mirthless jokes, the object of pity.

It also made him an excellent supplies controller. Give him a room full of sacks of wheat and he could count them in an instant; not just estimate their number, but actually tally them in his mind. A boxcar of tinned pork, dried sardines, and canned milk? No problem for Sasha Orlov, the Calculator.

Sasha Orlov's final reckoning: *Three hundred and seventy-seven*. The number of steps from the tram stop to this corner near Saint Johannis Hospital. *Fifteen.* The number of vials of penicillin he was carrying with him. *Twelve, eleven, forty-four.* The expiration date of said penicillin—but that date was no longer affixed to the vials. *Twenty-five thousand four hundred and thirty-one.* The number of American dollars he had earned in the past four months selling illicit supplies. He dealt only in the capitalist currency.

Sasha Orlov was a rich man.

He was also dying.

Exposed to air, blood tends to coagulate. In minor injuries, small oval bodies in the blood, platelets, collect to form a plug in a blood vessel. Or in more serious injuries, platelets go on full alert, working in an intricate series of steps to ultimately convert fibrinogen to fibrin. This insoluble protein in turn forms a delicate microscopic latticework of fibrils within which the blood plasma and cells are captured, made inert. Free flow ceases; clotting begins.

Sasha Orlov's type O blood was working to expectation, coagulating in brackish puddles amid the mortar and building debris of what was once a ground-floor apothecary with three more floors of apartments above. The blood was steaming in the chill November air, vapors rising from it like steam over a stove.

The problem was that Orlov's blood was clotting only *outside* his body. The arterial slashes at his throat would not be stanched, would not be plugged by hardworking platelets.

The blood did not look red in the darkness of night; it was a black inchoate field of muck against the lighter rubble. It wet the front of Orlov's thick coat. Above the turned-up collar of that coat, a gash was made from ear to ear, deep enough to rip through skin, muscle, arteries, and trachea, exposing white gaping cartilage and allowing the blood to spurt free at an alarming rate.

The killer looked down at the body, watching closely as the blood slowed from a fountainlike spurt to a trickle, a pulsing flow that followed the autonomic reflexes of the now dead body of the Russian soldier.

Orlov made a hissing sound. It did not come from his mouth; rather it was gas escaping from his belly, pushing out through the new opening in the trachea.

The killer watched and heard all of this, oblivious to the world around, to the voice of a child crying from a cellar not fifty-five yards away from this murder scene.

The first of many, the killer thought, feeling warmth inside, a coursing glow of sweet warmth.

The killer leaned down and placed the neatly cutout page of a novel into the dead man's right hand. Words were underlined on the page—a message, a warning. The dead man's hand was still warm, the fingers pliable, the pads of the fingers spongy to the touch. With a sudden flash of inspiration, the killer took the page of the novel back, slashed several quick marks at the bottom of it with the scalpel, writing in blood. Then the page went back in the dead soldier's hand.

While still crouched by the body, the killer wiped the blade of the scalpel on the Russian's coat, then carefully wrapped it in the purple scrap of velvet kept for that purpose, and stowed it in a coat pocket.

The killer stood once again, alert now. Ready to move away before being detected, back into the night.

Despite the biting cold, the killer's face was glowing with warmth, energized by death, sporting a grin at once ironic and self-satisfied.

"It says here you were incarcerated in Flensburg."

The American paused, expecting Beck to reply. Beck did not comply with the invitation. Instead, his mind was on the food parcel his mother had brought to the prison that afternoon. A whole Pressburger sausage, three oranges (unheard of this time of year!) with only a little browning on their dimpled skins, two Suchard milk chocolate bars with raisins, a tin of Norwegian sardines in oil. *Fell off a truck,* his mother answered when asked their origin.

Beck regretted the question now; not because it was rude,

but stupid. Where *would* such things come from but the black market?

His mother did not look as if she were getting enough food for herself, and here she was bringing food to her forty-five-year-old son who seemed to have gotten himself into trouble again.

Up to two years ago, Beck had been more accustomed to dishing out trouble to others. Such is life.

"Is that true?" the American persisted.

Beck shot him a weary look. So young, so fervent, so damn healthy. The Americans all appeared to have been raised on a pure vitamin diet. They were enormous. This one not so big as the others, Beck determined, but aggressively healthy looking nonetheless. As if he had just gotten off the squash courts or out of an Olympic-size swimming pool. This American's cheeks radiated warmth; his body sat energetically forward on the chair as if he were about to set off on a marathon. And his face: Such innocence should only be found in Gothic church frescoes. Masaccio, perhaps? Yes, from the church in the Oltrarno. *My God, what is its name? Have I completely forgotten all the little joys of my former life?*

"Flensburg. That was a camp for German political prisoners, if I am not mistaken," the American army captain said, leafing through his file. He suddenly looked up from the papers in his lap and fixed Beck with a steely gaze: "You seem like you might've been an honest cop. You want to help yourself out here or not?"

Perhaps not so innocent after all, Beck concluded.

"And how might I do that?" Beck said in English, obviously surprising his interlocutor. The American had been using a very proper school German. Beck's English came from the time he spent as a student in London, not long after the First World War. They were building a better world then, one in which cultural exchanges were encouraged. However, Beck's English was not so much the result of exchanging culture, but bodily fluids. Lisa was her name, a nurse at Charing Cross Hospital. Pubs

10

and fog and a tiny bedsit that smelled of sex and tea. That was a time.

"First of all, you can help yourself by telling me why you were in Flensburg," the American said.

Beck got up from the seatless toilet bowl where he had been perched when the American entered, pulled up his pants, and yanked the chain on the overhead tank, flushing the bowl. *So much for a quiet release of bowels*, he thought.

Beck took a seat on the cot—the only remaining available place in the six-by-eight-foot cell. He sat as upright as possible but was, of course, lower than the American, who was strategically perched on the lone hardback chair by the door. Beck was no stranger to the subtle psychologies of interrogation; he, in turn, fixed the American with his own concentrated gaze.

"Would you like to hear the expurgated or unexpurgated version?"

"The truth will suffice."

Irony. Beck had not credited the young officer with such a facility.

"Let us say, then, that my Gestapo colleagues and I had a falling out over who was really in charge of criminal investigations in the Nuremberg district. That argument manifested itself specifically and, finally, in a needless and idiotic order. I refused to institute it at Kripo; ergo, I was a political criminal."

"The order?"

Beck hesitated, blew air out, shrugged. "To shoot on sight any Jew caught in the district after the final transports had been sent to the occupied territories. It seemed a senseless piece of cruelty. Those people would be sent to their deaths once captured anyway. Why make my Kripo personnel complicit in their murder?"

The American officer was silent, staring at Beck with those innocent but not so innocent eyes.

"Not exactly what you wanted to hear, eh? Not exactly drawing a line in the sand for morality."

"So you admit knowledge of the death camps?"

"Of course. All of Germany knew. The news was not broadcast on the weekly Hitler family-hour broadcast, but we knew. Anyone who says differently is, well . . . I understand there are no more Nazis to be found in Germany now. Emigration must have been fierce since the end of the war."

This brought the edge of a smile from the American.

"Look," Beck said. "I think you have the wrong man with me. I've got nothing to give you. Nobody to inform on. We've had a dozen years of informing against one another; we're all soul sick of it. Sick of kids selling their parents to the Gestapo because they were too strict. Of jealous neighbors shopping old Frau Meyer on the second landing because she had half a cube of black-market butter."

The captain listened to the speech, then recrossed his legs. He picked at invisible lint. The view slot in the door in back of the American opened, an eye peered in and then the slot slid quickly shut, causing a sudden puff of air to hit the back of the captain's neck and make him jerk.

"They like to make sure we are *safe* in here," Beck said with heavy irony. "After Ley's suicide a couple weeks ago, security's been tightened." He was referring to the Nazi labor leader who had wrapped a towel around his neck and hanged himself from the pipe over his toilet. "They want to ensure there are some Nazis left to go on trial." He cast a rumpled smile the American's way. "And I still think you're sniffing at the wrong dog with me. I *hire* snitches; I don't play that role myself."

"I'm not asking for that sort of collaboration, Herr Beck. Others may, perhaps, but not me."

I, Beck wanted to correct. His usage was British; he found American English almost quaint.

The American waited a silent moment and then looked at his file once again. Beck wondered if he really had any information there beyond directions to his billet and a list of names. Something about the way the American was conducting this interview made Beck wonder if he hadn't been a cop himself.

"Can we get back to Flensburg?" the American asked. "I assume you were liberated with the advancing armies."

Beck let out a small laugh. "Hardly. The advancing army in question was Soviet. Our jailers left in advance of their arrival. As did we prisoners. Not a nice prospect being captured by Ivan."

"And so you made your way back here. To the American zone."

"Back *here*," Beck emphasized. "To my *home*."

Beck did not want to go down that road—did not want to tell the American how he'd come home to find it had been obliterated, as was almost all of the inner city of Nuremberg, in the Allied bombing raids of January and February of 1945. The street where he had lived—gone. His apartment house at 23 Breite Gasse—gone. A pile of rubble, scraps of blackened brick and mortar with the detritus of family possessions scattered here and there. He hadn't the heart to even look for a memento. The charred remains of the dozen apartments that had once stood there. Gone, along with his wife of fifteen years, Helga, and their ten-year-old daughter, Lisabette. Had his wife ever known of the secret betrayal involved in their child's name? Not Elisabette, but Lisabette, in memory of his British nurse.

No more betrayal now—all gone.

"And you found yourself in prison once again?"

"That is an interesting way of putting it," Beck replied. He would really like to relieve his bowels now. His three days of constipation seemed about to resolve itself quite abruptly and violently.

The American consulted his files again. "It says here that Chief Inspector Reinhard Manhof denounced you for Kripo collaboration with the Gestapo and had you rearrested. Is that the case?"

"If that is what is says there, it must be so."

Beck had lost all patience now; his bowels were denying him any pretence of *Geduld*.

"Captain . . . ?"

"Morgan," the American offered.

"Precisely. Captain Morgan, may we please simply get to it? I will not do a he-said-I-said denial about that idiot Manhof. Suffice it to say he is now chief inspector, a position I held before him for eight years. And I am, conveniently for him, in jail. Neither do I have the will to inform on former members of the Kripo nor the documentary proof to implicate any of my former Gestapo 'colleagues' in their true crimes."

"This isn't about that. . . ."

Beck put a hand up to halt the American.

"And if this interview is not to that end, then it is surely to sound me out about working for your intelligence services. Right? No need to confirm. Prison gossip is notoriously speedy in such matters. Wartime allies are falling out, no? The Soviets make better friends in time of need than in time of peace. And America can use the expertise of people who have been fighting Communism at its borders for almost three decades. Something along those lines. Isn't that what all this elaborate charade is about?"

"You tell me."

"I frankly have no time to tell you. I need very badly to make a return to the sacred precinct in which I was disturbed upon initiation of your visit. And as there is very little privacy afforded in these accommodations . . ."

"I'll wait outside, then," Captain Morgan offered.

"No need to," Beck replied. "Earlier, you said I seemed to be an honest cop. Not a bad assessment. With the emphasis on *cop*. Not a *spy*. Not an intelligence officer, or whatever it is you euphemistically call it. There is no way I can be of service to you. You have a crime you want me to help solve, come back. We'll talk. Right now I've got more important business."

Captain Nathan Morgan walked down the long hallway of the witness wing of the Palace of Justice. All about him he could hear the rhythmic tapping of prison Morse code. Morgan knew many varieties of such code, but this one was unfamiliar to him. Each prison had its own system. They could be talking about anything from his visit to what would be for breakfast tomorrow. Or maybe it was something more vital, information smuggled from outside being passed along to the right correspondent. A spoon against the plumbing pipes.

The clacking reminded him for a moment of his nighttime listening post in Bern during the war. Spinning the dial of the short-wave radio through the ether over Europe and listening to the cricketlike cacophony of clandestine keymen tapping their coded messages from Paris to Berlin to Moscow and back. The Red and Black Orchestras, the spy cells of every country in the war and neutrals, too. The buzz of telegraphed traffic filled Morgan's nights for months.

His introduction to the world of spying.

Morgan thought of former Chief Inspector Werner Beck as he approached the control point in the witness wing. Something about the man stuck with you. Not his physical presence, that was for sure. A long, rangy fellow who looked badly in need of a good meal. His sandy hair thinning on top and also in need of a cut. A cop's eyes, though. Morgan had grown up looking into a cop's eyes. He had also lived with a pair of them staring back at him from the mirror for many years. He knew the things that went on behind those gray eyes of Beck's.

Major Hannigan was waiting at the final set of gates.

"You find what you were looking for?" the senior MP asked as he ushered Morgan out of the wing. The question held the same animosity the man had displayed earlier when Morgan had come to him with his orders in hand.

"Not exactly," Morgan confessed.

"Shit, those old boys aren't going to get off their asses to help out anybody. Half of them should be in the other wing, anyway."

Hannigan meant the defendant wing, along with Göring and company. Texas, Morgan guessed. Or somewhere in the

Texarkana. Hannigan had been away from the region for a time, but the twang clung to him like a creeping vine.

"It might come down to that," Morgan allowed.

"Hell of a way to finish off a war," Major Hannigan said as Morgan was leaving. "Babysitting a bunch of goddamn murderers." He said it as if it was Morgan's fault.

Morgan knew the kind of cop he was: the bullish sort to beat out a confession from a prisoner. To take him in a back room with a length of hose and work him over so it didn't show on the prisoner's face. No scientific investigative techniques for a man like Hannigan. He represented the criminal justice system in its most primitive form: Don't do wrong, or you'll be sorry.

"Babysitting," Hannigan muttered again at Morgan's back, obviously applying the term to his dealings with Morgan, too.

Hell of a way for me to finish it off, too, Morgan thought. Recruiting the dregs of the Nazi state to play spy for America. But Donovan himself had ordered it, his last command before Truman closed up shop on the OSS. Necessary evil, Donovan had called it. The Russians were doing the same thing, gobbling up whole spy networks in their eastern zone of Germany, recruiting the bloodiest-handed SS, Gestapo, and SD officers around, if they had files to share or agents in the field.

Now attached to Military Intelligence, MI, Morgan was in Nuremberg on that recruiting mission, that *necessary evil*, something any shiny-pants bureaucrat could be doing. Peacetime spying wasn't going to be much fun, he figured. Not after the action he had seen during his three years with Donovan and Dulles.

Morgan humped on the overcoat he'd left at the entrance; made his way through the warren of corridors and offices attached to the prison wing; and finally got to the main entrance and exited the arcaded front. A young GI on duty snapped to attention when he saw Morgan's bars. The kid looked about old enough to be sitting in a high school algebra class. The men who'd fought the last months of the war, who'd been at the Battle of the Bulge and who'd helped to liberate the camps, were largely gone now. Rotated back home. Inexperienced kids like this pimply-faced private were what was left to "babysit" the final days, to watch over the coming trial of war criminals.

Morgan turned up the collar on his woolen coat. It was cold out, with a dampness in the air that went right into the bones.

In the distance, he heard the wail of a Military Police siren and wondered what the fuss was.

His own cop intuition told him Nuremberg was a good place to be a criminal. Everything had broken down there. Morgan had the statistics by heart: Of the 130,000 original dwellings in the city, only 17,000 had survived the bombings of last January. Only a third of the original nearly half million population remained. There were still 30,000 bodies trapped beneath the rubble, giving off a stink that made a skunk smell like Chanel No. 5. Blue bottle flies the size of a baby's fist swarmed in clouds over the rotting corpses.

There was limited electricity, public water, or transport, and barely any mail or telephone to speak of in the several months after the end of the war. The local government was a joke, and the occupation authorities were the only thing between the city and total anarchy. Three months earlier, OSS analysts had declared the place among the dead cities of Europe. But the accident of a huge Palace of Justice complex, inexplicably untouched by Allied bombing that had leveled the rest of the inner city, made it the venue for the trial of the century.

There was the further confusion of shared authority between the Allies themselves *and* between the Allies and the German police who had only started operating again last month; the complete absence of societal controls—women who would screw for an orange, displaced men who'd murder for less; a lack of records to track known criminals.

A cop's nightmare.

November 10, 1945
Croydon Airfield, near London

The "C" in C-47 stands for cargo plane. Kate Wallace found that out too late.

"If you don't mind my saying, you don't want to take the train," Colonel Jensen told her Saturday morning after he'd issued her press credentials at the Savoy, temporary office of the U.S. Army Information Bureau. "By the time you get there, the trial could be over."

Jensen emitted an asthmatic gurgle that he thought passed for a snicker. He was a good ol' boy. Kate had known lots of them in her life, also knew how to handle them.

"So, you have a better solution?" she asked with a hand on her hip and a frank, direct look—not a hint of coquettish charm.

Jensen brightened at the question. "Hitch a ride with us. Plenty of room in our C-47."

That afternoon, as arranged, Kate met the colonel at Croydon outside of London. The plane was a big, clumsy-looking craft, and they entered it through its belly. The penny began to drop then: no mid-flight tea service; no copies of the London *Times*. There was a crew of two and three passengers—

the colonel, herself, and a lawyer from Ohio. William Stanton was the lawyer's name, and he seemed in a daze when he introduced himself. Part of the team preparing the conspiracy case at Nuremberg, this lawyer had literally missed the boat in New York, and had been trying to catch up with his team ever since. He'd hopped transports to Newfoundland, and from there had a harrowing ten-hour flight to Iceland, and finally on to England after a three-day layover in Reykjavík. Stanton, in his three-piece blue suit and Windsor collar, didn't look like the sort to enjoy exotic travel. He kept his fedora on over his shock of red hair for the entire flight.

Besides the five of them, there was the cargo. The plane had been loaded in London with stenographic and office equipment meant for the proceedings at Nuremberg. Kate began to get an indirect idea of the devastation wrought on Germany simply by examining the store of goods being sent across Europe. Obviously, there was no paper, no envelopes, not even any furniture to be had in Nuremberg, for this plane contained it all. There were wooden crates with stencil marks to tell handlers they contained Gestetner duplicators and purple-blue duplicating ink; boxes full of law books; cartons of paper and pens and even paper clips. There were office chairs disassembled and crated up and metal bookcases stored on their sides and strapped to the bulkhead. And one large box the size of a small oven filled with U.S. Army–issued condoms. It said so right there on the box in one-foot letters.

The colonel made a point of turning that box as they boarded, with the stenciled side to the bulkhead.

Then they settled in for take-off, cinching up makeshift webbed belts on the wooden benches that were bolted to the side of the plane. The three of them were just cargo, like the rest; no civility of high-back chairs to stretch out in. The plane taxied for a moment, then hurtled down the runway, rumbling and bumping and lurching into the air, barely missing a startled black-and-white cow frozen in mid-chew at the end of the runway. Kate, looking out the tiny window in back of her, carried the image of the cow's startled eyes, its jaws once again working on the grass, into the air with her.

Then a steep climb and a green sward of English pasturage cut horizontally across the bottom of the window, the top triangle filled with gray foreboding sky. The composite looked strangely like some New York abstract painting.

"This will be good," the colonel assured her with a paternal tap on her knee that lingered an instant too long. She nodded a noncommittal smile at him as the Channel appeared, black and choppy far below.

At 10,000 feet, oxygen thins out and the ambient temperature hovers around zero on the warmest day. Kate soon learned that such phenomena were not factored into the travel arrangements on their cargo plane. She quickly became as cold as she'd ever been. The blue duffel coat she was wearing was hardly sufficient to ward off the freezing temperatures inside the plane, and her legs, covered in useless silk stockings under a woolen skirt, were trembling, her knees quite literally knocking against each other. Down the bench, separated from the colonel and herself by a box of envelopes and file folders, the lost lawyer mumbled to himself. "I respectfully submit . . ." he said aloud, though obviously he did not mean to.

Kate was even colder than on her eighth birthday, the one her father always thereafter called the San Juan Bautista Birthday. They threw a skating party for her at the Pennsylvania estate in February. The ice was not as thick as it should have been, and she broke through at the edge of the pond, sinking slowly into the bone-chilling water as the other children looked on in mild amusement.

Pulled out by distraught servants and by her laughing father, Kate had taken hours to warm up, sitting in front of the fire in the massive den, bundled in blankets and eiderdown, sipping on hot toddies that her father insisted would warm her up. She'd gotten drunk as a loon, but had eventually warmed up. She smiled at the thought.

What had she been thinking of to travel by this plane instead of the nice cozy train? There she could have had first-class sleeping accommodations and a dining car with damask table-cloths, candles and silver and glassware gently tapping against the table with the rhythmic movement of the wheels over rails.

Here . . . But her thoughts were interrupted by the return of the colonel's hand on her knee. Paternal an hour earlier, now it was distinctly groping. His fat college ring with its garish blue stone glared up at her from below the hairy knuckle of his third finger as she looked down in surprise, almost shock. Then the hand made a steady march upward under her skirt to her thigh, onto the tops of her silk stockings, and beyond to her bare skin.

Her voice would not come at first, so ridiculous was this, so uncalled for, so damned annoying and unbelievable. The lawyer muttered, "Might I respectively submit . . ." once more, and was not looking their way: He had other demons to purge.

The colonel leered in her face, encouraged by her silence. He nudged his hand farther upward until his fingers hit the elastic edges of her panties. This finally brought breath to her voice.

"Just what do you think you're doing, Colonel?"

She had promised herself she would make it on her own in her journalism career—make it on her own in the world. Not trade in on her father's name, prestige, power. A hard-earned degree at Columbia journalism, cum laude, and her writing samples from the school paper had won her a job at *The Out-look*. Her skill and tenacity had kept her there for three years, graduating from copyediting to writing features. Her energy and growing savvy had convinced Ed Sloan, her editor, that *The Outlook* needed a correspondent at the Nuremberg Trials, prob-ably *the* media event of the immediate postwar era.

This I have done all on my own. And now all it takes is a way-ward hand for me to want to cry for daddy, she thought. But she didn't. She merely repeated her question to Jensen who was now involved in near obstetric groping.

"What do you think you're doing, Colonel?"

Still he said nothing, merely grinned at her lasciviously. She

21

could smell alcohol on his breath. *Why didn't I notice it before?* she wondered.

"Do you have any idea who my father is?" she finally blurted out in a panic, feeling like a fool. The lawyer was too busy with his rehearsed apologies; she was on her own here.

"I'm not really sure parentage is relevant to this situation," Colonel Jensen said, with a little rasp to his laugh as his breath came more quickly. The nostrils on his pockmarked nose flared, and he nudged a forefinger under the elastic bottom of her panties.

"Bertram Wallace," she said, suddenly composed and sure of herself, glaring at him. You wouldn't think that this was a young woman with a man's hand up her skirt. "Senator for Pennsylvania. *The* Bertram Wallace."

Her feelings of discomfort and near defeat at resorting to the invocation of her father's name were more than compensated for by the look of piss-your-pants terror in the colonel's eyes as he registered the name. If eyeballs could speak, his were saying, "Oh my God!" His hand was pulled away with an alacrity that all but made a sucking sound. The offending member having disappeared, the colonel himself did so as well.

But not before he fished out a long woolen coat for her, which Kate draped majestically over her crossed legs. The colonel and the muttering lawyer made a fine pair down at the far end of the bench.

"So, what are you doing in Nuremberg?" the young British woman asked Morgan. There was just the edge of a slur to her oh-so-proper BBC English.

He examined her slowly: the heavy tweed jacket and matching skirt, ivory-colored silk blouse open at the neck revealing just the hint of cleavage, sturdy walking shoes, blonde hair falling shoulder length with bangs in front, and a complexion that finally made him understand the meaning of "peaches and cream."

"Let's just say I'm here on orders." He threw back the neat

shot of gentian schnapps—an acquired taste from his Swiss years—and presented what he considered his mysterious look.

"I'll wager you're a lawyer. They're thick on the ground here." She giggled. She was on her third gin and tonic. At least there were three glasses sitting on the bar in front of her. Morgan had no way of knowing if the bartender had cleared away earlier victims.

Morgan shrugged noncommittally. The bar at the Grand Hotel was packed this Saturday night with an international contingent of officers in uniform and bureaucratic types in suits speaking the language of the victors: English, French, and a smattering of Russian, though most of the Soviets kept to themselves in their own compound. Voices echoed off the high ceilings, rattled around the walls encompassing this ballroom-size boozer, and overall deflected attention from the damage done to the place in air raids. The ceiling molding was gone and chandeliers sold off in pieces. But at least it *had* walls, which was more than could be said for most buildings in central Nuremberg.

"You're the quiet type, aren't you?" the British woman persisted. "I like them quiet."

Someone's secretary let off the leash for the night, he thought, *or a member of the translation pool.* She was tipsy but also right: Morgan was the quiet type.

It suited his purposes.

A French lieutenant standing on the other side of the blonde suddenly whispered something in her ear, and now her giggle was transformed into a throaty, sensual, animal laugh that let Morgan know the man had not proposed a game of bridge.

"You're a cheeky one, aren't you?" she squealed turning toward the amorous Frenchman, patting at his lapels as if dusting dandruff. "I like them cheeky."

Another whispered intimacy from the Frenchman, and this time her peaches and cream turned to cranberry. She returned his pleasantry in her own raspy whisper, and soon the two of them were walking arm in arm out of the bar. She did not bother to cast a backward glance at Morgan. So much for liking the quiet ones. Seemed the blonde liked them breathing best of all.

Morgan ordered another schnapps and downed it, surveying the room. Lots of red faces, bright eyes, eager—and sometimes slurred—voices. An MP on the other side of him at the bar, making the rounds, had stopped in for a nightcap and was complaining to the bartender—an Englishman named Toby—that he'd had to pound the beat like a cop the past couple of nights. Something about a murder the day before yesterday, throat slit like a slaughtered pig.

Morgan paid little attention: Nuremberg was full of rumors. The place thrived on gossip. Latest word had it that Göring was a hermaphrodite: breasts of a woman and a schlong like a bull. Truth, swear to God. Straight from the guard who watches him bathe twice weekly at the Palace of Justice.

He thought about what the woman had said: the quiet type. So quiet he'd lost an easy night of enjoyment. No work involved, only a few nice words to her. That's all she'd wanted. A joke, a tease. She'd have toppled into bed with him; it was just those few kind words.

About such things, however, Morgan could not dissemble. Perhaps an odd trait in a man for whom almost the whole of his life was an act of dissembling, if not outright deception. That's why he and the OSS had been such a match. *Born to be a spy.* That's what Dulles had written about him in his final evaluation to Donovan. *The boy was born to be a spy.*

Deception comes easily when you were born Morgan, né Morgenstern, in the oh-so-Gentile world of Ohio. You learned quickly to join in the Yid jokes. To talk of kikes with your buddies, who knew you only as Nate Morgan. To excel at sports because that was something Jews weren't supposed to do. No temple for the Morgans.

His dad was a beat cop in Cincinnati who worked his way up through the ranks to detective. And nobody called his father Sy. Not even his mother. It was always Morgan, or Detective Morgan.

So it was with Nathan Morgan. He was called Nate, Morg, or Morgan. Later, it was Detective Morgan for him also. But never Nathan.

He'd gone to Harvard. The only child, his parents had saved every penny for his schooling. And he had done well there: Harvard Crew as an undergraduate, third in his graduating class from Harvard Law. A *real* Jew would probably have finished first.

And suddenly, after law school, he realized something was wrong. This was all too pat, too formulaic. The summer after graduation, he interned at Tate, Tate, and McGee, a powerful Boston law firm where he did the gofer work of checking deeds, wills, and trusts. It had all been very polite and dignified, *and* boring as hell. Offers were coming his way: Wallace, Fenton, and Smith in New York liked his résumé, they wrote. An interview was arranged. He was on his way toward an eventual partnership and a home in Connecticut like other successful, assimilated Jews.

Then he finally understood something about himself: He did not want to spend his days in courtrooms *or* boardrooms. He wanted to be on the delivery end of the justice system—to catch criminals, not prosecute or defend them. *Being a cop was in the blood,* he told his parents.

His father had tried to look disappointed when his son told him of his decision.

All that money spent on your education and you're going to be a cop?

But Nathan knew his father was proud of him, of his decision. It was a validation for the elder Morgan. His son following in his footsteps.

But not exactly in his footsteps. It was the police academy for Nathan Morgan, not a slow, work-your-way-up-through-the-ranks process. And then he was snapped up by the New York City Police Department upon graduation. He was made a detective at a midtown Manhattan precinct. Homicide. Where the real action was.

Jews don't become homicide detectives.

The sudden pop of shots from outside interrupted Morgan's reverie. Military men all around him, lately so accustomed to such sounds, stood stunned with drinks in their hands, and the bar grew deathly silent. Then, with no further gunshots heard, the drinkers went on with their meaningless chatter. Not Nathan Morgan. He made his way through the crowd, out into the cold night air. A gust of wind whipped powdery snow flurries about.

On the street, a small group of GIs huddled around a body. Shiny black boots protruded from one end of the grouped soldiers. Morgan elbowed his way through the group of men, who made way for him once they saw his bars.

"What's going on here?" he demanded when he reached the center. On the ground lay a GI, obviously dead: A head shot had penetrated his left eye socket and exited in the rear, taking off half of his cranium. Another GI stood, his .45 service revolver in one hand and the other arm wrapped around the blonde from the bar. She and the Frenchman had obviously not hit it off well.

"Nigger called my girl here a tease," the soldier with the drawn weapon said. "Nobody calls my girl names."

Only then did Morgan register the fact that the dead GI was, indeed, a Negro.

"Let's have the gun, soldier." Morgan put out his hand.

The shooter wasn't much more than a kid, but he was tough. Oh, he was going to show them how tough he was, Morgan figured.

The soldier stepped back. "No way. I ain't serving time for killing no nigger."

"The gun," Morgan said, his eyes fixed on the soldier's. *You don't need to be doing this*, he told himself. *That's what the MPs are for.* But it was too late for that; his cop instincts had taken over.

The soldier wasn't going to go peacefully, Morgan suddenly understood. His eyes told Morgan that. They were wild, darting back and forth, looking for the best way out. The other GIs grouped around the body slowly edged back; they could smell it too. Violence. Panic. Fear.

"I'm asking you once more. You might have self-defense here. That's a plea, you know. Get yourself a witness or two. Hell, not worth making mountains of trouble for yourself."

Morgan tried to smile; his face was caught in a rictus of his own fear. *Keep talking,* he told himself. *Smooth a way for the kid.*

The soldier's eyes narrowed. "Self-defense?"

"Sure. Happens all the time. It's wartime, you know. People go off." He nodded toward the black man lying at their feet.

A cunning smile broke across the soldier's face. "Yeah. That's good. Self-defense."

"So just hand over the gun, and we'll get you a good lawyer. Right?"

A nod from the gunman. Then sudden suspicion. "Why should I trust you?"

"Hey, I know the law. Just give me the gun and we'll get this settled."

The blonde had been trying to wriggle out of the soldier's grasp and now saw a way to freedom. "He's right," she said. "He was in there drinking with all the bigwigs. Must be a lawyer or something. You do like he says now. It'll be all right."

A flex of his jaw muscle and the kid lifted the gun. *This is it,* Morgan told himself. *You stupid ass. Leave this work to the MPs.* The kid leveled the weapon at Morgan's chest for a moment, then twirled it around on his forefinger and handed it grip-first to Morgan's still outstretched hand.

"What the hell's going on here?" The MP from the bar made his way to the scene, tossing soldiers aside as he pushed to the center of the crowd.

Nice timing, Morgan thought. He handed the gun over to the military cop.

"The private's weapon," he said, indicating the young GI. "He shot this man in cold blood. Take him down for it."

"You bastard." The young GI made a lunge for him, which Morgan parried with a knee to the groin and another knee upward into the nose as the kid doubled over. He could feel the crunch of cartilage as the kid went down.

The men watched in awed fascination, and the MP merely raised his eyes at Morgan.

As the MP secured his prisoner, the blonde sidled over to Morgan. "I *do* like the silent type," she said. Her sudden confrontation with death had sobered her up, but Morgan still wasn't interested.

"You should choose your friends more carefully," he said and spun around to leave.

The soldier, handcuffed now and struggling to his feet, called out after Morgan.

"Fucking Yid. Hitler should have killed you all."

Now how did that cracker know I'm Jewish? Morgan wondered. A tiny snowflake drifted into his ear, immediately melting and sending a shudder through his entire body.

November 11, 1945
Nuremberg, Germany

Sometimes Private First Class Bill Todd thought he could eat an entire long horn steer and the hell with such senseless preliminaries as cooking it. Like his father said, "Hungry enough to eat the asshole out of a skunk." Of course, his mom had always complained when Dad said it. "Rectum," she would say. "Eat the rectum out of a skunk. That's more polite, dear." To which his dad and Bill would sing in unison: "Rectum, hell it killed 'im."

For the last two and a half years, ever since being conscripted into this man's army, Private First Class Bill Todd had been hungry. There was never enough to eat. Until these last years Todd, six feet four inches and thick as a steer himself, had never given much consideration to food. It was always there. The family ran a ranch out in Montana, not far from Missoula, and what they didn't raise themselves and slaughter, they could trade with neighbors to get. There was always plenty of beef and mutton and pork, eggs from their own range chickens, and stewed chicken when the layers got old. And there were plenty of spuds and cabbage and carrots and dried beans from the Pollocks on the eastern side of the Muddy Draw. Milk came from the MacDermots, so cool it would bead the glass and with a thick skim of fat on top.

Christ, the thought of it drove Private First Class Bill Todd nuts. All but oblivious to the delights of food before, now after nearly 900 days without enough, he had developed a sybarite's concern for it. It was uppermost on his mind when he awoke in the morning, the last thing he thought about when he fell asleep at night.

K-rations were a joke; barracks grub not a whole lot better. What was that tonight? Some piece of spongy pink former part of an indescribable animal floating around in a mess of boiled cabbage. Jesus, we were lucky to win the war eating that kind of slop. If we hadn't bombed the Nazis into the Stone Age, hell, the U.S. Army might have gone down to defeat because of ptomaine. Todd thought it might be the French guy, Napoleon, who said an army travels on its belly. Leave it to a Frog to figure that one out. Make Todd the commander in chief, and he would be sure GIs got proper food. Thick, juicy T-bones, mashed potatoes stirred up with a little cream and butter, baby lima beans heaped in a gorgeous green pile, a dollop of butter trickling down and forming a yellow film over each and every one of those beautiful little beans.

Christ, man, you got to stop this, he told himself. *You'll go nuts thinking this way.* Other guys, they had pictures torn from girlie magazines taped or thumbtacked over their bunks; if he could have his way, Todd would put a picture of steak and potatoes and lima beans up there. But he knew they'd laugh him out of barracks if he did.

So he put the food out of his mind, dug his hands deeper into the pockets of his fatigue jacket that was too damn tight in the shoulders and too short in the arms. His wrists were always freezing. Two and a half years in the army, one and a half of those spent in Europe, and it seemed he was always cold and always hungry.

Outside of the churchyard, the street was deserted. Hell of a time for a meet, he thought. Hell of a place to meet. The old tombstones scattered all over the place gave him the creeps. Then another thought: *Have to clean up my language when I go home.*

Home. Boy that has a good sound to it.

Todd had re-upped, skipped his rotation back home, to do a final stint at Nuremberg. Most soldiers with his service record—Normandy, the Battle of the Bulge, the liberation of the death camps—were already boring their old friends at the local with stories of their exploits in the big war. Not Todd, though. He wanted to get something more out of his tour of duty than chilblains and a clap on the back. There was money to be made in Nuremberg. That's why he wasn't home in Montana right now, fueling up on steak and potatoes.

He turned his left hand palm-up, checking the watch he wore with its face on the inside of his wrist to protect it. His mother had given it to him before he left for the army. The glowing numerals told him it was just past eleven. That'd make it early afternoon on the farm, he figured. No work today, a Sunday. They'd just be finishing up Sunday lunch, probably a pot roast. . . .

Stop it, for Christ sake!

Todd had stayed on in the army to get himself a little nest egg so he could maybe get his own section of land. That nice piece down by Willow Creek. Plenty of water. Good grazing land. He had ideas, good ideas, about raising a new breed of sheep he'd come across in England when they were getting ready for the Normandy invasion. Ginny would like that. Him having ideas. Ginny had finished high school. She read books.

Ginny MacDermot and Bill Todd were an item. They'd been meant for each other ever since grade school. He was doing this for Ginny, for them. His dad, the prairie populist, would call what he was doing a little redistribution of wealth. Nothing so bad about that. He had a buddy in the quartermaster's section. A touch on supply. The crap he carried in the pack on his back now was nothing Todd found so priceless—tins of Spam, packs of dried milk, parcels of flour and oatmeal, some medicine, even three bottles of Scotch whiskey. Todd was not a drinking man, and the rest of it—well, it was food you gave to babies or old folks with no teeth in their heads to chew.

Eleven o'clock was the meet, his buddy had told him. So where the hell was the son of a bitch? It's freezing out here.

Todd stomped up and down the slush-filled paths of the deserted churchyard, trying to warm himself. Snow had stopped this morning, but it was still cold enough to turn a guy's nuts to brass.

Steps sounded from the street in back of him, and Private First Class Bill Todd turned, peering into the darkness. Not a street light around; hardly a standing house left in the bombed-out district. The approaching figure waved, and squinting into the blackness, Todd waved back, tentatively at first.

It was a good kill. A clean kill. The big, dumb American never even knew what happened. Just looked at me out of those startled eyes, and then down at the blood gushing over the front of his jacket as he tried to speak.

But there was no voice. The killer had seen to that. The scalpel dug deep, cutting down through layers and layers of skin and muscle and into hard cartilage. The soldier stood there for several instants, his mouth making soundless words, his hands grabbing his throat as if choking himself.

No tourniquet could stop that flow of blood.

Now the American lay in a crumpled heap where he had fallen, next to a tombstone marking the grave of Elfriede and Heinrich Mauthner, loving husband and wife who departed this earthly plane on January 12, 1931, and March 15, 1937, respectively. May their souls rest in God's grace.

The killer read the inscription carefully and sighed. This soldier would have his very own inscription for others to read: the page cut from the novel this morning with certain words underlined and a slash of initials in the crimson ink of the victim's own blood at the bottom of the page.

Words to keep you wondering, the killer thought, placing the page in the American's right hand.

November 12, 1945

"So that's it?" Hannigan boomed. "All your beautiful detective work and you're telling me what I know already? That this fucking Russian was dealing black market."

Chief Inspector Reinhard Manhof sat across a scarred expanse of desk in the Kripo office. Hannigan, energized by an early-morning visit from his immediate superior, Colonel Adams—PIA Adams, for "Pain in the Ass"—had made the trip down the rabbit warren of hallways in the old justice building to Kripo himself. Didn't want the German creeping around his own office—which he had requisitioned from Kripo to begin with. And here was Manhof stuck into a space the size of a broom closet without a window and barely a door. Hannigan had not wanted to deal with the man's hangdog expression looking at his former offices and their wide expanse of windows. Not much to look at out the window anymore, but it was a window, nonetheless.

Hannigan had flogged off the murder of the Russian Orlov on the German police, but now that a GI appeared to be the victim of the same killer, there was defecation all over the fans in Nuremberg.

"There is little to go on, Major Hannigan." Manhof spoke a fussy, correct, school English that irritated the shit out of Hannigan. "Both victims were found in the Sebald district to the north of the Pegnitz. Whether that is significant or not, we have yet to determine." He held his hands in the air as if measuring invisible valences. "The Russian was found near Saint Johannis Hospital, or what remains of it, and your American was discovered late last night in the churchyard of Saint Johannis. The minister there has insomnia, you see. A stroll around the grounds at midnight usually calms his nerves."

"Don't imagine he got much sleep last night after his little walk," Hannigan interjected.

Manhof nodded in agreement. "But the coincidence of Saint Johannis is intriguing, no?"

"You've got to die somewhere." Hannigan waved an irritated hand at him. "What else you got?"

"Well, there is the similar modus, as well. The slashed throat."

"Our medico, Haskell, says it could be the same weapon. He's not sure. Tell me something I don't know."

The German paused for a moment.

"There is also a similar possible motive. Your American was carrying a knapsack full of food of various types. The Russian had a pocket full of drugs."

Hannigan felt a sudden alarm. "That wasn't mentioned in this morning's report."

"No. It seemed insignificant at the time. But the goods have been impounded. I noticed, however, a possible connection when reviewing the elements this morning."

"What're you saying, Manhof? Both these boys were black market?"

Again the upraised hands of the German. He was what the textbooks call nondescript. *The sort of guy*, Hannigan thought, *who could go into a bank, shoot the tellers, take a million bucks, and the customers wouldn't be able to describe him.* Bland. A non-face. Two distinguishing features Hannigan could discern: a mole on his left cheek near the nose, and dishwater-blond hair thinning on top with a comb-over. *Vanity, there,* Hannigan thought. He prided himself on such observations.

"We are not ruling out black market involvement," Manhof said importantly.

Hannigan slumped into a chair that creaked under his weight. "So probably not Werwolves," Hannigan sighed, referring to the bands of holdout Nazi terrorists still operating in parts of Germany. "That would've been better. Easier to sell. I don't want to have to be the one to tell Colonel Adams that we're experiencing a little gang warfare over black-market turf."

"Maybe you won't have to," Manhof said. "The Russian, it seems, was dealing in drugs badly out-of-date. Your Captain Haskell was good enough to give me the results of tests. You see the implication."

"Dissatisfied customer," Hannigan said.

"Another possibility."

"Anything else?" Hannigan was looking for another explanation—anything but the black market for a dead GI.

"There is the curious similarity in these notes left in the dead men's hands. They appear to be from the same book, but I am afraid I'm not much of a reader."

Hannigan had not heard about the note with the American victim. The report he'd read was as full of holes as his socks.

"I don't fucking need this."

Hannigan had sent over an evidence package on the Russian to Manhof when he decided to include the Germans in the investigation, to spread the possible blame. This included the first bit of paper found in the Russian's hand. Now Manhof picked up two separate pages, both yellowing with age and both neatly cut out of a book. From Hannigan's vantage point, the pages looked to be from the same book: Size, coloring, and typeface all matched. Manhof displayed the front side of the pages to him, and Hannigan could see the same quick, rusty slashed marks at the bottom of each. Groups of words were underlined in black ink on each, seemingly at random. That both pages bore such underlined passages reinforced the idea that the pages bore a code of some sort.

As if reading his thought, Manhof shook his head.

"The words make no sense put together. '*Unklar, Hand, sterben.*' " He read off the words in order of appearance, and then skipped toward the bottom of the page: " '*Messer, Christus, tot.*' No sense to them in either of the notes. Articles, verbs, nouns. A mélange."

"What's it saying?"

"You mean the text itself?"

Hannigan nodded.

"They are still being formally translated."

"Give me a ballpark translation."

Manhof shrugged his shoulders. "My English leaves much to be desired."

"Humor me."

Manhof shrugged again; a gray man in a gray world. "The first one talks about a weapon, *Gewehr*, not a pistol but longer . . ."

"Rifle."

"Precisely. Or how is it? Carbine. Yes. A carbine that fires twenty-four rounds. There are two people talking, but from this passage it is unclear who they are. No names are given. It would seem to be the American West, however, for one interlocutor speaks of this weapon being the death of the Indians. 'They will be shot down like coyotes,' " Manhof translated. "And at another point, this same interlocutor seems to accuse the other of murder. 'Not just one murder, but mass murder.' "

Hannigan watched the German as he looked up from the page to him.

"Somebody's having us on," Hannigan said.

Manhof shot him a quizzical look.

"Pulling our leg. Teasing us."

Manhof made no reply as he referred to the other page, the one taken from the GI. "Much the same sort of text here, as well. It would seem to describe a knife fight between an Indian and a white man. Something about a battle to the death."

Hannigan struggled to his feet.

"That's real fine. So what we got here are two murders by the same bastard. It looks like our boy likes to leave his calling card, but me, I vote for red herring here. Something to take us off of the real scent. This smells to high heaven of black market. But somebody wants us to think different. To think there's a wacko loose in Nuremberg. We don't bite, though. See?"

Manhof nodded, but Hannigan was far from sure that the German understood what he was talking about.

"Okay, I'll spell it out. Talk to the friends of these guys. See what they were doing out at night. Did they talk about meeting anyone? Shake down your informants. Find out who's running the market from the German side, if you don't already know. Maybe you've got a Fritz or Hermann out there pissed off at the competition. Maybe we've got people in the DP camp who bought bad drugs from Ivan, sour milk from our GI."

Manhof smiled, placing the pages of the book on top of the two separate files. "The Russians are being, shall we say, less than cooperative. They refuse to deal with German police."

"Okay. I'll put some of my men on that end. Meanwhile, you get onto the others. The black-market angle, the displaced persons camp, any witnesses that might have seen, heard, even smelled anything, for Christ's sake."

"We have three officers in this bureau, Major."

"Well get them out there asking questions then."

"And there are other cases for them to work on. More than three thousand missing persons in Nuremberg, to start with."

"Those people are either dead already or they'll wander back eventually," Hannigan said, his voice rising in volume. "So you can't do too much about those three thousand, can you? Now we've got two murders of Allied soldiers. We don't want any more. Understand?"

Manhof shrugged. "We will approach it with diligence, Major."

"See that you do. Extreme *diligence*."

Life is a chicken coop, Hannigan told himself as he slammed the door to Manhof's cubicle in back of him. *You get pecked; you peck somebody else.*

Greilauer was a quiet suburban residential area on the northern outskirts of Nuremberg. Here, there were substantial homes of the city's favored: managers, lawyers, doctors, a smattering of aged nobility. The war had passed this district by; none of the scorched-earth destruction of the inner city to be found in Greilauer.

Here, there had been no war: no heaps of rubble, no stink of rotting flesh, no swarms of flies, no maggots the size of slugs crawling out of the sewers. Here, in Greilauer the lime trees were still in autumn foliage up and down the block; a matron in a tweed suit and fox wrap strolled her standard poodle along the wide expanse of sidewalk. Twin cypresses sentineled the bottom of the long front drive; the villa itself was from the late nineteenth century, with several turret rooms topping the stone façade. It looked like a fortress with its copper roof turned green with aging; ivy crept up the south side of it; a bay window gave out onto the front garden.

But there were not so many managers as before. Not so many wealthy German doctors and lawyers in residence. Many of the villas had been requisitioned by the Allies to house the numerous staff in town for the trial. Justice Jackson, lead American prosecutor, was billeted at a formidable old stucco home on Lindenstrasse farther away to the northwest in Fürth. Other high-up legal staffers were fortunate enough to share smaller rooms nearby; some of the female secretaries and translators lived in dormitory settings fitted into the precincts of old Biedermeier villas.

On Bubergasse, just up from the little Protestant chapel,

stood the stately home of General von Prandtauer, a turreted, neo-Gothic gray affair squatting on massive grounds. The general was dead; his widow now took in visitors of Nuremberg, those with connections and some modicum of power.

Kate Wallace had connections, but very little power. She had been destined for the fusty confines of the old town palace of the pencil magnate Faber-Castell. It was there that most of the international journalists were housed; a snake pit of media types all competing for the same story. Dumb luck and the intercession of a highly embarrassed and frightened Colonel Jensen had saved Kate from that fate.

Last Saturday, when the plane landed in Nuremberg, Jensen had done everything he could to cover up his bumbling pass. To make it go away, before Senator Bertram Wallace made *him* go away. That included giving up his prime billet at the Prandtauers to Kate. The spoils of war.

She was now, on this Monday afternoon, quite happily cosseted in the turret room at the top of the villa, her Underwood set up on the Biedermeier breakfast table, a half-finished cup of coffee at her side.

Below, as she looked out her window, she saw Baroness von Prandtauer at archery practice, heard the rhythmic *thwump* of arrows striking a distant target. It was a scene out of her own childhood at the Pennsylvania estate.

She turned from the window, looking again at the sheets of A4 paper containing her first piece from Nuremberg, fresh out of the typewriter:

> *The smells hit you first: the chemical reek of Sterno cans heating the night's supper in primitive lean-tos and tents made from parachutes and scraps of old tarpaulin; an occasional whiff of burning autumn leaves from wood fires and the more acrid bite of coal fires amid the gray-black destruction. The sweet smell of water from the Pegnitz River; the even sweeter stench that catches in the throat and burns the eyes of rot-*

ting corpses—30,000 of them, the Allies estimate—moldering under the broken mortar and bricks that once made up the city of Nuremberg.

Then the sights, a vista unbroken by buildings, for 90 percent of the city has been leveled by aerial bombardment—more than 20,000 high explosives and incendiaries rained down upon Nuremberg on the night of February 20 and 21, 1945, just weeks before the armistice—and lies in heaps of rubble, which appear dusty under the Indian summer sun or glisten greasy-slick with lime under the late fall rains. A jagged edge of wall stands here and there, a ruin out of ancient Rome, revealing a cross-section of buildings, their floors layered like toy models, the shattered domesticity of their former occupants disgorged for all to see. The ruined floors with their contents spilling out like so many socks from an unclosed bureau drawer: a Turkish carpet furling its fringe over the edges of the jagged floor; a doll left crumpled and dangling, its tiny white apron soiled soot black; a chipped bathtub dangling halfway out.

Sounds of traffic, of jeeps, of tanks; of Peugeot bicycles churning in the still night, a chain clanking obstinately against chain guard, a brittle tinkling of its bell as warning to pedestrians, dogs, an ambassador's black Cadillac, and a general's darting Rover. The polyglot mix of languages: German, French, English, Russian, Polish. A mélange of Europe gathered in this former commercial crossroads. The whispered urgencies of sexual negotiations in the ruins, the bark of military orders, the monotonic legalistic drone of witness statements.

It is cold this first fall after the end of the war. The bone-chilling damp reaches the people where they lie in their tents and makeshift hovels above ground, and in their bunkerlike cellars below the ruined earth. The cold is everywhere: in the broken stone, in the lethargic river, in the eyes of the people.

Kate took her blue pencil and crossed out a word here, a phrase there. *Tighten, tighten,* she told herself. *Just because it's impressionistic does not mean it can be flabby.* Professor Kramer's favorite dictum.

The sights, sounds, and smells she has gathered for this story were her own first impressions when driving in from the airport. Nothing could have prepared her for that first glimpse of a destroyed city. Aerial bombardment had been only a phrase she read in the newspapers until then. The reality of it was something quite different. To see those kids running through the ruins, chasing a rat as if it were a soccer ball—that had been a shock of recognition for Kate.

There were real stories here in Nuremberg. Yes, there was the trial to cover, and yes, it was important. The first time that there would be something other than rough victors' justice after the conclusion of a war. There would be, when the trial started on November 20, a score of men in the dock who all had a story; there were reams and reams of evidence. Their crimes must be announced to the world.

But there were also thousands of individual stories in the very streets of this ruined city.

Kate figured that she must be one of the luckiest journalists alive. A chance like this came only once in a lifetime. Her instincts had been right to come to Nuremberg. There were stories outside the courtroom and she would find them. She would make a name for herself here.

Baroness Elisabeth von Prandtauer—"Sissy" to her few intimates—was still at archery practice in the grounds to the back of the villa. She was impeccably dressed as usual. A tweed jacket and matching country skirt with just a hint of moss in the earthen beige to bring out the gray-green of her eyes; walking shoes handmade by Zeidlitz in Munich; her blonde hair French-braided and wrapped in coils on her head—she could not stand to wear hats of any sort. The morning air was crisp; dew on the back lawns of the villa; the hint of sun peeking through alder, apple, and apricot trees whose leaves were burnished gold in the autumn light.

She held the bow in her left hand, strung the wooden arrow in the gut string with her right. Flexing the string, she marveled once again at the craftsmanship of the bow, the pure beauty of design. Her late husband had given it to her as a wedding gift—their private wedding gift, for surely the others would not understand. In public, he gifted her with the Prandtauer collection of jewelry—the diamond tiara worn by the Prandtauers since Frederick the Great's day; the string of pearls that tugged at her neck when she wore them, each bead a miniature egg of luminescence; the emerald and ruby setting of the Francasi watch; the perfection of the diamond drip earrings. A bountiful glittering mass of jewels, gemstones, and precious metals.

She liked the bow better. It was, like the arrows, made of ash cut from the trees of the Buchholtz Wald on the Prandtauers' northern estates. Seasoned and worked by the finest craftsmen in Bavaria, the bow had the lines of a nineteenth-century woman held in firmly at the waist with whalebone girdles. She pulled the gut string to its full extension, loving the tug and sting in the muscles of her right arm as she did so. *Hold the bow firmly now, lock the left elbow, do not be over eager*—just as her brother, Gerhard, had always instructed. Just like the old days and the early morning shoots with Gerd.

The straw-backed target was illuminated by the afternoon sun, a golden pot of gold at which the baroness took aim. Sensing a sudden shift of wind, she drew the bow up a notch, holding her right hand to her cheek, sighting down the length of the arrow. She released as she would a harp string, gently plucked. The arrow whistled through the morning air, a graceful arc, a bidden missile. She heard the distant thump as it drove into its target, just right of center.

She loved the feel of the bow in her hand; it gave her power—power that had been taken away from her land by the conquering idiots. The conquering idolaters, lovers of freedom and democracy.

Freedom from what? she wondered. *Freedom to do what?* They surely did not know. Like the callow, young American girl who had taken her lovely tower room.

The baroness would like to put the girl's kewpie doll face on the target, send arrows to her rouged lips. They had no sense of honor, no sense of German history. They came with their chocolates and white teeth like the new gods of creation, these Americans.

God, what a world we now live in, Baroness von Prandtauer thought, *if they are to be the new rulers.*

Sometimes she wanted to weep for the loss of the Reich. Sometimes the sadness crawled over her and she wished to die rather than live in a world led by the new barbarians.

How could you have lost the war? she thought. *How could you have done this to us, subjected us to the victors' justice?*

Then, for the thousandth time, she cursed her husband for his weakness and perfidy. A traitor to the cause.

November 13, 1945

Beck was trying to keep warm in the prison yard. The guards took the prisoners out for morning exercise three times a week, whether they needed it or not. Whether they wanted it or not. *Exercise was something you did in lieu of living,* Beck thought. The Americans were as bad as the Nazis in this respect; their obsession with the culture of body and fitness was straight out of Hitler Youth posters.

Prisoners from Beck's wing were all gathered in the wet, cold yard, breathing vapor bubbles into the gray sky, looking like clowns in their striped flannel prison suits that were too thin for the temperature.

"Come on, Fritz," the guard said to him. "You need to move around some. Get the blood flowing."

Beck would have liked to share his thoughts on the efficacy of such exercise, of where, in fact, the guard might insert such blood flow, but thought better of it. Privileges such as receiving care packages from relatives had been revoked for less. He elbowed himself away from the wall he'd been leaning against and joined the flow of men walking like dumb sheep in a circular pattern around the yard.

Beck countered the hypnotic rhythm of scraped boots against gravel, the whisper of arms brushing against waists as the men lumbered along, by setting his own pace. He kept to the outside of the pack and stretched out his legs as he moved. *Our guard wants exercise*, Beck thought. *Well, he shall have it.*

Beck did not notice that one of the prisoners had come up next to him and was now keeping pace with the longer-legged ex-chief inspector, only with great difficulty. His short legs churned to keep level with Beck.

"I thought it was you," the man said, slightly out of breath.

Only then did Beck notice his companion. There was something familiar about him, but a shaved head—lice preventative—muted remembrance. *Humans, both men and women, looked so similar without hair,* Beck thought. Quite odd, really, that hair should give definition to our features. Mostly, it seemed to hide our features, but all you had to do was shave it off to see how important it was to physical definition. Also, something about the acrid smell of the man—a mixture of sweat and bad breath—tripped Beck's memory switch. Yet Beck still could not place him.

"It's me, Inspector. Rollo. Remember? Eh?"

Beck did remember now. Rollo, one of his primary snitches from before the war, a man who had his hand in much of Nuremberg's organized crime. Rollo was a maker of deals, a super-fence, a fixer. No breaking bones for Rollo. Not personally. But he could have it arranged for a price.

Beck did not slacken his pace. "I won't say I am happy to see you. Nor am I surprised by your presence in this lovely establishment."

Rollo laughed at this. "I see you haven't lost that sense of humor, Inspector."

Beck had never been more serious. He increased his pace, and Rollo almost had to run to keep up with him.

"Look, Inspector, you got to slow down. I need to talk."

It was how Rollo had always initiated contact before the war when he had information for them. *I need to talk,* whispered over a phone, and Beck had almost been able to smell the man over the line. The phrase brought it all back. Beck slowed down and Rollo caught his breath.

"I'm not really in any position to be buying information now." Beck grabbed the material of his own prison uniform at the chest between thumb and fingers. "I'm not just slumming, you know."

Rollo nodded. "I'm not selling. Yet. I need some advice, is all."

"Plead guilty," Beck joked. "Ask for clemency."

A shake of the head from Rollo. "I'm serious here. I've got some information that the wrong people don't want to get out. Get me? I don't belong here."

"None of us belongs here, Rollo. The world is a highly unjust place." He picked up his pace again.

"That goddamn Manhof, he's not a fair man, you know."

The mention of Manhof's name made Beck slow down once again. "How do you mean?"

"Not like you, Inspector. You made a deal; you always stuck to it. A gentleman, that's what we called you. A man you could trust. But this Manhof, he says one thing, does another. Got me in here for protective custody. I mean can you beat that?"

"Believe me, Rollo, I know exactly how you feel. So what is it you want to tell me?"

"Look, this information. I was wondering, should I try to shop it to the Americans? Can you trust them? This is very sensitive stuff, you know what I mean?"

"No, Rollo, I do not know what you mean. Maybe you should just tell me instead of playing at all this mystery."

Rollo put a hand to Beck's sleeve to slow him down even more and was just about to speak when the guard shouted at them.

"No talking in the yard." The big guard stood slapping a long billy club into the palm of his left hand, shooting a menacing look their way.

Rollo pulled a face at the man, then turned back to Beck. "I'll get word to you, okay. A message. I need advice."

Then he faded into the flow of the rest of the prisoners, joining their rhythmic shuffle, a stoop-shouldered little man with beady eyes and fetid smell. He had been a good snitch, Beck remembered. Not one of the best, but sometimes his information had been valuable. One thing about Rollo, however, Beck reminded himself: He did enjoy inflating the value of his information. Rollo was a great one for drama.

Later that night, Beck lay on his back on his cot, right hand on his chest and his left brushing the cool stucco wall. This was a tactile form of counting sheep, for Beck could not sleep in his tiny cell, not with the light on overhead and knowing that the view slot would be opened at least once an hour to make sure the prisoners were all alive. It had been like this since the suicide of the Nazi labor chief Ley; lack of sleep was catching up with him. He rolled over to his side, pulled the sheet up over his head to block out the light, and for awhile he dozed fitfully.

Commotion out in the hall woke him up, however, just as the guard was looking into his cell. The same commotion caused the guard to leave his door quickly, and to leave the view slot open. Beck got up from the cot, went to the door, and looked into the corridor. Panicked voices came from the far end of the hall, a shout. Running feet passed his door. A muttered, "Goddamn, our ass is grass," as another guard rushed by.

Minutes passed. Beck kept his eyes glued to the peephole in his door, fascinated by what was happening. Like the effect of lack of hair on physical features, his days had become featureless by lack of event. This was the best thing to happen since his successful bowel movement several days ago.

Then there was movement from down at the end of the hall. He could hear the shuffle of boots in the corridor, cursing voices. He peered far to his left and saw four of the guards coming his way, each carrying part of some object between them. As they approached one asked, "Where'd he get the stuff?" and from another, "You know where we're going to end up now?"

Then they were passing his door and Beck could see the

object they were carrying between them, two gripping the arms, two holding the legs.

It was Rollo. His head was dangling, his face was purple, and his tongue protruded his lips. One eye winked shut and the other, opened, looked straight at Beck. Sightless.

Then somebody from the other side slammed the view slot shut, clipping Beck's nose in the process.

November 14, 1945

On Wednesday morning, Kate ran into Colonel Jensen in the downstairs breakfast room at the von Prandtauer villa. The colonel acted as if he did not recognize her at first, but Kate perversely would not let him off the hook. She brought her coffee and kipfel to his table, smiling as she sat down. He had a spoonful of dripping, yellow egg yolk halfway to his mouth, and stopped his arm in its journey as she seated herself.

"Miss Wallace," he said, sputtering the plosive endings. The yolk dripped a fat, viscous drop onto the damask tablecloth, hardening instantly like candle drippings.

"Go ahead with breakfast, Colonel. I just wanted to thank you again for giving up your room. So comfortable."

The colonel had been relegated to a maid's room under the eaves.

"Don't mention it." He finally inserted the spoon, munching on the boiled egg. He dug in the freckled brown shell held in the blue-on-white onion pattern eggcup for more, but came up with only the concave remnants of the white from the bottom. He kept his eyes averted from hers. She was actually beginning to feel sorry for the big fool.

"Truce, Jensen?"

He looked up like a pet basset recently reprimanded.

"That would be wonderful, Miss Wallace."

She thrust her hand across the table at him. He stared at it for a moment, then wiped his hand on his napkin, grabbed hers effusively, and pumped it till she winced.

"Sorry."

She shook her head and took an exploratory nibble of the breakfast roll.

Now that the breach had been mended, Jensen turned effusive: "And what are you up to today?"

No sugar, not much butter in the roll, either, Kate decided. But there was flour. She swallowed hard. They were joined in the breakfast room by another of the "guests" at the villa, a British woman dressed in drab khaki, her chinless face pinched into a look of perennial disapproval. Kate nodded at her, smiling. The woman looked at her blankly, then at the colonel by way of hello.

Kate turned back to Jensen, finally fielding his question.

"I'm not really sure. Actually, I'm at loose ends. My first story's been sent off and now I am at that dead zone between stories. Though I bet you've got one for me."

She said it in jest, but Jensen took it all too seriously.

"You bet I do. And it comes in one word. *Werwolves.*"

Great, she thought. *I think I liked him better as a foe than as a friend.* She smiled at his statement.

"As in lycanthropy?"

The colonel shook his head, then pushed his plate away and took a final sip of the coffee.

"No. As in German terrorist. Hitler Youth stay-behinds and Volkssturm units. Stupid teenagers most of them. If they were in New York, we'd call them juvenile delinquents, but here, in Germany, they try to glorify their exploits by calling themselves Werwolves. And they are, pardon my French, a giant pain in my arse."

Kate suddenly found herself interested. "In what way?"

"They're magpies. Steal anything not nailed down. Leave a supply dump unmanned for a minute or two, and boom, your stuff is gone. Food, clothing, weapons. You name it, they steal it."

"For the black market?"

"Partly. But mostly it's to supply their own troops. These guys—and women, too—are fanatics. They plan to fight us to the death. In the Black Forest, the Harz Mountains, and the Thuringian Forest, they're still thick on the ground. But they're controlled from the urban areas and they operate small cadres in the cities, too, cutting phone cables, setting up decapitation wires across the roads, attacking soldiers."

Jensen's face grew redder and redder as he warmed to his topic. He began fidgeting with the college ring on his third finger, agitated at his own story.

"I'm listening, Colonel," Kate encouraged him.

"'The SS set them up back in '44, and now they're a power unto themselves. They terrorize honest Germans who work with us, prey on lone soldiers all over Germany, and generally make my work in supply a hundred times more difficult than it should be. But who's talking about them? Nobody. Suddenly, everybody's got tears in their eyes for the poor Germans deluded by their mad leaders, and aren't we going to show the world how bad those leaders are? Isn't that what this whole trial BS is about? To let the German people off the hook, and hang the leaders. But there's plenty of small-fry Germans still fighting the good fight. There's your story for you."

Kate had never heard of the Werwolf brigades and wondered just how much Jensen liked to exaggerate.

As if reading her suspicions, he said, "Look, there's this guy I know over in GHQ, he was in charge of routing Werwolf squads out of Bavaria last summer. He could tell you stories that'd make your hair stand on end. They're kids, some of them not older than ten or twelve. They ask a GI for a bar of chocolate and shoot his head off while he reaches into his fatigues. Cool and mean as hell. Never blink at you. It made this guy cry to go after those little kids, some of them no older than his own at home. After all, it's the adults he wanted, those giving the orders. But it's the kids with the guns and Panzerfaust, bazookas bigger than them, who are doing the damage."

A young redheaded man came into the breakfast room, his eyes averted from the others there. He joined the pinch-faced British woman at the only other available table. Suddenly, Kate recognized him—William Stanton, the lawyer on Kate's flight from Croydon Airfield.

This realization distracted her for a moment, but then she looked closely at Jensen

"Does this friend have a name?"

Brave Indians do not flinch from the pain. Brave Indians are able to withstand abuse, beatings, even torture.

Under the covers, it was dark and cool in the middle of the afternoon. Only their two sets of breathing. Faster now, not regular breathing. Not just inhale-exhale. But quick and urgent like a dog on a hot summer's day.

Brave Indians never tell secrets, either. They take their punishment with eyes closed, faces impassive. And later . . . Well, later is just that. Another time to play.

Brave Indians are always ready to play. They keep their weapons in tip-top shape.

The scalpel, cleaned of any trace of blood, was returned to its home in the purple velvet wrap. *The French soldier looks like a brave Indian*, the killer thought. Peaceful now, a smile on his face above the gaping wound. The killer was sure of that smile.

November 15, 1945

"Thanks for meeting me, General. I know you're a busy man."
Colonel Adams stood as his guest for breakfast approached the
corner table at the Grand.

General "Wild Bill" Donovan—founder of the OSS and
part of the prosecution team at Nuremberg—was, in fact, not
busy at all. He'd just been given his walking papers by Justice
Jackson, chief U.S. prosecutor for the upcoming trial. "Your
services will no longer be needed here," the man had told him,
as if he was some shoeshine boy you could send packing.

Donovan took the chair offered by Adams, the one with its
back to the wall. Long habit.

"No problem, Geoffrey. Takes my mind off other matters."

"Yes." Colonel Adams sat after Donovan, pulling his chair
in tight to the table. "I heard. Sorry. I think the man's making
a mistake."

"That makes at least two of us," Donovan said. "Relying on
documents instead of witnesses. He'll put the world to sleep
with that approach. What we need is for teary-eyed mothers
to take the stand and tell of their sons and daughters murdered
by these criminals. To have a young woman testify how Nazi

doctors sterilized her with their so-called experiments. For survivors of the camps to tell the world what the Nazi death machine was really like. But what are we going to get instead? Documents. Boxes and boxes of documents. They've got tons of them stored here, Geoffrey. This trial's going to be flat as Kansas without the human element."

"Exactly," Adams chimed in.

A waiter in white jacket and black tie brought a silver service of coffee. The rich aroma seemed to calm Donovan momentarily.

"What will you do now?" Adams asked. He would take it slow at first, demonstrate his own compassion.

"Only thing I can do. Go back home. Go back into private practice. Truman doesn't want me or the service I built for the country. Says he doesn't want some 'American Gestapo.' Sheer effrontery. Goes to show the man's never seen the Gestapo in action. And now they tell me they don't need my services at the trials. So . . ."

"We'll all be going home soon, General."

"Yes, well . . ." Donovan stirred nonexistent sugar into his coffee with a tiny silver spoon. "I somehow imagined I would end this war on a higher note." He took a sip of the steaming coffee, then peered at his tablemate over the tip of the cup.

"Sorry to inflict my woes on you. It sounds as if you've got your own troubles."

Adams, who headed security for the upcoming trial, cleared his throat; it was the invitation he'd been waiting for. The waiter brought their bacon and eggs, forestalling his presentation.

"I took the liberty of ordering for both of us. Hope you don't mind, sir."

Donovan shook his head. "I never mind a good breakfast, Geoffrey. Especially when someone else is paying." He laughed with a surprisingly high trill.

Adams waited for the waiter to get out of earshot before continuing.

"There's been a third murder since I talked with you last night."

Donovan tipped his head toward Adams, blowing air between moistened teeth. "Same fellow?"

"It would appear so. Same method. Rather grisly in fact. French lieutenant, this time. So now we've got the Russians *and* the French breathing down our necks, wondering what we're going to do to stop these heinous crimes in our sector. And I've got the heads of the Allied Control Commission boring me a new orifice over this. It makes us look bad, General. Very bad. Those same CC heads asked me how we can expect the Germans to trust us to run their country if we can't even find a killer in Nuremberg."

"Press gets hold of this story and it could well upstage events in the courtroom," Donovan added.

"Exactly. I knew you would understand, General."

"Plus, I imagine you're taking flak from Washington over this?"

"How did you know that?"

It was apparent Donovan felt in his element now—the *Magister Ludi* teaching the junior officer. Just as Adams wanted it to go.

"Why do you think we've got some of my former OSS officers here, Geoffrey? Vacation? Hardly. They're working the prison, looking for recruits for military intelligence. The former enemy, right? But the climate is changing in Europe. Enemies and allies. Murky line now that the hostilities are over."

"I could not have put it better myself," Adams said, smiling as he stuffed a forkful of egg—a trifle on the runny side—into his mouth.

"So Washington is crawling all over you about public relations, I suppose. They're telling you it's okay to put the Nazi bigwigs on trial. A sort of national expiation of sins. But if Mildred and Clarence out in Nebraska start reading about some crazy killer running around the ruins of Nuremberg killing off the conquering soldiers . . . Well, then we're going to have a public relations problem of the first magnitude convincing those same folks to welcome Germany to the banquet table as our next ally."

This impressed Adams. He'd never doubted that the general had a mind for analysis, but the factoring of Adams's problems over coffee and eggs in the Officers' Club showed real acumen and political savvy. Adams began to wonder, indeed to worry, if perhaps the general had political aspirations of his own. It was clear Ike did. And Adams was already calculating the political ride he could get from his tour of duty in Nuremberg. But they didn't need too many old warriors flooding the political pool.

"Public relations," Adams muttered. "You're exactly right there, General. Washington's made it abundantly clear they don't want news of these deaths leaking back home. We've got a press blackout on them, of course, but it's only a matter of time before some hotshot puts a scoop above national security interests. Plus there's nothing much we can do to control the foreign press. We're under the media microscope here. Did you know there's more than five hundred journalists here from thirty-some different countries? We need to solve these murders before, as you say, they upstage the trial itself."

General Donovan nodded his head at this, then sighed.

"Worse luck for you."

Adams wanted to push this interview forward. *A name. Give me a name.* But he waited, allowing Donovan to come up with the idea himself.

"I can see you're caught between a rock and a hard place," Donovan said, now attacking his breakfast with real vigor. He ate a great mouthful of the food and sighed contentedly. Other officers at surrounding tables were aware of his presence, casting wary glances his way. Word had gotten out about Justice Jackson's decision to dismiss the former spymaster as a cantankerous busybody. To send him home. And these other officers wanted to avoid contact with him now, as if to avoid contamination.

Adams would normally have done the same, but he had use for the man. *Gently now*, he told himself. *Get him around to it.*

"The worst of it, I'm stuck with a staff bordering on incompetence," Adams prompted. "My security officer here, Major Hannigan, is a former prison warden, not an investigator."

"Makes it hard," Donovan agreed through a bite of Dutch bacon.

They ate on in silence. Finally, Adams realized that the old fox was not going to make it easy for him. The stares of his fellow officers in the dining room were beginning to get to Adams; he did not want all of Nuremberg to know he was consorting with a general in disgrace. He should have asked him to the office, but that was just as bad with adjutants everywhere and the prying eyes of secretaries.

"Look, General. I'll level with you. I badly need a professional investigator to handle this."

Donovan looked up from the ruined egg yolk of his second egg and smiled. "I thought you'd never ask, Geoffrey. I'm your man."

Adams's heart sank in his chest, knocking against his spleen, drumming on his belly. How to explain now that he was after advice, not the general himself?

Donovan easily read the disappointment in Adams's face, and chuckled to himself.

"My little joke," he said. "Why not just come out with it, Geoffrey? You know as well as I that Nate Morgan is here recruiting for intelligence. You don't need me to give him the blessing. He's no longer part of my organization. Nobody is, not since Truman made us disappear last month."

Adams was relieved for an instant, then on guard again just as quickly.

"A word in the ear at MI could help with a reassignment."

Donovan looked at Adams long and hard. "You wouldn't be planning to hang this boy out to dry would you now, Geoffrey? To save your ass by putting our wunderkind inspector from New York on the case?"

"I need help here," Adams said with what he hoped was proper humility. "We're all on the same team, General. We all want the same result. And if there is somebody with special skills in Nuremberg, then it makes sense that we are able to utilize him."

Donovan continued looking at Adams, as if examining his very soul. Adams felt himself go red at the examination, but finally Donovan nodded.

"I'll see what I can do, Geoffrey. I'll let you know this afternoon before I leave town." He wiped his mouth with the starched white napkin before placing it on the table neatly refolded. "But don't fuck with the boy, okay? He's a good one. One of my best men in Switzerland."

Adams shrugged as if nothing was further from his intentions. He stayed seated after Donovan took his departure. Eyes in the dining room remained averted as the general walked out the door.

He never made things easy, Adams told himself. The general had no idea how to simply play the game. That was his problem. His accusations still stung; Adams smelled a rank body odor from his own torso, despite bathing that morning. The general had a way of making a man break out into a sweat.

Nonetheless, Adams smiled at his tiny triumph. He now had someone of prominence onto whom he could dump this case. Someone who had the trust of those in the Allied Control Commission, and in Washington, to come up with the goods. Somebody far enough removed from Adams so that it would not be *his* derriere in the wringer if the investigation were less than successful. After all, it would be Donovan who had the man transferred from MI to security. It would be Donovan's last order before leaving Nuremberg.

And even better than that was the fact that it would be Morgan himself. Adams had the man's file right there in his briefcase. The reports of his early successes in New York as the detective who broke the Lombardi kidnapping case and became a *Life* magazine cover cop overnight; his exploits as an OSS operative in Switzerland and his undercover ops in occupied Europe. The boy was indeed a magazine cover—the right person to carry the investigation along. He might, in fact, actually solve it. But if he did not, and if the press got hold of the story, it would not be Colonel Adams they would write about; not Colonel Geoffrey Adams, future senator from Connecticut, who couldn't bring home the goods, but General "Wild Bill" Donovan and his former agent Captain Nathan Morgan.

And the final ace in the hole for Adams: Morgan was going to be the perfect flak jacket. After all, who would accuse a Jew of incompetence now, after the six million? Captain *Nathan Morgenstern*—Adams had done his homework on the man—was just too good to be true.

Adams flagged down the waiter and got a snifter of Napoleon brandy to go along with the last of his coffee.

Morgan got word that afternoon from his Military Intelligence superior that he was being transferred to security, Nuremberg sector, ASAP. By four fifteen, he was in new offices requisitioned for him at the Palace of Justice, the fifth staircase. About as far away from the prosecution teams as you could get, but not far enough from Major Hannigan, it appeared.

The moving crew had just finished up; they'd lugged in a couple of heavy metal desks, file cabinets, a conference table, a corkboard, two typewriters, paper, pens, pencils, a sharpener, and four wobbly chairs. A man from communications was stringing the wire for a phone.

When Morgan agreed to take on the investigation, he told Adams in no uncertain terms that he was going to be independent on this, not working under or for Major Hannigan. He'd need an office, a small staff. Colonel Adams just nodded his head, said he'd take care of Hannigan.

Obviously, he hadn't.

"So they brought in the hotshots," Hannigan said as he barged into the office.

The communications guy gave Morgan a glance, but continued his work, head down. He was a corporal and didn't want any part of the world of commissioned officers.

"Please come in, Major."

"You didn't have enough on your plate recruiting those Nazi scum, you have to come horning into my investigation?"

Hannigan stood barrel-chested and puffed up like a rooster, his face beet red and fists clenched at his side. Morgan had dealt with bullies like him all his life. In the schoolyard, at Harvard, with the NYPD—blueblood or redneck, the stance was always the same.

"I actually had no choice in the matter, Major. Security requisitioned me from MI."

A partial truth. Adams had given him the choice, but when he'd learned Donovan himself had recommended him, Morgan could not refuse.

"You fancy college boys figure I can't handle this case, that it?"

Morgan looked from Hannigan to the serviceman installing the phone to remind the major they were dealing with classified information. Hannigan was too dense, too wound up to get the drift.

"So they take the case away from me and put a *captain* on it. I hear you're some sort of ten-dollar cop in civvy life. A real crime buster."

Humor him, Morgan told himself. *He is the superior officer here.* It was his rational voice talking. But there was another voice, his own anger, talking to him, as well. *You made it clear you weren't working with this pig farmer. Adams knows that. Adams needs you, not this pumpkin-headed idiot.*

Morgan clenched his jaw, chewing on his anger for a moment longer.

"Is there a question here, Major? Can I help you somehow?"

Hannigan's beet red turned to an enraged purplish color.

"You insubordinate little shit."

Morgan turned to the communications man. "Will you please excuse us, Corporal?"

The man was happy to get out of there, stuffing his pliers

and wire cutters into side pockets of his cargo pants with the alacrity of a shoplifter at a Macy's white sale. He didn't wait on the other side of the door, either, but headed down the hall to a neutral corner.

Morgan waited for the door to close in back of him, then eyed Hannigan with a cold, level stare. He'd been dealing with bullies like Hannigan all his life. Now he was just flat-out tired of dealing.

"A little bit of truth time here, Major. I've been assigned this case, whether you like it or not, because you've proven yourself incompetent, unimaginative, and irresponsible."

"I'll have you up on charges, you little kike bastard."

Morgan stilled his fists. "You know, you really should watch that fat mouth of yours. Okies like you give it away every time by the language. Did you know that? You want to trade racial slurs, fine. Let's do it. Go cry to Adams—he's the one who fired your sorry ass."

The bravado was leaking out of the man now.

Morgan shrugged. "I'm only advising you here, Hannigan, if you understand what I mean. You don't come blustering into a man's office threatening to have him up on charges unless you've got some authority. And frankly, Hannigan, you've got about as much authority left in Nuremberg as a dogcatcher. You should be thanking me—you probably are, but figure you've got to put on this outraged act, to defend your manhood, however questionable that is."

The pinched up anger on Hannigan's face was being replaced by a squint of suspicion.

"Don't think too much, Hannigan. It's bad for the brain. What I'm telling you is *I* know and *you* know that you're happy to be rid of this case. It's the sort of ballbuster that can ruin a man's career at your time of life. All you want is a comfortable position after the army bossing some small-town cop force, right? Maybe back in Texas where you can round up the Negroes and Mexicans when anything goes wrong and make the rest of the town happy. You're doing you're job. Am I right?"

61

Hannigan continued to peer at him like he was some kind of modern devil. Morgan figured his guesses were all too close to the truth.

"And here you are handed a case of multiple homicide and you don't even know what the hell that is, do you? You haven't been doing squat with this case, so you should thank my ass, pardon the expression, instead of barging in here wanting to kick it. I'm taking the heat off of you. You're out of the loop; you're safe. No egg on your face."

"I did my best," Hannigan finally protested. But there was little conviction to it.

"I'm sure you did," Morgan said flatly. Bear baiting was fun only when the bear remained enraged. "I've got your files on the case and I'll go over them tonight. If I've got questions . . ."

"Yeah, sure," Hannigan said, his fists still clenched. Morgan wondered if he slept that way.

"This Manhof. How is he?" Morgan knew how to play good cop, bad cop. Complicity now. A little bridge building.

Hannigan snorted. "Shit, he's a German, what am I going to say?"

"Does he know what he's doing?"

"Said he was going to be checking out the black-market angle, the DP camps."

Morgan nodded. In other words, the usual suspects. *Let's hope it's that simple*, he told himself.

"I'll have a talk with him."

Hannigan nodded. "Yeah. You do that."

The man is pitiful, Morgan thought. *Doesn't know how to extricate himself.* Bluster gone, he had nothing left.

"Well, thanks for stopping by, Major Hannigan. You've been helpful. Colonel Adams emphasized the necessity for a smooth transition."

A crisp salute, which Hannigan automatically returned, and then he was gone. Morgan poked his head out the office, spied the communications man lurking down the far end of the hall, and waved him back in.

"Don't worry, Corporal," Morgan reassured him as he reentered the office. "All clear now."

"Yes, sir."

There wasn't much in Hannigan's files. Seemed the major had delegated most of the investigation to Manhof. It took a map for Morgan to find his way to the Kripo office. They were even farther afield from the prosecution people than he was. Manhof was gone for the day—it was after six—but his desk sergeant, a fellow named Hoffman, was on hand. He looked skeptical about Morgan taking the files, but a call to Hannigan's office convinced him. Morgan smiled at the worried bureaucrat as he gathered up the evidence bags, the folders, the lists, even Manhof's notes on the case, and packed them into a wooden crate for the trip back along the labyrinth of hallways to his own office.

The Palace of Justice was not a place in which Morgan would like to spend the night—dimly lit hallways, the ghosts of other criminals. He knew that Gestapo had its offices there during the war, and imagined there were interrogation rooms that still had the smell of fear and death in them. Not much heat in the wing, either—infrastructure was a mess in the city and what little there was in the way of amenities was reserved for those developing the prosecution case. The closest office to Morgan's was that of the German defense counselor for Kaltenbrunner, the scar-faced SD chief who'd replaced Heydrich, which let Morgan know how low the murders he was supposed to be investigating were on the priority list at Nuremberg.

Gloomy thoughts, though Morgan was anything but gloomy. He was playing games with himself, trying to reign in his own excitement. His work in Switzerland had been demanding enough, even dangerous at times, but truth be told he had missed investigation. There was a part of him that would always be a cop.

Getting back to his office, he set the crate down on one of the desks and started to go through the files, to familiarize himself with the killer who had cut the throats of three servicemen thus far, the most recent, a French lieutenant, just last night.

By eight fifteen, his eyes hurt—he would need more lighting in his office, which had no exterior windows—he was cold, and he was famished. He took care of the last of these infirmities in the canteen near the courtroom on the first floor. Some lukewarm soup with bits of greasy ham hock floating in it, a plate full of beans and more ham—which he left partially unfinished—some sliced white bread and margarine, and the cavity in his belly was filled. Two scalding cups of coffee warmed him up. Eyestrain was a different matter, but he figured some streetwork might counteract that.

According to Hannigan's notes, they were proceeding under the assumption that the murders were black market related. This assumption had been called into question with the death of the French lieutenant, who had no apparent links to such traffic. Nothing found on the body; nothing found on the scene. Of course, that did not mean the killer had not simply taken away such evidence.

So it was a matter of process of elimination. Go through the obvious motives, eliminate them one by one until you came to one that could not be eliminated. Gruntwork detection. Tomorrow, Morgan and the staff he had yet to recruit would requestion all those who knew the victims, look for any common threads between the three. Try to establish a link, a pattern to the murders. Try to decipher just what the hell the importance of the pages from a book was. But tonight, Morgan could work on a lead that Manhof had on a "to-do" list.

He was right: The street was a palliative to the eyestrain. Too much buttwork lately—Morgan missed investigating in the field. He felt better just getting into the requisitioned jeep—with a roof for protection from the elements and booby traps—and turning on the ignition. According to some notes in Manhof's file, one of the centers of Nuremberg black-market activity was near the old Hauptmarkt. Good sense of irony there. The old central market. It, like most of the rest of

Nuremberg, now lay in ruins. Morgan drove his jeep down the Fürther Strasse toward the middle of town, along the darkened streets. His headlights cast ghoulish shadows on the fragments of buildings left standing to both sides of the road. He crossed the Pegnitz by the Fleischbrücke, one of the few bridges left standing in the city, and parked by the bombed-out ruins of the Frauenkirche, then set out on foot for his destination.

Morgan was a student of history; he knew that this was the one-time ghetto of Nuremberg before the expulsion of Jews in the fourteenth century; that the church there was built on the foundations of the old synagogue. More irony for those in search of it.

Morgan could not quite accustom himself to the level of destruction that confronted him each time he set foot into the streets of the city. Not just a building destroyed here or there, but entire blocks of buildings reduced to rubble. Everywhere the eye looked were the crumbling facades of buildings, like a Wagnerian stage set of the *Götterdämmerung*. Not a straight architectural angle left in the city. Not in the center, at any rate. Churches, bridges, public buildings, and apartment houses all in ruins.

The Hauptmarkt was deserted that time of night. At least it appeared so at first sight. Then, as Morgan continued walking along the perimeter, women beckoned from the remains of doorways or from behind the edge of half-destroyed walls. "*Du, Schatzi. Komm.* We will have some fun."

They looked like wraiths in the gloom, their faces haggard and drawn from hunger; the daily food allowance was barely enough to keep a person alive. He felt sudden shame at the beans and ham he had left on his plate at the canteen. More food than any of these women had seen today, in all likelihood.

One of the women displayed a wizened and sagging breast to him; another lifted her skirts to show him bare skin above bagged-out silk stockings. The sight of the woman's pubic hair was shocking. The main market had become a meat market of the basest sort.

He hurried past the women—there were a dozen or so in all—telling himself that he would not retrace his steps past them to return to his jeep. Near where the square exited into the Burg Strasse, just opposite the Schöner Brunnen memorial, which had miraculously not been destroyed, Morgan found what he was looking for. A crude shack had been built on a section of wasteland just off the main square.

Brazen, he thought. According to Manhof's notes, this was an ad hoc administrative center for Nuremberg's black market. The Germans owned the streets at night—at least that's what Manhof's report had to say about it—and the Allies were complicit in this: They could not supply enough food, clothing, or other essential materials. It was felt that the black market was at least a market. The raw edge of capitalism, but capitalism nonetheless. Distribution was distribution. So this little shack with its activity was known of, but allowed to exist, so long as things did not get out of hand. So long as they policed themselves and did not start some turf war.

The uneven flicker of lantern or candlelight showed through heavily waxed paper that served as a window in the top portion of the door. The shack had been assembled from salvage: The walls were put together from what looked to be the sides of carts; the roof was a strip of metal crudely ripped along the edges; the door was elegant enough to have come from a city palace.

He had no need to knock; the door opened as he approached. There were chinks between the sections of wood that made up the walls providing peepholes to the outside. There was no surprise to his visit.

"Good evening, Colonel." A ragged little man stood in the doorway, blocking Morgan's entrance. Like a caricature of a refugee, he wore rags around his feet and a winter coat at least two sizes too large for him. His head was enormous for such a small body, and his grizzled beard and salt-and-pepper hair seemed about the same length. The man gave the impression of a midget with a bowling ball on his shoulders.

"May I help you, Colonel?"

It was the Bavarian custom to inflate one's rank, Morgan knew. An old trick of cabbies and butchers to cadge a tip. For another mark, he'd make Morgan a general.

"No need for compliments, friend," Morgan said in his rather formal, rather Swiss-inflected German. "I'm not here for goods, but for information."

The gnome did not appear surprised at Morgan's use of the language. Instead, he expelled breath in an exaggerated sigh that almost knocked Morgan over with the halitosis reek it carried with it. Not just the stink of unwashed teeth, but the deep, internal stink of organic illness and decay.

"Well, I've none of the former and scant little of the latter, so it is fortunate for you . . . Captain."

Morgan caught the trace of a smile on the man's globular face.

"Let's be straight here," Morgan said. "I haven't come to cause you trouble. Business is business, no? What I need to know is if there has been a little competition lately. Some animosity, shall we say, between suppliers?"

The little man puffed his lips. "Information can be an expensive commodity."

Morgan shook his head. The same the world over. He looked over both his shoulders in turn before reaching into his wallet, drawing out a crisp five-dollar note, and handing it to the man. The gnome took it delicately between forefinger and thumb, closing his eyes as he tested the texture of the paper, the rub of the ink.

"I'm not passing counterfeit," Morgan said.

The man opened his eyes with something near shock registering in them.

"Nor would I accuse you of such, Captain. I just love the feel of money, you see. Something of a hobby of mine. And two such fine pieces of paper rub together far better than one. Like making love—always done better in company."

When he smiled, he showed black pegs where his front teeth should have been.

Morgan drew out another five-dollar bill and handed it over.

"Lovely," the man said.

"Now can we talk?"

"But of course." But he did not move from the threshold; their discussion would be held *alfresco*.

"About competition. Freelancers."

"Yes." The man had to pull himself out a reverie with the dollars; they could buy him several weeks' worth of food. "The person you really should talk with would be a chap called Rollo. Very knowledgeable is Rollo."

"And where might I find Herr Rollo?" Morgan peered into the shack over the man's head.

"Oh, not here, I'm afraid. In fact, he is currently a guest of yours. I mean of the Americans, in general. Kripo arrested him several days ago. Last I heard, he was in the Palace of Justice."

November 16, 1945

The next morning, Morgan was still smarting from the wild-goose chase to the Hauptmarkt. He'd taken one of the bills back from the gnome before leaving. It had made the man squeal, and the whores had berated him as he hurried back through the main square, forgetting his resolution to avoid them on his return to the jeep. He'd gone home from there, to his billet at the Grand Hotel. Not as grand as it sounded—a former maid's room at the top of the establishment. In the daytime, he could see sky through his partially demolished ceiling, and had to put numerous pots and pans about the floor whenever it rained. And it was tiny. Morgan was only five feet nine, but still he kept knocking his head on the cantilevered ceiling at one end of the room. But at least it was a place to rest his hat at night.

He was back at the Palace of Justice by seven thirty in the morning. It had been too late to check on that Rollo fellow last night, and now he could conference with Manhof at Kripo before going to the cells. That's what the old buzzard had told him last night: Kripo had lifted Rollo. But there had been no mention of Rollo in Manhof's notes.

Manhof was at his office early, too. A good sign. Introductions were made, a tepid handshake, but intelligence showed behind the man's eyes. *Maybe this is a man I can work with*, Morgan thought. Such hopes were soon dashed, however, when he questioned Manhof about Rollo.

"How was I to know Hannigan would be removed from the case?" Manhof's tone was defensive, obviously so, even to himself. He tried to soften it with: "Major Hannigan put the case largely in my, how do you say, thighs?"

"Lap," Morgan offered, but was not amused by the linguistic slip. He had the feeling that Manhof knew the idiom perfectly well and was only trying to score points. Beneath the inspector's somewhat fawning façade, Morgan thought he detected something harder.

"Yes, lap. Of course. Thus, what notes I had were rather for myself, you see."

"I'm not blaming anyone here," Morgan said. "I just wanted to know about the Rollo matter. What've we got on him? Why was he lifted?"

"Not much I can tell you there, I'm afraid. Especially now that he is dead."

"What?"

"You didn't know?" Manhof turned his limpid eyes on Morgan, all innocence.

"No. I only heard about the man last night. Now he's dead?"

"Cyanide. A rather clumsy mistake by the guards, it would seem. They somehow overlooked a capsule he must have brought in with him."

"What was he in for?"

"Conspiracy, of course. In the transport of the Jews. Rollo was an infamous street snitch in his day. He could tell you the whereabouts of any criminals who had gone underground, as the Jews did during those insane times. Submarines."

Morgan shook his head, unfamiliar with the term.

"That is what the Jews who had gone underground were called. 'Submarines.' Rollo liked to call himself the 'Depth

Charge.' He could sniff out anybody. Did quite well for himself with the Gestapo."

"But he also had a connection to the black market?"

"Of course. Rollo was connected to anything that had illegality attached to it. Imagine a magnet and its attraction for iron filings. That was our Rollo vis-à-vis criminal activities."

"And what did you get out of him about possible turf wars?"

Manhof shrugged, an expansive gesture for this otherwise motionless creature.

"He was not, shall we say, forthcoming."

"So you squeezed him by arresting him on these old charges. A bargaining chip."

"That is one possible interpretation."

"Why wasn't he picked up before, then? You obviously knew where to find him."

"Manpower, Captain. That is our great difficulty in the new Germany. We do not have enough of it. Of men, there are a multitude, of the able-bodied . . ."

Another shrug.

Morgan suddenly did not like the man. The mole on Manhof's left cheek was a problem; Morgan found his eyes continually wandering to it. Where else to focus on the man's nondescript face? But it was far more than the man's features. Manhof was the obsequious sort, the passive-aggressive type. He spoke politely, but underneath, Morgan understood that the hardness he'd discerned earlier was actually animosity. Morgan had experienced this so often in his life because of ethnicity that he always had to guard against the easy assumption. But it was not his Jewishness this time; more likely the fact that Manhof's case was being usurped. The ball was going back into the American court. Hannigan would have been a much better colleague for a man like Manhof, who could work around him, oil him, lie to him sweetly.

No. Morgan did not care for Chief Inspector Manhof. Which was too bad, he could use the help. He needed to fill out an investigative staff ASAP.

"And how far have you got on the DP angle?"

Manhof smiled at him with eyes that were partially dead.

"Again, Captain, we are three in this office."

"Interviews with colleagues or friends of the victims?"

Another shrug. "The Russians have been less than cooperative."

Morgan did not say what he was thinking, what he had said
to Hannigan: *What the fuck have you been doing then?* Instead, he
nodded.

"I'll get back to you." In the next millennium.

Manhof titled his head by way of response. "Any assistance
we can provide . . ."

Morgan didn't wait for the rest.

Manhof watched Morgan make his way out of the overfreighted
office.

He did not like the looks of the American. It was not just
that Manhof was racist. Sure, he could tell the man was a Jew,
but it had nothing to do with that.

No, it was worse.

It appeared the man had brains. Even spoke a modicum of
German, with a Swiss accent no less—which also worried Manhof. Switzerland meant espionage. This Captain Morgan had
more to him than he let on.

So close now. Could a nothing like Rollo really begin to unravel
the carefully laid plans?

A nonentity. A blank.

Rollo.

He bit the inside of his cheek hard enough to draw blood.
He did not even realize he was doing it until he tasted the brass
of blood in his mouth.

Men talk in prison. They have cellmates; they have buddies
watching their backs in the yard. Some of them are so eager
to talk, they'll bend your ear waiting in the chow line. At least
that's how it was in Sing Sing. Morgan figured some things did
not differ with a change of borders.

One handy thing about the Palace of Justice: The prisons were in the wings to the back of the main building. It took Morgan half an hour to track down Sergeant Willie Cooper, who had been lead watch the day Rollo died. He was on break, hunched over a low table that was about big enough for a kindergarten student, warming his meaty paws around a steaming metal cup of coffee.

"No," Cooper told him, "the prisoners did not have bunkies. Solo suites here."

Of course. Morgan should have known that from his own questioning of prisoners. But Rollo must have talked with somebody, hung out with one prisoner in particular.

"Now that you mention it, the boy did have a little conference that day in the yard." Cooper blew ripples on the surface of the scalding coffee.

"Could you hear what he was talking about?"

"Wouldn't have meant anything to me if I could've," Cooper said. "Speaking Kraut talk."

"You remember the other prisoner?"

Cooper took a timid sip of the coffee, his eyes instantly watering.

"Damn. The only thing they do heat around here and it'll take the roof of your mouth off."

"Sergeant?"

"Yeah. He's one of those politicals. The guys you've been talking to."

"Name?"

Cooper blew out moist air to indicate that was a pretty dumb request.

"How about cell number?"

"Sure."

Cooper gave him the number and Morgan was halfway out the door when the sergeant said, "Saves the taxpayers the trouble."

Morgan thought about it; no reply was necessary.

"We must stop meeting like this," Beck said to him as Morgan came in the cell.

Morgan did not feel in the mood for polite banter.

"I hear that a criminal named Rollo was talking to you in the yard the day he died."

Beck directed his right hand to the hardback chair and seated himself on the cot.

"We shared a few words, yes."

"He's dead, you know. Poisoned himself."

"I saw," Beck told him, pointing to the door's view slot.

"Manhof tells me this Rollo was a major snitch. That he sniffed out underground Jews for the Gestapo."

Beck considered this. "Is that a question?"

"Did he?"

"If Manhof says so. He is the chief inspector now, after all."

"*Did* he?" Morgan repeated.

Beck sighed. "Our friend Rollo was capable of about anything. Except bodily harm. He didn't go in for that sort of thing. I mean, not personally."

Morgan was silent for a moment, trying to put things together.

"May I ask what your interest in Rollo is, Captain? Surely, you were not trying to recruit a man such as he. America cannot be that desperate."

Morgan ignored this. "What did you talk about?"

"It was quite brief. In fact, Rollo indicated he had information that he might want to sell to you folks. Information that others badly wanted. Rollo always had information for sale. Expensive information. Rollo had a high opinion of his sources."

"You had connections with him before?"

"Before the war, yes. He was a long-time *employee* of Kripo. Not in our pocket, mind you, but when it suited him, when the price was right, he could deliver information. Not always reliable, though."

"And the nature of this information he might have had for sale?"

Beck sucked his teeth in a *tssk*-ing sound. "The guard on duty would not let us talk any further. I assume they are afraid that we will plot a breakout. Escape to where, I ask."

"Anybody else you know with connections to the black market?"

"You have a large number of questions for me, Captain, yet you ignore the only one I have for you. What is your interest in Rollo? He was not really such a remarkable creature, after all. A common hoodlum, in fact."

"I need information on the black market. I was told he was the man to see."

"So your duties in Nuremberg have changed? You are now playing policeman, cracking down on the horrible black market. Searching for the German Al Capone. Well, he doesn't exist, Captain. Except for those men that go on trial next week. Those are our versions of Al Capone. The well-regulated society, you see, must have its criminals as heads of state. We could not allow crimes of their magnitude to go forward in the private sector. State-sanctioned violence, Captain. That is what we Germans are famous for."

Morgan sat listening to Beck go on, watching him closely. *He's a cop, all right*, Morgan told himself. And one with a philosophical bent. It was the same sort of self-irony Morgan's father used on himself when he was disgusted that a criminal was getting the better of him.

"And no, to answer your question at long last. I have lost contact with the situation here in Nuremberg from long absence. I have no connections to the black market."

Morgan continued looking hard at him. He'd read the man's file again after their last meeting.

"Rollo was your snitch. He was in here for turning in Jews. You're in here for turning in Jews. . . ."

"Ergo, I must have somehow magically killed the man so that he would not provide evidence against me. Is that it? Slipped him a little bar of chocolate laced with the poison of preference. I confess, Captain. You are too smart for me. You have discovered my awful secret. Arrest me."

Morgan suddenly had enough of all the dancing around. He reached his flash point.

"Shut up, okay. I'm not in the mood for jokes today. What is it with you people? You treat all this like it's a carnival. A big joke."

" 'You people,' meaning Germans? No it is no joke, Captain. I can assure you of that. But faced with certain unbearable facts, one tends to take refuge in the absurd. Haven't you ever found solace there?"

"My solace is tracking down criminals, Inspector."

"Ah, I knew it from our first meeting. Another policeman."

"I didn't think you claimed that distinction anymore. All too absurd for you."

Beck did not go on, but cast a more thoughtful look Morgan's way. They continued to stare at each other for several seconds. Beck broke it off first.

"There's not much help I can provide you, Captain."

"In fact, your refuge in the absurd has allowed you to be railroaded into prison. Made you so helpless that you have to accept food from your aging mother when it should be you helping her."

"You *have* been doing your research, Captain."

"Three years in intelligence makes a man obsessive about information. You can never really have enough. Never know enough."

"Information and knowledge are separate things, Captain."

"One can lead to the other. For example, you tell me that Rollo did not go in for the bodily harm stuff personally. Sounds like a physical coward to me. And physical cowards do not take their own lives. See, and you say you have no information for me." He smiled bitterly at Beck.

"I wondered about that, too," Beck said, suddenly thoughtful. "Rollo was, to be sure, a physical coward. He told me he was being held under protective custody, which means Manhof was probably trying to squeeze him for information using the conspiracy charge as leverage. But that's a powerful indictment in Nuremberg, Captain, even if trumped up. And in Rollo's case, it was probably true. It's a charge that can bring the death sentence. And fear of the hangman's noose can inspire bizarre behavior."

"Doubtful he was going to swing. Not any more than you."

A slight nod from Beck. "But Rollo was the panicky sort."

"Did you do it?"

Beck looked up at him. "Kill Rollo? Please."

Morgan shook his head. "Turn over Jews to the Gestapo?"

Beck squinted at the far wall, unlocking his eyes from Morgan. "No more so than other policemen," he said after long silence. "Kripo, for the most part, was kept out of that operation." Beck once again focused on Morgan. "Gestapo didn't want to share the fun."

Morgan was not expecting quite so blunt an answer. But there was reassurance in Beck's brutal honesty.

"Millions have died, Captain. Why do you concern yourself with this one minor criminal? Can you really care that much about the black market? It serves, after all, a minor distributive purpose."

Morgan thought for a moment, then said to himself, *The hell with it*, and went with his instincts.

"I'm going to take a chance on you, Beck. I need some help, and you clearly need a life. I'm going to tell you something that does not go beyond the walls of this cell, not unless you personally go beyond these walls with it."

Without waiting for Beck's agreement, he told him what he knew, laying out the murders in strict chronological order, filling in all the details he could remember, and those were numerous.

Beck sat listening in silence, nodding every now and again at some detail, rubbing his knuckles over a three-day growth of beard.

When he was finished, Morgan looked at Beck closely.

"So. You interested?"

"What is it you're offering?"

"For you to be a cop again. To get out of here, for the time being anyway."

"Sounds as if I'm exchanging jailers."

"Plus your mother gets out of the DP camp, has a clean room in a woman's hostel, regular food."

"So much information, Captain. Your head must ache at night."

"Is that a yes?"

Beck nodded. "I admit it is unseemly for a grown man to be receiving care packages from a woman so aged she must wrap her legs to hold in the varicose veins. I accept your offer, Captain."

PART II

November 16, 1945

Morgan had to create his own detective squad—it was that simple. There wasn't going to be any help from Manhof on this, or from Hannigan. He could requisition the odd MP, but they were the sort of big-boned boys who were more comfortable keeping the peace than tracking down criminals. So he had to do it himself.

He liked the challenge. He hadn't felt this alive since the end of the war, since his last mission into occupied France.

By that afternoon, he had secured Beck's release. Colonel Adams balked at first, but Morgan reminded him of his pledge of support: *Anything you need. Just ask.*

"Well, I need a pro here," he told Adams. Someone who knows the ground. Someone who has worked multiple murders before—but this he did not tell Adams, did not mention to Beck, even. That was the assumption he was beginning to work under: that these three murders were only the beginning. And Beck was one of the best men in Europe on such cases, had lectured at Interpol in Brussels on the subject before the war. Morgan had done his homework.

"He could be a war criminal," Adams had countered.

"Aren't we all?"

So he got his man, and by four that afternoon, Beck was seated in quite another part of the Palace of Justice, freshly scrubbed and shaved and fitted out in khakis, out of which his white wrists jutted and ankles showed, and which bagged on his shoulders and hips. It was all Morgan could come up with for clothing at short notice; the man could not go about the office in his striped flannel prison outfit.

But Beck was not complaining. He set to reading the files gathered thus far, occasionally looking up at Morgan with squinting eyes, shaking his head.

Morgan had not said anything to Beck about the possibility of a multiple murderer simply because he wanted the man to draw his own conclusions. *What we have here are three deaths, some similarities in MO, some possible connections to the black market. Let him take it from there,* Morgan figured.

"Busy man," Beck finally said, sitting back in his chair. "Three murders in one week. All of them men, and all of them armed, it appears. Implication?"

Morgan nodded at him. "Right. That's confirmed by Haskell's report." He tossed photos of the wounds to Beck across the table from him. "Notice the depth of wound from the victims' rights to lefts. They're deeper at the right, at the point of incision, and the skin then feathers out toward the exit on the left, where the wound is also shallower."

Beck looked closely at the photos and the accompanying medical examiner's reports on all three victims.

"Consistent with a frontal slash," Beck said after a moment's consideration. "You take a man from the back, and the exit end will be much deeper than entrance. You'd be pulling the blade toward yourself at the end, no matter which hand you used."

"Right. So these victims saw the perpetrator coming at them."

"There was trust," Beck said. "No fear. No expectation that they were about to die. No struggle."

"No *indication* of a sign of a struggle at any of the scenes.

Then again, I didn't get a chance to see the crime scenes, either. But at the very least, there was no evidence that any of the victims even made an effort to draw their weapons."

"A meeting, someone they knew or trusted," Beck said, still gazing at the black-and-white glossies of the ruined necks. "Someone who could get close enough to them to do this."

"That might support the black market angle," Morgan said, thinking out loud.

Beck made a noncommittal humming sound.

Morgan didn't believe it, either, but didn't like Beck's attitude.

"If you have a better suggestion, please share."

"What about victim number three? At work on the French prosecution case, they tell us." Beck picked up the flimsy on the French victim provided by the French military authority. "Lieutenant Jean Grammond, twenty-nine, of Poitiers, France," he read. "A law clerk researching documents pertaining to war crimes." He looked up from the paper to Morgan. "This does not sound like black-market involvement. And he was found in a totally different area than the other two. South of the Pegnitz this time, near the main train station."

"A mistake, perhaps." Morgan offered, playing devil's advocate. "The wrong victim?"

"Everything is possible, my friend."

It was said like a dismissal.

"Alternate theories then," Morgan prompted.

"Well, I see Manhof and this Major Hannigan proposed rousting the DP camps for possible lunatics. Which displays their deductive abilities quite well. One would assume those poor wretches would be killing Germans, not Allied soldiers."

"Anything is possible, my friend," Morgan mimicked.

"Point taken. What seems more likely to me, however, is a Werwolf lead. I see this mentioned in Major Hannigan's report, too. I heard rumors in prison. These men are real. Insane, perhaps, but all too real."

"There was Franz Oppenhoff, the mayor of Aachen," Morgan remembered aloud. "Murdered in March because of his 'collaboration' with the occupying forces. And last month a GI with his head cut off by their piano-wire booby traps."

"So we take them seriously," Beck agreed. "And then there are these rather bizarre calling cards left behind by the murderer." Beck picked them out of the litter of other papers on the table.

"I think there may be a crude code involved in the underlined words," Morgan told him. "I haven't had a chance to examine them more closely."

"We need to find their origin. Perhaps there is a meaning in the book they came from. Or, perhaps it is, as our predecessors thought, merely a false trail to keep us from the obvious—black-market turf battles."

"And," added Morgan, "we need to rule out our Frenchman's involvement in any way with the black market."

"But we have to have more manpower to do that," Beck said. "I think I know somebody that might interest you. A fellow by the name of Imhofer. Wieland Imhofer."

Morgan nodded, waiting for more, staring at the German.

"What?" asked Beck.

"What do your instincts tell you?"

"You surprise me, Captain. I did not believe modern American forensics took instincts into account."

Morgan did not take the bait. He sat silently, waiting for more.

"Well," Beck finally responded, "I now understand why you wanted me. I've got experience with this sort of thing, haven't I?"

"What sort of thing would that be?"

"Multiple murderers, of course. And yes, to your unspoken question. I think our murderer will kill again. And again and again, until we stop him."

November 17, 1945

Wieland Imhofer was sitting in the office Saturday morning when Morgan arrived. He and Beck were having a friendly chat over wurst sandwiches, the smell of which almost turned Morgan's stomach. Nobody should eat garlic before eight in the morning.

It was pouring down outside, and Morgan tossed his sodden cap and coat onto a free chair. No coat or hat racks yet. If they were lucky, there wouldn't be enough time for such amenities. Imhofer's left sleeve was pinned to his shoulder; there was air where his arm should have been. *A vet*, Morgan told himself. Imhofer looked too old for this war, but then, toward the end, Morgan knew, Hitler was taking them out of the old folks homes, out of the Realschule, and giving them guns for which there were scant bullets.

Morgan extended a hand to the man. "Captain Morgan," he introduced himself.

Imhofer rose with effort, bread crumbs rolling off his coat.

"*Es freut mich,*" he said.

Morgan glanced at Beck, who shrugged. "Wieland doesn't speak English. But then we do not need his services for English lessons."

Imhofer smiled at Morgan and continued chewing on the bun and wurst. The man was about as wide as he was tall and had the appearance of a down-at-heel gumshoe in New York. The sort who might share an office on the Upper West Side, with pipes that clanked in the winter and a permanent frost of grime on the windows.

Beck and Imhofer finished their repast and their discussion, and Imhofer, who never took his heavy coat off, stood, donned a crushed homburg, and bid Beck and the captain adieu.

"Wiedersehen, mein Herren," he said gaily as he left the office.

Morgan gave Beck a look as if over the frames of nonexistent reading glasses.

Beck smiled to reassure him. "Not to worry. I've detailed him onto the black-market angle. He knows the city. He knows the players. He'll produce."

"Just what kind of cop are we talking about here?" Morgan finally asked.

"Wieland was in private practice before the war."

"Practice, as in medicine?"

Beck smiled at this, finishing the last of his bun and wurst, moistening a fingertip to blot up every last crumb on the table.

"As in private detective."

Morgan groaned.

"Not to worry," Beck said again. "As in a very competent private detective. His caseload is full now with all the missing persons, but he's agreed to help us out on this."

"How much did you tell him?"

"Enough."

"You do remember this case is on a need-to-know basis? It's not to get out to the press."

"Wieland needed to know, okay? Besides, he has a linkage of operatives throughout Germany. In the absence of any real official policing going in Germany now, men like Wieland are invaluable. And best of all, he has his own farm just outside of

Nuremberg. Fine sausage, he and his wife put up. Sorry I did not have any to share."

"Don't mention it. Not quite my meat of choice. And what kind of detective runs a farm on the side?"

Beck shrugged. "Is there a law that they must be hard-drinking loners? Wieland's a family man." Beck laughed at a thought. "Eight children. Can you imagine?"

"It must have been hard on his family when he got called up."

"Wieland? In the army? Hardly."

"What happened to his arm?"

"Oh, that," Beck said. "That was back in 'thirty-two, three. Somewhere in there. Caught in a winch. No, Wieland had a fine war on his farm."

So much for my deductive powers, Morgan told himself. "I think it's time for a drive," he said.

Neuenhausen Displaced Persons Camp was six miles to the south of the city. The rain was coming down hard all through the drive, bouncing off the canvas top of the jeep, whipping into their faces occasionally by sudden gusts of wind. Beck did not hold out much promise for this line of investigation. Yes, the inmates, or rather inhabitants, of the camp were close enough to Nuremberg to get into the city, even by foot. Searching for one madman among those thousands would be, however, like looking for the proverbial *nadel im heuhaufen*, needle in a haystack. But still it felt good to be on the road, to be out of the ruined city. To see buildings standing whole and undamaged for a change.

Beck looked at the gray landscape unfolding outside the jeep like some black-and-white travelogue at the cinema— something to precede the latest sunny offering from Hollywood. Suddenly, he felt a lightness he had not experienced since he was a young man off to university in Heidelberg. Dressed in his clownlike American fatigues, he was suddenly a person out of time. The ghosts of the bombed-out city were left behind for the moment; their sadness dissipated by a sudden liberation from all that history. All that weight of former lives.

Suddenly, he remembered a gilt relief that had been in the ceiling of the reading room of Nuremberg's main library. It depicted the reclining figure of Roland, squire to one of the Habsburg princes whom the honest servant had persuaded *not* to spend the night in the amorous arms of some scheming minor baroness. Roland had persuaded said prince by staying up all night drinking with him, imbibing amounts so plentiful as to destroy all royal amatory impulses, passing out three times while the legless prince drank on, and rousing himself back to his duties each time. Thus *Dreimal Roland*, "Three-times" Roland as he was thereafter dubbed, saved, in all likelihood, much of the Habsburg wealth, for the baroness in question was already pregnant with another man's—a very poor man's—child.

For that antipriapic service, Three-times Roland had been knighted. Beck had never been able to study in that library's large reading room, never been able to place his books on the aged oak tables with the individual brass reading lights, without first looking up at Roland and smiling secretly to himself. That such a service should earn such an honor.

Now the reclining Roland was gone, obliterated just like his namesake, Rollo. Memories were thick in Nuremberg. Bombs had erased—released—some. Today, this morning, this moment, there was a feeling of freedom because of it.

Suddenly, Beck remembered something else. The first time he'd met Morgan, the man's cherubic face had reminded him of certain frescoes by Masaccio, yet he could not for the life of him remember the name of the church where they were. Now that name came to him like the name of a long-lost school friend. The Brancacci Chapel of Santa Maria del Carmine in Florence. He wondered if the frescoes, or indeed the church, even existed any longer, or if they, like the reclining Roland, so tired after his night's labors, had been destroyed by a careless bomb. Perhaps his memory was the only thing left of either. He laughed at the thought.

Morgan took his eyes from the road for a moment.

"You want to share the joke?"

Beck shook his head. "Just life, Captain."

Knighthood for managing to wake up three times. Not a bad trade-off, Beck thought.

And suddenly, something else clicked in his brain, something that had been working on him, preying on him, and now made all too much sense.

"Hold on," Beck said. "We've got to go back."

Morgan kept driving.

"We need to stop," Beck said, grabbing for the wheel.

"What the hell's gotten into you?" Morgan brought the jeep to a stop by the rutted side of the road. In a field beyond them, a farmer was driving a horse in the wind and rain, hauling the remains of a tree trunk, and leaving a brown swath in the green field.

"It's just come to me. The timeline. We've got to get back to Nuremberg."

Morgan eyed him warily, like a wild animal that just might bite.

"The first murder was November eighth, right?" Beck said as they sat in the chuffing jeep at the side of the road.

Morgan nodded.

"And then there was one on the eleventh," Beck went on. "And on the fourteenth. Why didn't I see this earlier?"

"You make it sound like it's a bus schedule. You think he's working in three-day intervals?"

"It's one of the few tangibles we have in this case so far. Three murders, three days apart. Some of these sort of murderers enjoy a pattern. The crazy organization of it."

"Which puts his next one . . ."

"Right, Captain. Today, tonight most likely, under cover of darkness."

Morgan put the jeep in gear, turning around sharply on the narrow road, bumping up and over the verge as he did so.

Beck's voice was suddenly deflated: "But what are we supposed to do about it? Close down the whole city? We can't very well impose curfew without tipping our hand to the media."

Morgan glanced sideways at him, a hint of grin on his face. "That may not be necessary, Inspector."

Kate took the offered piece of Black Forest cake gratefully, cut into it manfully with the edge of a silver fork bearing a coquille pattern at the tip of its handle. She ate with eyes closed, loving the tastes exploding in her mouth. Only a week in Nuremberg, and already she felt deprived of the good things in life.

The baroness smiled at her hearty appetite.

"You like it?"

Kate opened her eyes, beaming at Baroness von Prandtauer.

"*Like* is too mild a word. *Love* approximates my emotions at this minute."

The baroness gave an open-mouth laugh at this.

"We'll make it your wedding cake, then."

"Where do you manage the eggs?" Kate asked.

The baroness was seated across from her in what she referred to as the drawing room, in the British fashion. Heavily draped windows, massive oak furniture, and creaking parquet covered in wine red rugs; the room had a Victorian feel to it. She looked at Kate with large brown eyes, lifting her high brows conspiratorially.

"We have our ways, Miss Wallace."

They ate in a refined silence for a time. The baroness's invitation to Saturday tea had seemed a nuisance to Kate when first proffered. She could hardly refuse; after all, the woman was her landlady, so to speak. However, now, seated there with the woman, Kate felt strangely at home and at peace. The cake seemed an invitation to more than mere food. And Kate badly needed such creature comfort at the time. It had been a lousy week.

Jensen's lead about the Werwolf brigades had come to nothing. She had spent days tracking down the informant at GHQ, a man who, when finally encountered, treated her condescendingly, telling her that women didn't need to know about certain things. A throwback to a time when, perhaps, dinosaurs roamed the earth, Jensen's supposed informant was stolidly silent, angry that Jensen had given her his name. And Jensen was back in England now, so there was no leverage from that quarter. Kate had taken the lead as far as she could on her own, even insinuating herself at the local offices of the German Criminal Police, Kripo, asking after possible Werwolf-related incidents, but the man in charge there, a creepy little worm by the name of Manhof, was decidedly uncooperative and unforthcoming.

She finally had to write off three days of research as a dead end. There was a story there, she knew, but she could not get to it. Wearing trousers instead of a skirt, she would have gotten something. That was the most frustrating part of it all. She had been trained at the best schools, had brazened her way through an apprenticeship with one of the best editors in New York—Ed Sloan had worked with Mencken, had copyedited early Hemingway dispatches from Rapallo. And yet it signified nothing if she could not get the news, if people would not open up to her.

A week in Nuremberg and all she had to show for it was one impressionistic piece on the shattered city. What any cub reporter could turn out in an afternoon's noodling around on the typewriter.

The rest of the American press corps took her as a dilettante, she knew, not least because of her cushy billet. The male journalists had been solicitous when she showed up for the first noontime briefing at the Palace of Justice. Several of them wouldn't mind bedding her, and had told her so quite bluntly. Others obviously knew of her father, and did not want to risk getting on his bad side; these were servile, but contemptuous toward her. Others, who had neither items on their agenda, simply looked sorry for her: poor girl out of her depth on an international assignment. The other women journalists were the worst; they held her youth and connections against her. They took her for an ornament, not even worth the bother of an introduction.

A spot had been reserved for her in the pressroom at the Palace of Justice, between the correspondent for the *Times* on her left and the one for *The New Leader* on her right. Both seemed to believe that the pile of typewriter paper by her Underwood was their individual property. She had not a single piece of paper left to stick in her carriage.

But that did not really matter, as she had no story to file, anyway.

So much for her chance of a lifetime.

"Do help yourself to more cake or coffee," the baroness said, bringing Kate back to the here and now.

"It's really wonderful," Kate said. "I can't tell you how glad I am you invited me."

Muffled noises came from the dining room where two other occupants of the villa—a British woman, Beth, working as a translator, and an American lawyer, William Stanton— were having *their* Saturday tea of day-old rolls. Kate could hear through the closed door of the drawing room as the lawyer prepared to speak, clearing his nasal passages each time with a plosive burst of air through his nostrils. He made a *khhnn* sound when he did so, which quite took away from his pomposity. "William, but never Bill," is how he had introduced himself to Kate, forgetting that they had already met aboard the flight from London.

Neither of them interested Kate other than as caricatures, and obviously, the baroness felt the same way, for *they* had not been invited to afternoon coffee. The tiny rosewood table— inlaid with the same coquille insignia as on the silverware—was laid for two. The baroness merely raised her eyebrows at the murmurs from the next room.

"What wonderful story are you working on, Kate?" The baroness smiled at her with liquid gray-green eyes, which appeared all the larger with her blonde hair pulled back in a low bun. There was just the trace of a wrinkle or two at the corners of each of her eyes, and several more perpendicular to her bottom lip. Otherwise, her skin—of an olive hue that certain Germans had—was quite lovely. Kate estimated that she was perhaps late thirties or early forties.

"The trial gets under way on the twentieth, so I'll be focusing on that, I suppose."

The baroness looked vaguely disappointed. "I haven't heard your typewriter the past few days."

"I am sorry," Kate said, misunderstanding. "I hadn't realized the sound carried so."

The baroness protested: "No, it is not a disturbance. I was only wondering, the first few days you seemed so eager. So energetic. But lately . . ."

"Well, there's research to be done." She did not want to go into her failure with the baroness. "Background workups on the defendants. That sort of thing."

Normally, speaking with a German about the upcoming trial, she would be more cautious, more circumspect. In fact, she would not even bring it up for fear on stepping on someone's toes, if not memories or loyalties. But with the baroness, there was no such second thinking. General von Prandtauer, the baroness's husband, had paid with his life for his role in the July 1944 coup attempt against Hitler. The Prandtauers were examples of the "good" Germans she had heard so little about during the war in America.

So why not write about such people? Kate asked herself. *The ones who had resisted.* While the monsters go on trial and claim most of the column inches, there needed to be a palliative, a sidebar to iniquity, so to speak. Not a bad title, Kate told herself: "The Good Germans."

" 'That sort of thing,' " the baroness repeated Kate's last phrase, nodding. "Yes, I suppose there will be all too much of that sort of thing in a few days."

"I didn't mean to sound so callous about it all," Kate said, feeling color come to her face. "It must be very hard for you."

The baroness shook her head. "Why me? All of Germany mourns."

"I mean your personal loss. Your husband."

The baroness brushed the suggestion aside with a flick of her right hand. "He was a soldier. He knew what to expect." Her wonderful eyes focused on the intermediate distance for a time. "It's my brother I truly mourn." Her eyes fixed on Kate again. "He was not a soldier at all, but an artist. Gerhard was a true artist, yet he was lost with all the others on the Russian front."

Kate watched the baroness's eyes close down slowly, as if the memory was too bright, too painful to see.

"But I will not bore you with my family tragedies."

She stood suddenly, moving gracefully in her simple cardigan and woolen skirt to the pull cord by the Delft-tiled fireplace. Another Victorian element: the servants' bell. A few moments after pulling the cord, an elderly, skeletal servant named Falk arrived at the door in a black suit, and the baroness requested another pot of coffee.

"One so rarely gets to spoil oneself," she said to Kate as the domestic retreated.

Again the smile, the sparkling eyes, and the catlike movement—surprising for such a tall woman—as she returned to the love seat where she ensconced herself, folding the pleats of the pearl gray skirt under her legs as she sat.

A handsome woman, Kate thought. Almost beautiful, and comfortably elegant in manner as well as movement. She was one of those women who made Kate feel that she was too loud, too clumsy, too tomboyish. Yet Kate felt a strange sort of attraction to the baroness, as to a teacher or older, wiser cousin. Her beatific smile hid much, Kate was sure. It could not have been easy for the baroness after the death of those closest to her.

They ate more cake and talked of the latest party at the Grand Hotel, wondering coyly together which general was sleeping with which stenographer. Kate usually did not take part in such *kaffee klatsch*, but the baroness made it seem like intellectual chatter, not simple gossip.

"But such affairs are hardly fit topics for your magazine. We do need to get you writing again, my dear. And not dreary old profiles of Field Marshal Göring."

They talked pleasantly for some time of life before the war, of the endless round of social evenings and summers at the Lido.

"I was quite the athlete as a young woman," the baroness confessed. "A real, how is it you say, Bill-boy?"

"Tomboy," Kate offered, feeling a sudden connection.

"Exactly. I could swim for miles, especially in the Adriatic. The warm, buoyant water. It was wonderful. My brother and I would play together for hours on summer vacation in the Alps, like wild Indians."

She suddenly caught herself, then smiled at Kate. "Here I go again, boring you with old memories."

"Not at all," Kate said.

With the second pot of coffee halfway consumed, the baroness surprised Kate with a sudden change of topic.

"Maybe there is another story for you. But no, you've probably heard rumors about them already. Who knows, they may only *be* rumors."

Kate put her coffee cup down. "What rumors?"

"Well, now I think of it, it sounds silly. I mean millions have died, haven't they? What's a few more to the total?"

"You're teasing me, Baroness." Kate shot her a winning smile. "What rumors?"

"Everyone seems to know, even though it is quite apparent the Control Commission is trying to keep things covered up." The baroness gave a coy look around the room as if searching for eavesdroppers. Then in almost a whisper: "Murders. In the streets of this city. Several of them, by all accounts, and quite gruesome, according to my friends."

Kate sat in bewildered silence. She had heard nothing about any murders in Nuremberg.

"You mean you haven't heard about them? Everyone's talking about them."

By noon, Morgan and Beck had been able to contact British forces in Nuremberg. Brigadier Charles Nelson agreed to give Morgan a skeptical five minutes of his time.

"First I've heard of it," he said after Morgan gave him the essentials of the investigation. The brigadier spluttered his words as if homicide were a distasteful latecomer to a dinner party. They sat in his frigid office drinking tea that could wither the sturdiest houseplant if poured over it.

"Can't see what it has to do with our boys, either," Nelson added testily. "They do not fraternize."

Morgan kept his patience in check and tried his best to explain the circumstantial evidence leading them to believe that a British soldier might be the target of a murder attempt tonight, November 17. It was as Morgan had explained to Beck before they turned around in their jeep that morning: They'd had a Russian, an American, and a Frenchman. It was as if the murderer was working his way through the Allies. Now it was very likely the turn of the British. Narrowed things down a bit. No need to confine the whole of Nuremberg to quarters tonight, just the Brits, or let them go out in pairs. No lone British soldiers on the streets tonight.

Nelson rubbed a knuckle over his short cut, bristling Sandhurst mustache and muttered, "Quite."

But he looked far from convinced.

Finally, Beck, still dressed in his impossible khakis without trace of insignia or stripes, jumped into the fray. Donning his best British accent he said: "It's not on, you know, sir. Deaths are a damned shame. Blight on the entire Control Commission."

Morgan gaped in disbelief at Beck's Colonel Blimp accent, but Nelson definitely paid more attention now, his beady eyes searching Beck's sleeve for some identifying marks. None found, he contented himself with head nods in Beck's direction.

"Poor show all round," Beck went on in his fulsome South

Counties accent. "We've been given top priority, don't you know?" A wink was followed by a forefinger to the nose—word to the wise. An exchange of secrets here. The nudge of conspiracy.

"Full powers. Full cooperation to be extended. Straight from General Clay. That would be General Lucius D. Clay."

He emphasized the "D" and for some reason this energized Nelson; sent him scurrying to the phone and demanding that his men be confined to barracks tonight. Only vital services to be allowed out, and those were to travel in pairs or larger groups.

Beck raised his eyes at Morgan as they listened to the bark of orders into the Bakelite telephone receiver. Then they refused a second cup of tea: The first was already eating a hole in Morgan's gut.

Hannigan had proved a harder nut to crack. It took a phone call from Colonel Adams to get him to provide twenty extra street patrols tonight. If Beck was right about this schedule, they would need the extra men to stop the murderer from striking a fourth time. By two thirty, that had been arranged.

Later that day, Beck and Morgan sat in the office at the Palace of Justice feeling like they had put in a good half-day's work. An orderly brought up a late lunch for them from the canteen, and they sat chewing in silence for a time.

A visitor showed up at two forty-five: Imhofer, the detective, back with a report for Beck. Meanwhile, Morgan had already set up the notes in front of him and began to work on various transpositions of the letters underlined on the book pages left with each victim, for he was certain those words held a coded message. He and Beck had already tried to decipher a message from the underlined words themselves, which had come to nothing. *Unklar, Hand, sterben.* Twelve of them in all on the page found with the first victim. Now he took the first letters of these underlined words—one of the most basic encoding techniques—and tried to gain some meaning from them.

Let's start with the simplest trick, he told himself. The first bit of spy lore he'd learned in Switzerland. He filled the rectangular grids of a decoding table with the first letters in the order they came on the page, a separate grid for each page the killer had left with his victims. The twelve were U-H-S-N-P-C-I-U-H-M-C-T. He worked on a single transposition cipher, listing the letters in a three by four rectangular grid, trying to ignore the discussion going on between Beck and his private detective, trying to withhold judgment on the use of the man at all. *After all,* Morgan reminded himself, *Beck was the one to see some pattern to the murders. That's why you brought him on, because he knows the ground here.*

He went back to his work. Placing the letters vertically into the grid in order of their appearance in the text, he came up with a graphic representation of the coded letters:

U	N	I	M
H	P	U	C
S	C	H	T

Then transposing the letters by reading them horizontally, he came up with a new arrangement of letters: U-N-I-M-H-P-U-C-S-C-H-T.

Not very promising. Which meant that he was most likely dealing with something more complicated than a single transposition. *If* he was dealing with a code at all. But it was all he had to go on for now. Perhaps it was a double transposition, in which case he would have to find some key to know the order in which to place the columns; some word in these letters that would help him put order to the others. *If this is a code,* he told himself, *then it is clearly meant for us.* So there had to be a solution to it.

Beck and Imhofer continued their discussion while Morgan looked for combinations of letters to find a key. If he could find one word, he should be able to get the letters into their proper sequencing. The *U*s looked promising, not a common letter; and the *C*s looked good, too. The vowel before or after the consonant. It was like playing Scrabble. Except here he was looking for German words; and his German was not all that great. Alternatively, he knew, there could actually be a key word in the text of the book page itself that would tell him, by order of the alphabet perhaps, which column to put first, which second, and so forth to solve the anagram.

He worked for ten more minutes without success, then Beck and Imhofer came over to his desk, looking over his shoulder.

"Looks Swahili to me," Beck said.

Morgan nodded. "Me, too. It's the first cipher."

"Something you might want to hear, Captain," Beck said.

Morgan turned, looking up at the two of them. "Proceed," he said in German.

Beck nodded to Imhofer, who sniffed once then began his report in a lazy Bavarian drawl.

"Rollo was the head of the black market here, that's for certain. I've been talking to his friends and enemies all day. So nothing new there, but there is one bit I came up with. Rollo was petrified that he would be arrested by the Gestapo one fine day. That they would treat him to one of their special interrogations here in the cells. Rollo's friends say that he had a fail safe."

Beck raised his eyebrows at Morgan, who spoke again in German directly to Imhofer: "Let me guess. Cyanide?"

Imhofer nodded. "A tooth hollowed out and a glass capsule fitted in the cavity. The same friends told me that Rollo was delivering butter to the dentist's home for months afterward."

Not much, Morgan thought. But it did lay to rest the nagging doubt he had about Rollo's death.

As if reading his mind, Beck said, "I have to admit it bothered me that he died so conveniently after telling me he had information for sale. But then Rollo always had information to share. And he did inform to the Gestapo about Jews in hiding. Another bit of insurance so they would leave him alone. But when Manhof threw him into jail to put pressure on him, maybe he figured he should use his escape hatch before it was too late, before the guards did a thorough search of him and found the poison."

Morgan made a noncommittal hmm. He turned back to his cipher; the death of Rollo was hardly top priority.

From in back of him Imhofer said, "Rollo died because he knew something. Not because he sold some Jews. Rollo hedged his bets—a little bit of badness here and little there. Plenty of bad to go around with Rollo. But I guarantee you he wasn't in prison because of shopping Jews. Who gives a shit now? Not Manhof, that is for sure."

Morgan felt hairs go up on the back of his neck; the refrain of turning Jews in suddenly hit a nerve. He stood suddenly, looking from Imhofer to Beck.

"Who gives a shit, you ask? I do for one. And there's a trial coming up here in this very city in a few days' time that is a monument to giving a shit about such things."

"You misunderstand me, Captain," Imhofer said. "I was not being disrespectful, just realistic about the German attitude."

"Wieland hid a Jewish family on his farm for three years, Captain," Beck said.

"Let's not go into that," Imhofer protested. "It was not done to curry favor. They are friends, neighbors. Anybody would have done the same."

"He needs to know," Beck insisted. "And you're wrong, Wieland. Hardly anybody did do it." Then, directed at Morgan: "It brought the death penalty in Hitler's Germany."

There was uncomfortable silence for a long moment.

"I'll keep that information about Rollo in mind," Morgan finally said. Another silent pause. "I spoke out of turn," he added.

Imhofer shrugged. "Forgotten," he said. "One bit of advice, though."

"What's that?" Morgan said.

"Werwolves. They're involved in this somehow."

Beck had a large-scale map of Nuremberg thumbtacked to the wall, coordinating patrol zones for tonight. There were pushpins with bits of red fabric attached stuck in place for the location of the three bodies thus far. The first two were located close together in the Saint Johannis district; the third was across the Pegnitz River by the main train station, or what was left of it. Not much to be learned from that distribution of bodies, and with only forty men, twenty patrols, there was little that could be done but make the killer's job a little more dicey. It was a lottery, though. A game of chance that the distribution of these patrols might come across a killing in process.

The old town itself, bounded by the ancient city walls, was over two and a half square miles and took a good twenty minutes to walk one end to the other. That area in itself would be difficult enough to patrol, but there was no indication at all that the killer would confine himself to the precincts of the old town. The first two killings were well outside the walls near the Saint Johannis Hospital and in the cemetery of the Saint Johannis churchyard. Murder three was just outside the southern wall. That one bothered him. Its location. Only a block away from the Grand Hotel. It was as if the other two murders had taken place in symbolic locations. A hospital for someone selling drugs. A graveyard for death. The third murder in such close proximity to half the notables staying in Nuremberg for the trial was like a declaration. An announcement. *See what I'm doing? Look at me!*

Don't read too much into it, Beck reminded himself. *Not like the last time. Don't get into a* mano a mano *with this lunatic.*

He put his mind back onto practicalities. If they intended to patrol the whole of Nuremberg, they would have to cover nearly eighteen square miles of territory in a city with a prewar population of more than 300,000. *That will take some organizing,* he told himself.

These ruminations were suddenly disturbed by the entrance of young woman with jet-black hair and apple-red cheeks.

"I'm looking for Captain Morgan," she said, standing in the open doorway, her rumpled Burberry belted defiantly at the waist with a knot rather than employing the buckle.

Journalist, Beck registered immediately.

She looked at Beck and smiled guardedly; her English was American, the attitude moneyed. Her eyes went to the map on the wall. Beck pointed a bony finger at Morgan, who sat peering suspiciously at their visitor.

"Captain Morgan?" She directed her query toward him now. "I'm Kate Wallace with *Outlook* magazine."

She moved toward Morgan, hand outthrust, but he remained seated, ignoring the gesture.

She was not put off by this rebuff, Beck observed.

"I was told you could help me with a story I'm writing."

Morgan finally spoke. "And what story would that be, miss?"

She bristled at his condescending use of "miss," but kept her head. Beck was beginning to enjoy this.

"I understand you have a slight problem, Captain."

"Who sent you here?" Morgan asked suddenly, rising. Standing, he was almost eyeball to eyeball with the young woman, given a boost in height by her high heels.

"Major Hannigan," she said. "The head of military police in Nuremberg. But he told me you're the one who can help me."

Morgan looked sideways at Beck. *Hannigan,* his look seemed to say. Beck shrugged back at him, moving slightly to block the woman's view of the map on the wall.

"And just what is it Major Hannigan says I can help you *with*?"

She looked coolly at him. "These murders in Nuremberg, Captain. Haven't you heard?"

Beck knew they weren't going to be able to keep the case

under wraps, no matter what the American thought. Nuremberg, despite its size, was a village where gossip was concerned.

"No, miss," Morgan said, returning her own cool look. "I hadn't heard until now. Sounds like reporter gossip to me. Late nights at the Grand with nothing better to do than spin tall tales."

"Three of them, my sources tell me," she interjected.

"Sources now. Fine. Then perhaps you should check your sources, lady. I'm telling you there haven't been any murders and if you print to the contrary you're likely to find yourself on the next plane out of Nuremberg."

She lost the smile now, glaring at Morgan.

"Three murders," she said, suddenly turning and pointing her finger at the map that Beck's body now partially concealed. He smiled at her in his winsome way, but she was not amused.

"So what are you two doing here, then?" she said, spinning back to Morgan.

"Logistics," he said. "Planning for the trial."

Their eyes remained locked for another few instants. *Oil and water,* Beck thought. Like two cats squaring off to fight, looking for the weak spot; a hiss there, then a spit. All very civilized, of course.

"Now if you will excuse us, miss, we do have important work to be doing here."

She glanced down at the book pages on the table, at the sheets of anagrams Morgan had been working on.

"Logistics," she said. A firm nod of her head that made her long hair bounce. "Looks like a cipher to me."

Morgan spread his right arm toward the door. "I think you know the way out. You can thank Major Hannigan for me. It was a pleasure meeting you."

Morgan led her to the door and was about to close it when she turned to face him again.

"I will find out, Captain. If there's a story here, I'll get it."

He closed the door in her face, locking it this time.

Walking back to his desk, he muttered, "Rich bitch."

"That was well handled," Beck said, going back to his plan for police distribution.

Morgan shot him a hard look, but said nothing.

They returned to their respective work, Morgan hunched over the ciphers, Beck examining the map on the wall. The map showed no destruction. Built up areas were in pink; the map was mostly pink with some green patches for parks and cemeteries. *Should be gray*, he thought. Gray for rubble, gray for destruction. They had only a matter of a couple of hours until it was dark, until the darkness gave their killer the sort of cover he liked. The anonymity of the night.

It was all a gamble, Beck knew, finally deciding on the routes the patrols would follow. Four foot patrols for the old city; then send two motorized patrols to each of the eight surrounding districts: Stadtpark, Saint Johannis, Weidenmühle, Gostenhof, Galgenhof, Wöhrd, Steinbühl, and Lichtenhof. Two men to each patrolling jeep. Random patterns, no set routes; nothing for the killer to key off.

But Beck knew they were fighting a rearguard action. If someone is determined enough, inventive enough, perhaps even crazy enough, he can kill. Forty men in a city this size would not be able to stop him.

By ten o'clock, all patrols had called in a quiet night. Beck and Morgan were stationed at the office, using it as a semblance of command station. The patrols had been on the job for over four hours; it would be a long night.

Eleven o'clock call-in produced the same result, and Beck began to wonder if his killer had changed his schedule. If so, the Brits were going to be livid they had missed a Saturday night on the town.

At eleven fifteen, Morgan announced he was going to take a walk, stretch his legs, get some air. Beck could man the phones.

The stairs were narrow and confined, built during the 1913 remodel of the place. There was a faint smell of paint; much of the building had been undergoing repairs and renovation. Looking down, you could see wooden railings spiraling around the five lower stories.

The elevator was working, but on the ground floor the entrance was crowded; men had been waiting to take it.

The fire stairs felt good, taken slowly. They pulled at muscles in the back of the leg. The door to the sixth floor was not marked, but there had been five before, including the parterre, so it was safe to assume.

The door opened without sound; the hall was clear. But there had been all those waiting for the elevator in the lobby. *Caution. Look both ways. This is not the darkened streets of the city.*

The room was down two long hallways. Doors opened, but in distant corridors. The carpeting was thin, ragged at the borders. A maroon color with medallions of green and blue, but faded, worn.

A look to right and left in the corridor, then a knock at the door. Nothing from within. It was surely time.

Another knock. The shuffle of slippered feet from the inside the room now. The door opened slowly inward. The man was short and thick. He wore a brocade robe, tied with a tasseled bit of gold silk cording. His robe matched the maroon of the carpeting in the hall.

He smiled, showing a gold tooth in front.

"Good evening."

"Hello," the killer replied, entering the room.

Like cutting the drumstick of a Sunday chicken, the killer thought. *Find the right angle, the joint between the two parts of the knuckle, and then saw through.*

The killer extended the little finger of the dead man's right hand and worked the scalpel at the exposed crutch of skin and bone. A final cut and the finger came off at the palm. It was plump and hairy and had an emerald ring in a gold setting on it. The severed finger went into a special bag for the occasion.

Then the little finger of the left hand. The initial cut was easy, going through the flesh as through butter. When the blade struck gristle and bone, the killer concentrated more closely, probing to find the juncture of the third knuckle, bending the finger with such force that it popped out of joint suddenly, making the work easier.

The job was done in ten minutes. Another ten to clean up any traces of blood on clothing or shoes, washing up in the tiled bathroom with its enormous bathtub and row of expensive cologne lined up on a low table.

The page from the novel was left almost as an afterthought on the way out, placed under the forefinger of the right hand so that blood from the removed little finger would not obliterate its message.

Twenty-three minutes from knock to departure.

But there was more than simple satisfaction at a job well done: The killer was enjoying this. The hunt, the expectation, the first thrust of scalpel. This was living; all the rest was marking time.

Brave Indians do not flinch.

November 18, 1945

They were always told to clean their shoes before approaching. It was not so much a matter of finickiness on Dulles's part as it was solid technique. The Swiss police watching the entrance to Herrengasse 23 looked for such things: Muddy shoes could mean the visitor had come over the mountain passes from occupied Europe to pay a call on the American spymaster.

Herrengasse—Lords' Street: Every old city in Europe had one like it. Bern's was cobbled, arcaded; a world apart from any Nathan Morgan had ever known. Just as the book-lined study where the pipe-smoking Dulles received his guests, accompanied by a crackling fire in the large stone fireplace, was of another world. Morgan loved those meetings with the older man; not in need of another father, still he felt a familial pull. The man knew how to attract people to him, men and women, ally and enemy alike. It was no surprise to Morgan that Dulles would begin his own negotiations for the end of the Second World War with some of Germany's top military men. He had that way about him, that aura.

You wanted to please 101. They actually called him that at Herrengasse; Dulles's code name in OSS.

The first months in Bern were spent on late-night radio transmissions, encoding and decoding traffic from operatives Dulles had contacted in occupied France, fascist Italy, and among the resistance in Austria. Morgan had stayed at Herrengasse during those first months, and then he'd been made operational in the field. He was their bagman into Italy to deliver weapons or money or forged papers to the CLNAI, the Committee for the Liberation of Northern Italy, a ragtag band of anti-Fascists with a ten-dollar name. An assemblage of Christian Democrats, Socialists, and Communists who were at one another's throats more than they were at those of the Fascists and Germans.

Morgan would cross Lake Lugano to his contact man on the Italian side, a giant of a man who spoke few words, but who saved Morgan when he stumbled into a wolf trap one night. He had carried Morgan on his back more than nine miles to the CLNAI camp. A good man. A simple man.

He would meet with the other resistance men high in the mountains. The *carabinieri* there, except for one or two holdouts, had been turned by the anti-Fascists, no Germans present. These were nothing missions; except for a wolf trap, there was little danger involved. Exactly the sort of meet for a new agent to cut his teeth on.

He'd made half a dozen of the meets after the incident with the wolf trap, after his foot healed. Then came the Allied landings in 1944, the steady march of soldiers up the boot of Italy, the renewed squabbles between CLNAI groups as they caught the smell of blood, could see the end was near.

As Morgan sat and thought in the hard chair at the office in Nuremberg, he halfway dozed. His head nodded and then jerked up occasionally. He knew if he slept, he would dream it. Knew it would be there all too real again. Even if he did not sleep, it would still be there. The scene was emblazoned in his mind: the cave high in the Dolomites, the howl of wind outside, the occasional flurry of snowflakes drifting into the mouth of the cave and, like errant moths, momentarily catching in the flicker of firelight within, then disappearing as they instantly melted.

And the voices raised in anger that night, prelude to guns, he knew. This time it was no petty squabble over who should have the greatest number of bullets from the shipment, or which group deserved the largest number of lire from the OSS war chest.

No. That night they were speaking of a traitor. One of the CLNAI seen trading pelts with the local *carabinieri*; the policeman had later been captured and questioned. Yes, he bought more than pelts, he told them before they killed him. He bought the names of anti-Fascists, mostly Communists from the man, as well.

And where are those men whose names were sold? asked the weasel-faced leader of the Communist resistance. *Dead. That is where they are. We ask an eye for an eye. Or else this resistance movement is finished.*

Paolo was his name, the Communist leader. Morgan knew he was right; the other groups did, too. They all knew justice must be done. Yet they would not allow the Communists to carry out punishment. And none of them had the will.

Those Marxist pig fuckers will not kill one of our men, cried the leader of the Christian Democrats.

The comment brought more hisses, more anger. The flames licked the contours of the cave, incited and fed by such anger.

Men's hands went to guns, to knives.

Enough! shouted Morgan. *I will do it. I will carry out the sentence on this traitor. Where is he?*

And they pointed to the guide, to the man who had saved Morgan's life. Then they handed him a knife. It was not to be a bullet in the back of the skull, but the man-to-man death that was called for by the nature of the crime.

The action was frozen out of Morgan's thoughts now; all that was left was the pleading in his former guide's eyes; what he felt was the chaffing of the knife's cross-hatched metal grip, like a file in his hand as he gripped it tightly; what he could sense was the warm spill of blood as he hacked through the man's throat for the first time. But it was not deep enough; timidity had held him back, made things worse. Six men had to hold the giant on his knees as Morgan cut again, this time more successfully, and the blood spurted and spluttered into the fire, filling the cave with the burning stench of death.

Morgan never made the trip into Italy again.

Then his thoughts were jangled to a merciful close by the ringing of the phone in his office at the Palace of Justice.

Beck was sleeping on the table, hands on his chest like a carved relief on a sarcophagus. Yet before Morgan could reach the phone, Beck stretched out a long arm and retrieved the receiver.

"Beck here," he said with a voice two octaves deeper than usual.

He listened to the receiver and Morgan watched him for reactions. Looking at his watch, he saw they had sat, and partially slept, the night away: It was just past six o'clock in the morning. Dawn soon.

"When was this?"

Another pause.

"Yes, I see."

More silence from Beck. Morgan could hear a tinny voice from the other end. It sounded urgent, excited.

"No. Not the Kripo. We'll be right over."

He slapped the phone back onto the receiver, and rose like a long, lanky cadaver from the table.

"There's been another one. Change of venue this time."

Beck drove; Morgan looked the worse for wear. When Beck told him their destination, Morgan could only whistle.

"Unexpected, eh?" Beck said.

"Yes. That, and the fact that I'm staying there. Interesting."

Beck didn't ask what was interesting, but kept his eyes on the road as he sped toward the Grand Hotel.

Inside the lobby, things still seemed relatively quiet. Quiet, seeing that a murder had just been discovered in room 613.

The manager, a tiny bald man in a shiny morning coat, stood wringing his pudgy hands by reception.

"The military police said to call you," he said in German to Beck. "We really should call the German police, too, no?"

"No," Beck said quietly but firmly.

"This is awful, horrible. First the war, then this."

Beck wondered about the man's priorities. On a scale of disasters, a homicide on the premises hardly earned a ranking alongside the Second World War.

"Our reputation," the man moaned. "And we have guests from all over the world staying here."

"Perhaps you could take us to the scene, Herr . . ."

"Freytag," the little man said. "I am the managing director here. Such a pity."

"The scene, please, Herr Freytag," Beck coaxed.

They rode up in the elegant mahogany-paneled elevator with its velvet bench seat and leaded glass windows, and Morgan and Beck exchanged glances over the shiny pate of the manager, who was too busy dry-washing his hands to pay them any attention.

As the elevator jerked upward, Beck asked him, "Who discovered the body?"

Freytag looked up from his hands. "Our staff. Herr Krensky ordered breakfast to be served at six. A very early riser was our Herr Krensky. A businessman. Most important."

"And just what sort of business was your Herr Krensky involved in?" asked Beck.

But the little man could only shrug ignorance of specifics.

"A very important man. He paid a month in advance always, and in American dollars."

Freytag smiled at the silent Morgan as he said this.

The elevator finally lurched to a halt at the sixth floor, and the men exited, Morgan leading the way, Beck following, and Freytag mincing down the hallways in back of them, trying vainly to keep up.

Beck imagined they presented a rather odd tableau. He also

found it strange that Morgan should be the one leading them to the crime scene, but attributed it to the fact that the American had quarters at the hotel and was most likely familiar with the layout. It did not escape Beck, however, that Morgan was out for a walk last night, on his own. Beck's mind was trained to take nothing as given. He would check out Morgan's whereabouts during the other murders. Stranger things had happened than a policeman being found guilty of committing a crime. Skeptic or realist, Beck was never sure about his true nature.

Finally, after passing a warren of hallways, they came to room 613. A young MP was stationed outside the door, perhaps the one who had called in the crime. He and his partner—two of the extra contingent laid on last night—had coincidentally been in the hotel dining room when the maid had come rushing down from the room, hysterical and still screaming after having discovered the body.

The young GI saluted Morgan as he pushed past, gave Beck a sideways look in his ill-fitting khakis, not knowing whether to salute or call reinforcements.

"Inspector," Freytag called out in back of him, stopping him in the doorway. He shuffled up, hand holding hand, out of breath, with a glisten of sweat on his upper lip. "You will keep me informed, won't you? I simply cannot go into that abattoir again. Most unsettling."

Beck started to reassure the man that they would keep him posted.

"Such a mess. I am sure the carpet will never be the same. And we have such demand. Only this morning the Control Commission was seeking lodgings for a general."

Beck rolled his eyes and left Freytag in a frenzy of dry washing without an answer.

Inside, the electric light was on despite the fact that the day had dawned relatively bright. Gray skies but no rain. And it was cold. Somehow it seemed colder inside the room than outside. Beck gave an involuntary shudder.

Morgan stood over the corpse. Beck tried to avert his eyes

for the time, to take stock of the rest of the room first. No sign of a struggle; the room had not been tossed. Rule out burglary, he figured, unless the killer knew exactly what he was looking for and where to find it. This was drill to keep the devils at bay. Twenty plus years on the force and Beck still had not grown accustomed to the grim realities of death.

The GI keeping watch over the body had obviously not become inured to death, either. He stood solemnly, helmet in hand, some three yards from the body, determinedly fixing his eye on a spot on the opposite wall. Beck imagined he'd been in that position since calling in the murder.

Morgan was bending over the body now, and Beck moved toward what seemed to be the bathroom. Flicking on the light here, he was greeted by tiled brilliance. A quick look at the sink let him know the killer had cleaned up in here. They would have to dust for fingerprints, but he knew that would be a waste of time. How many sets would they find in a hotel room? And there would be scant little to match with since most records had been destroyed in Allied bombing raids. But there was security in routine.

They will need more warm bodies on this, Beck thought. Now that they had a crime scene, they would need people to brush for fingerprints, to take some still photos, to start questioning staff and guests to see if any visitors were seen. And they would need to get a medical man to determine time of death.

Drill. Pure drill to keep them from the inevitable. Nothing more to be learned in the bathroom but that the killer was the tidy type. *Doesn't pay to draw attention to oneself; there is no bigger attention grabber than a spray of blood on the clothes.*

Which set Beck wondering about the other crimes, the outdoor ones. No luxury of a tiled bathroom there. So how did their boy stay clean in such a messy occupation? And had they checked for blood other than the victim's own at the murder scenes? Perhaps the killer had been injured, had bled. It happened. Maybe they could get lucky.

He filed that one away for further consideration and went

back out to the bedroom–sitting room area. Morgan was still hunkered over the body and Beck let his eyes go there as well. The first things he saw were the hands and the missing pinkies. He squeezed down an impulse to retch, then followed the blood pattern up to the neck. Freytag was right: That carpet was ruined.

"Nothing has been touched?" he asked the GI, who quickly shook his head. Beck now saw why the soldier kept his distance; blood had pooled around the body, spreading and soaking into the carpet like ink in a blotter. Morgan had found one of the few dry patches of carpet to approach the body. Beck bent over, peering at the surface of the carpet to see if there were footprints. Lighting was bad.

"Would you please open those drapes?"

The GI gladly responded, moving to the wall-wide bank of drapes and finally finding the pull cord. The room was suddenly flooded with light as he drew the curtains back.

"Holy shit!"

The GI's exclamation made both Beck and Morgan look at him. He teetered on the edge of the room; there was no wall, merely a gaping hole that let out into free fall. Beck quickly moved to the soldier, who was caught in a vertiginous swirl, attracted to the six-story drop. Beck took his arm, pulling him back from the precipice.

"Nice view," Beck joked.

"Which explains why there isn't much smell here," Morgan said. He flexed one of the man's remaining fingers. "He's cold, but that doesn't mean much in these meat locker conditions."

The GI continued to look at the gaping hole in the wall.

"Who did that?" he finally said, then realizing how inappropriate the question was, he added, "sir."

"I believe it was your air force." Beck grinned, but the GI was not amused.

"Do we have an ID here?" Morgan asked. He'd patted down the man's pockets and found no wallet, no passport.

The question let Beck know that Morgan's German language ability had some gaps in it, or that he had been distracted on the elevator ride up.

"Krensky, the manager says. Someone very important."

"Right. That's what Freytag said. I mean real confirmation."

Morgan kept looking at the body, then suddenly plucked the book page from under the right hand.

"You can wait outside, Private," Morgan told the soldier. Waiting for him to leave, he sighed. Then, when the door was closed in back of the MP, he said: "This is just wonderful. He hits smack in the middle of the Grand Hotel filled with lawyers and journalists, and we're supposed to keep this quiet."

Beck shrugged; such considerations were secondary to him.

"Somebody must have seen our killer coming or going last night," he said.

"We have to establish time of death first. I'll get Haskell over here. He's our medical examiner."

They looked down at the body for a time.

"Any idea who he is?" Morgan asked. "I mean important how?"

"A man named Krensky who pays in American dollars? One good guess."

Morgan nodded. "My guess, too. Black market. So here we go again."

"You find anything near the body?" Beck asked, trying hard to keep his eyes off the wounds now.

Morgan held up the page. "Just our friend's calling card. What are we looking for?"

Beck pointed at the hands. "The missing fingers. I don't see them here. Which means the killer took them as a trophy."

"Or flushed them down the toilet."

"Yes," Beck agreed, but thought it unlikely. He saw the severed fingers as an escalation, as a demand by the killer to be seen and heard. Not enough to simply kill; he was mutilating now. Perhaps the press blackout on the crimes was angering him.

Maybe he was in it for notoriety. That had surely been the case with the Nuremberg Slasher—the damn silly name the papers had given Beck's nemesis before the war. Nuremberg's one big case of multiple murders, and Beck had been unable to solve it. The man had been obviously bent; he killed young women and girls. Strangled them, then took a small trophy from each of his victims: He cut off a nipple. Sometimes the right nipple, sometimes the left. But the Slasher had gloried in all the publicity he was getting. He took to writing letters to Beck to give him clues, to encourage him, to taunt. Even sent him one of the nipples in a tiny jewel box.

They had never caught the Slasher, despite Beck's work day and night. Despite half the police force of Nuremberg diverted to his capture. Fourteen victims—six of them in the summer of 1939 alone. And then had come the war with Poland on September 1, which quickly spread to all of Europe, and the Slasher was heard of no more. Beck believed the man was drafted, or joined up. Found his niche as a soldier, where killing was no longer forbidden, where killing was the accepted norm. He could only hope the Slasher was one of the many millions of victims of that war.

"He doesn't look British," Morgan said, breaking into Beck's thoughts.

"No. Not even vaguely." Beck had also been wondering about that. So regular in other respects, the killer seemed to have missed out on the progression from Soviet to American to French and finally to British Allied victims. Unless, again, such murders were only a ruse to cover up simple turf war battles. They would have to check Krensky out, but it seemed obvious to Beck that the man was fast and flashy money, and that meant some involvement with the black market.

"But you were right about the scheduling," Morgan added. "Which means we've got a problem. If he keeps to schedule, the next victim is going to turn up on the twentieth."

Beck waited for more; so much was obvious.

Morgan finally filled in the missing passage: "The day the trial starts. You think it's just a coincidence?"

Morgan fetched his Leica from the jeep and, using available light—there was plenty of that with the drapes pulled back—he documented every inch of the sitting room, and took pics of Krensky from every angle imaginable, being sure to throw in a couple of less disgusting head-shots for ID purposes. Meanwhile, Beck had found the man's stateless person passport in the wardrobe: Polish, one Victor Krensky, born Warsaw, August 12, 1903, occupation: businessman. No other papers though, no address books, diary, or appointment calendar. Nothing.

Beck then returned to the Palace of Justice to round up a local for a more thorough sweep of the crime scene. He told Morgan that one of the boys at Kripo was a doozey at lifting prints and picking up dust motes with a miniature pair of tweezers. Morgan relied on Beck for this—not his specialty at all. And Beck had seemed to relish the idea of requisitioning one of Manhof's men right out of under him.

Haskell arrived just as Morgan was finishing up, and gave a low whistle at the sight of the corpse on the floor.

"Time of death would be appreciated," Morgan told the medical man.

But Haskell was not sociable; Morgan had seen all sorts of reactions to death while working homicide in New York: the jokers from forensics who tried to conceal their own revulsion by stupid comments; the rookie beat cop who would spill his dinner into the nearest trash can; the ME who talked of Bordeaux vintages as he rammed a thermometer up the victim's rectum. Haskell was the overly professional sort who obviously felt speech was disrespectful to the dead. He pulled on green rubber gloves before going through the preliminaries.

"I'll check back in, then," Morgan said as he left, but Haskell was already bowed over the body, as if in prayer. Morgan made sure the MPs stayed on duty outside the room. Freytag had seemed very anxious to tidy things up and turn his room around to the next five-star general in town, but Morgan was damned if he was going to have their first viable crime scene mucked up; the MPs were his insurance against overzealous maids.

Downstairs, Morgan took the rolls of black-and-white to a film shop on premises. Opened by an enterprising Brit who had been rotated back home and then clawed his way back onto the first transport back to Nuremberg to set up some scam or other. How bad must it be in dear old Blighty that business opportunities seemed brighter in bombed-out Germany?

Smith was his name, and he had a corner room in the cellar of the Grand where he serviced the visiting press corps or the odd serviceman who wanted a memento—profile with the backdrop of devastation to impress the folks back home in Omaha, Brighton, Toulouse, or Moscow. Very ecumenical was Smith.

One look at Morgan's MI credentials wiped away the supercilious grin on the man's face—he had taken him for a memento seeker. *Not the usual job this a.m., or the usual price. And by the way, you mention anything about this murder, and we'll bury you.*

That got Smith's attention, all right.

By nine thirty, Morgan had his photos freshly developed and dried, with their frilly edges like some Brownie-captured outing to the Grand Tetons. He stuffed them in the inside breast pocket of his heavy field coat, and went back upstairs to find Haskell peering at a thermometer, half-frame reading glasses at his eyes. He pried out an estimate from him: somewhere between ten the previous night and one that morning. Impossible to be more specific, he said, until further tests. The cold from the missing wall delayed rigor; it also upset the normal cooling of the body after death. But there was about a three-hour window. Yes, he could stand by that.

Jesus, thought Morgan. *Not so much a window of time as a yawning chasm.* But he started making the rounds of staff, looking for anyone who'd seen Krensky last night, or better yet, seen Krensky in company. He batted zero for three with the receptionist, the bellhop, and the doorman, a grizzled hulk by the name of Karl. Nobody had seen anything; no Krensky, no visitors.

Morgan figured he would have to start rousting the inhabitants of the sixth floor, but that was the last thing he wanted to do. So much for their private little homicide investigation in that case.

As he was crossing to the bar, the two MPs came out of the stairwell maneuvering a stretcher between them. Krensky had been rolled into a sheet, leaking through at one end of the shroud where there was a pink rose of blood showing. Haskell followed the two bearers.

"There you are, Morgan. I'll get back to you with anything more definitive information I find."

Heads were turning in the lobby as the two MPs lugged their burden through the mid-morning rush at the coffee bar in the hotel.

"Couldn't you have wrapped him in a blanket at least? Gotten him out of here with a little less fuss?"

Haskell's nostrils quivered at the question, like those of a hound dog at a particularly foul scent.

"I am a medical examiner, Captain, not Houdini."

He left without further comment, his professional nose seriously out of joint.

Morgan sighed, continuing on to the bar where the British bartender was on duty. *What is it with these Brits?* he asked himself. *Things really must be bad in England.*

Morgan went to the bar, ordered a seltzer, and pulled out the headshot of Krensky.

"You know this man?" he asked as Toby the bartender delivered his fizzing drink.

Toby examined the photo briefly, wincing at it once he understood that the man portrayed there was not sleeping.

"That 613?"

Morgan nodded.

"I heard about it when I came on this morning." He looked at photo again. "Yes, he used to come in. Regular as clockwork.

Eight till ten almost every night. Left a fiver every time." Another glance at the photo lying on the varnished surface of the bar. "Looked better than that the last time I saw him, though."

"That was last night?"

Toby lifted his eyes toward the ceiling as if thinking, then went to the end of the bar and hauled a crate of beer into place in the cooler, still setting up for the day's trade.

He came back to Morgan, dusting his hands on the white apron he wore.

"No, not last night." He plucked the photo off the bar again, as if he could not get enough of the sight of death. Morgan looked at Toby's compact little body, at the way he moved jerkily and almost combatively. A bantamweight, Morgan bet himself. He'd spent time in the ring; that was for sure. You don't wear your nose toward the east like this boy without some real ring time.

"I remember his table was empty," the bartender said, nodding toward the one in the far left corner of the room. "No problems with his girlfriend on a Saturday night, and for that I was grateful. Even if I lost my usual fiver."

"Problems?"

"She's German." Toby tossed the photo down again like it was the hole card in a blackjack game. "It's off-limits here for them, but Krensky's the sort of bloke who's fast with his mouth and money. A tip here, a wink and nod there. Figures he's taken care of the problem."

"But he hadn't?" Morgan offered.

Toby shook his head. "Not half. A Frog officer recognized her. I assume from the trade, so to speak, and raised a stink about the *Boche* being served here. That was what, last week? Like he hadn't been *served* by her as well. But not here, *merci* very fucking much. So I had difficulties, yes."

"She have a name, this German girl?"

Another shake of the head from the bartender. "But a real stunner. Legs up to her shoulders, blonde hair, and a set on her that makes a man weep to look at."

Toby's eyes drifted to the ceiling once more, replaying his last vision of her.

"Ask Karl. He set Krensky up with her."

Karl, as in the doorman who had not seen anything.

"Your colleague did not ask me about any friends of the Pole, only if I had seen him last night. I simply answered his question. I did not see him."

Karl sat on a stool—the only bit of furniture available in the tiny room Freytag had made available for him at the Grand Hotel—and tried to avoid eyes. Two pairs of them—Morgan's and Beck's—sought his eyes out, for Beck had returned from the Palace of Justice with his Kripo crime-scene man.

"You're a very literal man, Karl," Beck said.

It was his interview. Morgan wanted no confusion this time, no possibility for misunderstanding or excuses from Karl about why he failed to supply information.

"So how about it? Who's the girl?"

Karl hugged himself with short, thick arms. The maroon, knee-length coat he wore as official uniform was frayed at the cuffs. Not as small for him as was Beck's uniform for him, but still tight around the chest, short in the arms. He kept his eyes straight ahead of him, one foot planted on the floor and the other on the bottom rung of the stool. It was all he could do to maintain his balance. Beck smelled the sour stink of early morning wine on Karl's breath.

"Karl?"

The man finally looked at Beck with rheumy, mournful eyes. The eyes of a much-abused dog. He was fifty but looked a decade older.

"Sir?"

"The girl. Are you going to tell us about her?"

"What do you want with her? She's a good girl."

"Karl, we need to talk with her, that's all. A few questions. Maybe she saw something; maybe she can help."

"She's a good girl."

Beck felt Morgan's eyes on him, a silent question if the man perhaps did not have a few dishes missing in his cupboard.

Suddenly, Beck lashed out at Karl, backhanding him off the stool. Kneeling over the startled doorman, he gripped the coat in two hands and lifted him so that his face was centimeters away from his own.

"Beck," Morgan said, moving toward them.

Beck ignored him, glaring into Karl's watery eyes until he finally made contact.

"I'm not a patient man, Karl. I guess you see that now."

"All right, all right," the man pleaded. "She's my niece. My dead sister's daughter. I didn't want to get her in trouble."

So why did you introduce her to the Pole? Beck wanted to ask, but instead said, "The address. Give me her address." Still gripping the prone doorman's lapels.

Beck didn't know how anyone could live in these cellars; he'd go crazy having to live underground. *Take me back to the cells at Justice first,* he thought.

No address as there were no street numbers to follow on Stumpergasse, just across the Pegnitz. But Karl's directions had been accurate enough: second bombed-out house beyond the half-destroyed chapel. No bell to lean on; no front door to knock. Beck simply lifted the iron hatch leading down to the cellar and called out.

"Fräulein Laurent? Is Hilde Laurent here?"

A shuffling from down the darkened expanse of stairs; the scratch of a match, the flicker of fire light showing the concrete steps down, then steadier as a kerosene light was lit. The soft pulsing of the light seemed almost welcoming, but still Beck felt a surge of claustrophobic fear sweep over him. Nobody returned his call.

"Hello. Anybody there?" he called down the steps.

A cough, then a clearing of throat. He could not tell if it was a man or woman.

"Let's go," Morgan said in back of him.

Beck felt sweat break out on his forehead, felt the prickle of hairs going up on his neck. This was all too familiar. Like the last time. Like his playmate from before the war. They'd found victim five in a cellar not unlike this one. A ten-year-old girl sodomized and eviscerated, hung up like meat to dry—awaiting them at the end of a trail of clues the son of a bitch had laid for them. A girl not much older than Beck's own daughter at the time. A sign on the dead body: "I know your address."

"Beck?" Morgan said. "You going down or not?"

Beck stood aside, sweeping his right arm like a maitre d' offering a table to a hungry diner. "Be my guest."

Morgan brushed past him, taking the steps at a rapid clip. Beck followed slowly behind, trying to rid his mind of the evil memory.

By the time Beck reached the bottom of the steps, Morgan was standing cap in hands with his back to a young blonde woman who was peering up at him from beneath a mountain of covers on a simple metal cot. A quick glance around the room: a metal stove that looked like it had not seen fuel in some time; water-stained walls with a line attached from side to side in one corner supporting a row of hanging sequined gowns; a concrete floor covered with a couple scraps of rugs obviously salvaged from others' misfortunes; a simple table and two Coca-Cola boxes as chairs, *gratis* the liberators.

Hilde Laurent was smiling at Morgan's discomfort; she obviously had nothing on but the covers. Morgan's face was growing increasingly red.

"Good afternoon, Fräulein," Beck said in German as he approached.

She turned her eyes toward him, taking in the cadaverlike anatomy, the ill-fitting uniform. His accent let her know he was one of them. Her eyes went back to the better prize.

Beck ignored this implied rebuff. He'd had years of such experiences to harden him. Of course, in those years, he'd also had a wife and child to go home to at night. In those years, he was lean, not emaciated. In those years, his suits were rumpled, perhaps, not ludicrous.

"Late night?" he said, sitting unbidden on the edge of the narrow cot. Hilde quickly scooted away from him, raising a yeasty gust of sex from under the covers.

"What do you lot want?"

Close up, she was older than one thought at first glance, mid-twenties perhaps, and not so pretty, either. There were dark bags under her sunken eyes. Anemia? *But then this type was surely getting enough meat, of every sort*, Beck thought.

"Sorry, I have no shiny badge to be showing you," Beck went on. "But my friend and I"—he nodded toward Morgan who had now taken himself off and was examining the clothesline of evening wear—"are investigating . . . a crime." He'd have to tell her eventually, but he held back for a moment, waiting to see her reaction.

"I didn't do it." She pulled the covers up so they nearly covered her head. The roots of her hair showed dishwater brown.

"No one said you did. We need some information, that's all. We aren't interested in the other." *Whatever that might be*, he thought ruefully.

She suddenly sat bolt upright in bed, the covers falling to her lap, her torso exposed in the warm light from the single kerosene lamp. Fake hair, bags under her eyes, but her breasts proclaimed her youth, her beauty. They jutted out from her chest with manic pride, the aureoles pink and soft looking, little buds of nipples standing up in the sudden chill.

"What *other*?"

Beck shrugged as if to say it was obvious.

"You fucking skeleton, what do you know about the *other*? You probably haven't had it in a year."

Wrong, he thought. *Two.* But he said nothing, letting her go on with her grumble.

"You don't know how hard it is for a girl these days. Your fiancé killed at the front, the shit-eating Russians with their paws all over you at any chance. A girl needs a job. A girl needs a protector."

"Like Herr Krensky?"

Her eyes narrowed at the mention of his name. She looked down, as if only now realizing she was putting on a show. As she did so, Morgan turned to see what the fuss was about, reddening again at the sight of her breasts. She caught his gaze; not much she did not catch, and slowly draped the sheet over her bosom. Her nipples showed through; she cast a smile Morgan's direction.

This one is as stubborn as her uncle, Beck thought.

"Like Herr Krensky," he prodded.

"Yes. So what? So I have a Polish boyfriend. Is that a crime?"

"If he's your boyfriend, why weren't you with him last night?"

Suspicion showed in her eyes. "What's going on? Did something happen to Viktor?"

"You weren't with him last night, were you?"

Her glare burned into him. "No. He had business, he said. An important meeting."

"A black-market contact?"

"Viktor's an honest businessman. He runs a nightclub. I know nothing about the black market. Is that why you're here?"

A nightclub. *Good one that,* Beck thought. Cellar clubs that served watered wine, green beer, and stolen gin. Day or night, they were open throughout the city. In the cellars, it was eternal nighttime. A curtained section for the card tables, another curtained area for quick copulation. Passed as entertainment in the new Germany.

"Who was he meeting?"

She shook her head so adamantly that her loose hair waved about her head.

"I'm not saying anything else until I know why you're here."

"Your boyfriend is dead," Morgan said suddenly in his passable German from across the room.

She acted as if she had not understood, sitting up more stiffly in bed, gripping the covers to her chest.

"Did you hear, Fräulein?" Morgan said. "Krensky is dead. Murdered last night. We think it is the person he had an appointment with. We need your help."

"No. You're wrong."

"Any information," Beck encouraged her.

"Viktor can't be dead. It must be somebody else."

"No mistakes," Beck said. "Who was the meet with? Did he have any enemies?"

Then she began to cry, letting loose of the bedclothes and exposing her torso again. Her sobs came in large waves that shook her entire body. The grief seemed real, but something didn't fit.

Beck waited for a break in the waterworks. "What were you up to last night, Hilde?"

She peered up at him between strands of greasy hair. "What do you mean?"

"Where were you? What were you doing when your boyfriend had this meeting?"

"You mean do I have an alibi? Stupid." She spit the word out. "Viktor was my protector. I would never want to hurt him."

"Simple curiosity. Indulge me." The smell of sex was still strong from her.

She squirmed in the bed, scowled at him. The sudden tears had also passed.

"That is my business."

"Quite literally, you mean?"

"Pig."

Perversity made him want her to admit it.

"So you were turning tricks while your lover was being killed?"

"Beck." Morgan's voice was sharp. "Enough."

She looked at Beck with crude shrewdness now.

"*Beck*. I know you. Mr. High and Mighty from before the war. Chief Inspector Beck with his mug always plastered in the papers."

Beck rose from the cot.

"You and your big murder investigation. But you never could catch him, could you? He made you look a real fool, didn't he? And look at you now. A bag of bones doing the dirty work for the *Ami*'s."

Beck made no response, simply mounted the flight of stairs to the drizzle awaiting above ground. He sucked in the flinty air like a swimmer emerging from a dive.

Morgan came above ground a moment later, squinting into the daylight.

"That was productive," he said, echoing Beck's comment the night before about the way he handled the female journalist.

Beck made no reply, looking around the street at the devastation, at the unreal quality of it. He could not recognize a single landmark in this city he had grown up in.

"What was she talking about back there, Beck? What murder investigation?"

Beck sucked in more air.

"I thought you were the great one for information. Don't tell me you never heard of Beck's Waterloo? That's what the press dubbed it anyway."

"Look, what I know about you is that you lectured on multiple murders before the war. I could care what crap some journalist came up with. But I don't need mysteries from guys I'm working with. You've got a problem here, you tell me. You've got an attitude because of some other case you didn't clear, that's your problem, okay. I don't want it impinging on this case. I don't want you carrying the carcass of another investigation into this one. Understood?"

Beck finally saw a familiar sight: the Burg in the distance, at the north end of the old town. The castle had miraculously escaped most bomb damage. Why should its sight so cheer him now when he had found it so vulgar before?

"You listening, Beck? I don't need you going off on people like that Laurent woman. You antagonize them, they bite back.

They don't cooperate. Even if she knew who he was meeting, you think she'd tell after you rubbed her face in her own rotten morals?"

"Do you have a point to make, Captain Morgan? Are you saying that I do not know how to conduct an interrogation? That you and your colleagues in New York never turned a suspect's or witness's anger to advantage?"

"I just don't want to have to second-guess my partner."

"Then don't."

"And one more thing. When I took my walk last night, I went to a *Lokal* not far from the Palace of Justice. Had one beer and talked with the *Wirt*, an old duffer named Heinrich, who wants to change his name, now that Himmler is out of fashion."

"Why are you telling me this?"

"And the first murder, the Soviet, Orlov? I was talking to you in your cell when that happened. I guess I've got similar alibis for the other murders." Morgan fixed Beck with a hard look.

"I saw the way you were watching me at the hotel this morning. One cop to another, Inspector: Don't play poker. You haven't got the face for it."

Beck repressed a smile. He wanted to hold on to his resentment for a time. He began walking in the drizzle, which was now turning to rain, walking away from the jeep. Morgan let him go.

Kate sat between Henry Brandt of the *Times* and Pierpoint Phipson of *The New Leader*. Both men still seemed to think that the stack of paper by her Underwood belonged, in fact, to them. But they were no longer so greedy as to leave her none. A small stack was in place today, Sunday. A slow news day. The paper was brownish with large chunks of wood fiber pressed into it, like some sort of overgrown toilet paper. It was what passed for typing paper in Germany now; not the sort of paper that you made a stand over; not the sort of paper that launched a thousand ships. But still it was her paper, and Kate had swallowed her pride long enough vis-à-vis Brandt's and Phipson's poaching. It had kept her away from the pressroom at the Palace of Justice since she had arrived in Nuremberg, had cost her insights and leads and story contacts. But no longer.

Here she sat at her assigned seat—the name Wallace printed in thick black calligraphy with the W bleeding and feathering in the porous cardboard used for the identity card. This card had been bent into an inverted chevron and placed next to her typewriter. As she sat down, the men to the right and left reacted with a start as if a flock of mallards had just flown over their blind; she had accompanied her father on enough bone-chilling early morning outings in Pennsylvania to know the feeling, the exhilaration and absolute shock at the arrival of the prey.

Kate rolled one of the pieces of paper into the carriage of her typewriter; the men made a studied effort at ignoring her. Phipson's hand shot out automatically toward her pile at one point, then hesitated mid-flight, retreating to his own mudgy pile.

"I don't think we have had the pleasure." Brandt, to her left, said suddenly. Tipping a nonexistent hat her direction, he sat in suspenders and white shirt rolled up to the elbows. A double-breasted suit coat hung over the back of his chair. His tie was a muted burgundy vomit pattern; his hair thick on top and growing out of his ears, his nostrils, from under the front collar of his shirt with alarming fecundity.

"No, we haven't," Kate allowed.

The comment shut Brandt up for a moment, then he let out a piercing honk of a laugh that turned heads from clacking typewriters.

"Brandt here," he said, punctuating the admission with another honking laugh. "And the chap your other side is Mr. Pierpoint Phipson, Esquire. Just call him Dock."

The correspondent for *The New Leader* ignored the banter and continued pounding away on the keys of his typewriter.

Brandt wiped the underside of his nose outward with his right index finger to demonstrate Phipson's snootiness.

"Don't mind him. He's a good old son, but just hasn't realized it yet."

"As long as he leaves my paper alone," Kate said, suddenly fortified by Brandt's puckish demeanor.

Which brought another bit of honking approval.

"Where have you been keeping yourself, my dear? The old pressroom's been dreary enough without you."

Kate smiled at this, then clacked in a name slug at the top of her copy, but had no idea what was going to go below it. Still two days until the trial opened. Should she prepare opening-day copy? The faces of tyranny in the dock, and all that sort of thing?

"I imagine you've been off being very investigative, haven't you, my dear? Sniffing out the ghosts in the cupboard, that sort of thing? Not like us old dogs gathered round the press briefings of the Judge Advocate General's Office, reprocessing swill from the prosecution case. Will they or won't they be found guilty? My, oh my, that is a difficult one. Rather keeps one on the edge of the seat, now doesn't it?"

"I suppose it sells newspapers."

Brandt glowed at this, finding a co-conspirator. "You hear that, Dock, old son? The lady has a gift for irony."

But Phipson would not be brought out.

"Well, please do tell, Miss"—he craned his neck to get a look at her name card—"Wallace. What is it you have been getting up to? The trial is about to begin, and you only now make your appearance. Is it the smoking gun you seek? The Hitler order for the camps, which everyone here seems determined to find. Or the murder? Do tell. Though it would hardly be fair to do a knock on that. We've all signed off on it, zipped lips, buttoned flies. That sort of thing. The American brass have pleaded national security, and we must obey." He saluted her.

Kate looked at him with a steady gaze. "Murder?"

"Oh, you are good. Too good for the magazine trade. Hollywood, that should be your métier. 'Murder?'" Brandt raised his voice to falsetto. "But, of course, you have heard of it. Everyone in Nuremberg has. Who could miss a murder at the Grand Hotel?"

That was all she needed to hear. She gathered her purse and grabbed her coat off the back of her chair. She did not bother saying good-bye on her way out.

Beck walked for ten minutes before a jeep pulled up in back of him.

He did not turn around, thinking it might be Morgan; he'd had enough of the Captain for the time being. Then a voice called out: "Need a lift?"

He turned to see Wicland Imhofer sitting in the backseat of his requisitioned jeep, a private in front who was just tall enough to see over the steering wheel. Attached to the front was one of the cow-catcher constructions to ward off decapitation wires strung across roadways.

Beck smiled and hopped in back with Imhofer, quickly ascertaining that the man had already made progress on the most recent killing. This without even being told to do so by Beck. More effects of Nuremberg the village.

"Krensky dealt mostly in women from what I've found out so far," Imhofer explained as the driver worked his way clumsily through the gears. "He had a string of cellar nightclubs throughout the city. And he worked with black marketers for his drink supply. Whether or not it went deeper than that, I'll find out soon. But according to his bodyguard, Krensky wasn't a big player in the black market."

This woke Beck up. "Bodyguard? Krensky needed protection?"

"Personally, I think he just did it for effect. Made him feel important. The guy's a cousin of his from Lvov. Talked to him this morning—he's got a crib at one of the nightclubs. Only incrementally more intelligent than this." Imhofer patted the metallic side of the jeep. "Makes an upstart from Poland look a regular swell to have a bodyguard."

Beck asked the obvious: "So where was *he* last night?"

"Mitya—that's the bodyguard's name—had the night off. Krensky's orders."

"Which means he was not expecting trouble. Same as our other victims."

Imhofer nodded, pulling a sandwich out of the inside pocket of his voluminous coat and offering part of it to Beck, who shook his head.

"Just goes to show."

Beck looked at him. "Show what?"

"You should always expect the worst." Imhofer bit into the sandwich with a snarl, chewed for a time, then finished the thought. "That way whatever you get will be okay."

A true Bavarian Catholic, Beck thought.

They let him out at the Grand Hotel: Imhofer was off to interview a man about a possible Werwolf link in Nuremberg, but he was being secretive about it.

"It may turn out to be nothing. We'll see. Local black-market contact set up the meet."

Beck waved him good-bye from the entrance to the hotel; Imhofer was still gnawing on his sandwich.

Things had grown more frenetic in the lobby of the Grand since earlier in the day, but Beck figured that had nothing to do with the murder. Rather it was the effect of the impending trial: the biggest tourist attraction since the bombing of Dresden.

He took the lift to the sixth floor. The MPs were gone but Perlmann, the crime-scene specialist he'd hijacked from Kripo, was hard at work. On hands and knees, he was humming something out of Puccini when Beck entered the room. Perlmann was always humming something out of Puccini, even during those years when Wagner was the preferred flavor. Beck was no opera fan—Baroque chamber music was his addiction—but wondered that Perlmann never ventured to other composers. A little Verdi, say, or Mozart. But no, Perlmann hummed Puccini as he picked bits of whatever out of the carpeting with his tweezers. He did not hear Beck enter.

"Anything?" Beck asked and Perlmann jerked his narrow head up at the question. He had a refined face, delicate features. He looked much more like a curate than a cop. All but his belly, that is. That part of the body made Perlmann look like a gourmand, but where he got the ration coupons to feed that portly middle, Beck did not know. The contrast, however, the ascetic facial features against the sybaritic paunch, was startling the first time you met the man.

"Everything," Perlmann answered, going back to his labors seeing it was only Beck. They had worked too long at Kripo before and during the war to stand on ceremony, but Beck could tell this morning he was pleased being seconded out of Manhof's supervision if only for the time being.

"Too much." Perlmann bagged a loose hair and stood slowly, arching his back and wincing. "Getting too old for this damn job."

"Too much of what?"

"It's like a train station in here. I've got at least twenty sets of prints, the markings from seven different pairs of shoes." He sifted through one of the pockets of the while lab coat he wore. "And this. Found it stuffed down the toilet. Messy job."

Beck took a look at the contents inside a sodden paper bag. It was a rubber glove with the tinges of blood still on the index finger.

"I know how squeamish you are about such things, so I'll save you the trouble," Perlmann said. "It's surgical and not over large—your boy's got little hands. Doubt we'll be able to trace derivation. Been a high need for surgeries in the last years. I'll run a check on the blood to see if it's a match with the victim's. If there's enough there for a test, that is. And if it hasn't been corrupted too much by the contents of the toilet."

"Better you than me," Beck said, filing this new piece of information away to help build a profile of their killer. He was hoping the angle of the cuts would be able to help them with the height of their killer. Haskell might be able to help there.

"That it?"

Perlmann shrugged. "Yes, one more thing. Get a new suit, will you. You look like a clown."

Perlmann was right, of course, Beck allowed, staring at his reflection in the cracked mirror in the hall while waiting for the

elevator. Looked like a damned idiot in the cast-off fatigues.
He no longer enjoyed the sight. And the effects of lack of sleep
were equally unkind: bags under his eyes large enough to carry
a new wardrobe. His features were haggard; he was badly in
need of a shave. He could use a nap and a bracer—schnapps
would do.

He was able to satisfy the last of these wishes by a quick
trip to the bar of the Grand—one thing his clown uniform
got him was entrance without the usual hassle of "no Germans allowed." When the British bartender set the shot glass
in front of him, Beck suddenly realized he had no money. He
flashed his letter of appointment—Morgan's idea—at the man.
The Brit shrugged.

"So what? That'll still be a dollar."

So close yet so far. Beck left the drink untouched and walked
out of the hotel a chastened individual.

Two hours later, he was sporting a charcoal double-breasted
suit with the subtlest of gray stripes; a sparkling white shirt
and somber, businesslike gray tie; and a fedora that smelled of
pomade. His shoes were Italian, already broken in; in his pocket
he carried a small roll of bills.

Debts called in; debts repaid. *Lovely thing, debts,* he thought.
No sleep, but a shave and bath had done wonders for his mood.

Frau Henzig was to be thanked, also one of her clients
whose clothes had been left behind when he failed to return
from the Russian front. The good Frau ran the finest brothel
in Nuremberg in a lovely eighteenth-century chateau that
escaped the bombing in the suburbs. Beck had been her protector for several years, keeping vice from shutting her down
in return for the odd piece of information that she could supply. The bill ran to her favor; today was payback time. After
she had stopped her laughter, that is. Clapping her hands, she
tittered in delight at his skinny wrists popping out of the khakis and high-water pants showing his boot tops as he stepped
out of the Mercedes he'd requisitioned at the Grand—Morgan's letter was good for something, apparently. But it was

more than simply past debts: Frau Henzig was already working on new ones.

"I'm the wrong horse to back, you know," Beck had told her. "Manhof runs things at Kripo now."

But she only smiled at this, brushing the lapels of the suit clean with a boar-bristle brush that made a shushing sound over the material.

"I know my horses, Inspector. I'll place my bets accordingly."

Now, as the sun was setting, he sat with his mother in her tidy room at a sanatorium on the outskirts of town, not too distant from Frau Henzig's establishment, relishing the comforting silence between them.

She was the first to break it.

"I must say, Werner, our fortunes have changed rather abruptly." It was her first mention of the move from the DP camp. "You are not doing anything illegal, are you?"

She wore a quilted housecoat and sat snugly in an overstuffed armchair upholstered in a pattern of large pink peonies. She was so small and fragile she looked like a mere stem of these bounteous blooms.

"You hurt my feelings, Mother. I am an honest policeman, much abused."

She chuckled. It had taken her decades to accept his profession. She'd wanted business for him, like his father.

"Do honest men dress so well these days?" she asked with feigned innocence.

"Honest men with favors due to them."

They sat for a time as the dusk settled outside. He would have to be going soon; the driver in the Mercedes was surely growing restive, as Captain Morgan would be, as well.

"I think about your father more the longer he's been dead," she said suddenly.

He made no reply.

"Do you think that is normal?"

Beck had no idea what normal was. He tried never to think of his wife and child.

"It's been four years now, just past the anniversary of his death. What a day to die. Your father would not have appreciated the coincidence."

Beck looked at her, a tiny presence in the great chair, almost disappearing in the darkness filling the sitting room she'd been allotted. His father had died on the ninth of November.

"I hadn't thought of it that way."

"He was no friend of them, you know." Her voice faltered, struck a quaver.

"No."

"To die on the anniversary of the Munich Putsch." She shook her tiny head.

You have to die on some day, he thought, but said nothing. His mother had been merely counting time since his father's death. And then she'd been bombed out of her home the same night as . . . No. Beck would not think of them.

"Do you think it was a sign?" she asked.

"No, Mother. Merely a coincidence."

And then suddenly another coincidence came to mind: The first of the four deaths he was investigating had occurred on the night of November 8, or the early morning hours of November 9. Was that a sign? Was that of any importance or just more blind coincidence?

"Werner?"

"Yes."

"You seemed so far away."

Then, as he was preparing to leave: "Why do you never talk of your poor wife and child? It will poison you to keep it bottled inside."

Morgan had napped briefly in the afternoon, but otherwise had spent his time at the office working on what he was increasingly sure was a coded message. He had looked in vain for key words that would make some sense out of the jumbled letters. Intuition helped in such matters; led you to the often used article or pronoun that could serve as a key to the rest, but with German he had no such intuitive feel.

He looked at the transcription table for the first message again:

U	N	I	M
H	P	U	C
S	C	H	T

In the absence of some key to the code, he'd been playing around with different permutations and combinations of the columns all afternoon. Following a pattern of four-one-two-three, that is placing the last column in the first position, he thought for a moment he had come up with something. The word *Munich* leaped off the page. But then he just as quickly knew he was mistaken. The German word for the Bavarian capital was *München*. Try again.

When Beck finally arrived, Morgan's stomach had been growling for at least half an hour. He tried not to act relieved to see the man again, but could not conceal his amazement at Beck's physical transformation.

"I didn't know the lotto was back in operation."

Beck hung a deep blue cashmere coat on the back of a chair, laid a relatively new fedora on the table, and sat down without comment or explanation of his absence.

"I've been doing some thinking," he announced. "About what these murders might mean. Are you a student of recent history, Captain Morgan?"

"I try."

"Then you tell me what happened on the night of November eighth and ninth, 1923."

Morgan squinted at Beck, wondering where this was leading.

"What? The Hindenburg burned?"

Beck raised one eyebrow. "Second guess."

"All right. That holy of holies, the Beer Hall Putsch. Hitler's claim to fame."

"Very good, Captain. And it was a holy day of sorts for Nazi Germany. Fifteen years later, it was celebrated by the destruction of Jewish businesses all over the country. The shards of glass from damaged storefronts were heaped so deeply in the street they called it *Kristallnacht*. That day became the most important of the state holidays during the Reich. The holiest of holy days, in fact. The Munich Putsch."

"Wait a minute."

Morgan looked back down at the four-one-two-three transposition he'd created from the original:

M	U	N	I
C	H	P	U
T	S	C	H

"Damn, it's there. You're right."

Beck got up from the chair and hurried to look over Morgan's shoulder.

"MUNICH PUTSCH," he read, stringing the letters horizontally.

"I ignored it because it was partly in English," Morgan explained. "But that's got to be it."

"Very tidy," Beck said, still looking at the transposed message.

"That means we're working with a four-one-two-three pattern," Morgan said, growing more excited. "Normally, you'd find a key word in the text to give you the pattern, but we've stumbled onto it by pure dumb luck. Now let's hope it fits the other coded messages."

He quickly laid out the eleven initial letters from the page found at the second crime scene, leaving one blank space in the grid. After reconfiguring the columns according to pattern, he came up with more English: "WELCOME HOME."

"What's that supposed to mean?"

But Beck behind him sighed heavily as if all was suddenly clear for him.

"Try the third," he told Morgan.

In another few minutes, he'd transcribed that code as well: "CHAMBERLAIN."

"That's it then," Beck said. "Don't you see the significance of these? It's like a concise history lesson of modern Germany. A stations of the cross of the high points of the Nazi rule: the Munich Putsch, the *Anschluss* with Austria—a homecoming to the Reich. And then . . ."

"Czechoslovakia," Morgan added, excited now. "The sell-out by the British prime minister. The policy of appeasement. Hitler won the country without a shot being fired."

Beck nodded. "And what comes next?"

The next one, found at the scene of the crime at the Grand Hotel, was harder to work out. There were only nine letters in this, and it took both men some time to figure out where to put the blank spaces. It was Morgan who finally saw it.

"CASE WHITE," he all but shouted.

"Exactly," Beck confirmed. "The code name for the invasion of Poland and the beginning of World War Two. And"—he looked squarely at Morgan—"victim number four happens to be a Pole."

They both stared at the decoded messages for a time.

"Our killer is obviously educated," Morgan finally said. "He has a knowledge of English; he has a crazy pattern to his killings."

"And he knows cryptography. He's making it easy for us. Not depending on the fact that any Germans might be involved in the investigation. He is handing the clues to you, Captain. He wants you to follow his trail."

"Where's it leading, that's the question," Morgan said. "What's the next high point in Nazi history?"

Beck shook his head. "You pick. But according to the killer's schedule so far, the next murder should come on the twentieth. Just two days away."

Morgan thought about this for a time. Finally, "You think that's what this is all about? The trial?"

But Beck made no response to this.

By nine fifteen, Morgan had called it quits for the day and headed to the bar at the Grand for his usual nightcap. *More sleep, less booze,* he counseled himself. But when the French bartender—no Toby tonight—asked his pleasure, he ordered a double Scotch neat. He'd offered to buy Beck a drink, but the German had begged off.

"Not too eager to serve Germans there," he'd told Morgan.

Beck was off to his lodgings at one of the few other standing hotels in the city, the Terminus. Where they served Germans, apparently.

Slow night in the bar—Sunday. Not as if there was a regular workweek in Nuremberg, but old habits die hard. People from around the world were programmed for the Monday through Friday grind. Not even years of war had disturbed that ritual. A group of French at one table and some Brits near the recently situated dartboard—so out of place in the mahogany and brass of the bar. Thumping one another on the backs at good throws, spilling their beers. A few solitary Americans hunched over the bar spaced several feet from one another. Allies.

He saw her reflection in the mirror over the bar, walking in so casually and self-contained. The suit cut snug but not tight; a little furl out at the bottom of the skirt, just below the knees. Not bothering to look this way or that, but homing in on a table and sitting with her back to him. Compact and well groomed and, he had to admit it despite himself, damned appealing. The reporter woman who'd come to the office the other day.

Her black hair was curled under at shoulder length and glowed lustrously in the dim light of the bar. Sure of herself, but not brash. Just sat there waiting for the bartender to take her order like she was used to giving them. He pulled his service cap back on and down low over his eyes. He didn't want to have to duck any of her questions tonight.

Morgan finished his drink and was about to leave for his attic quarters when he noticed, in the mirror, one of the Brits approaching her table. The guy sat unbidden and she cast him a noncommittal look, half amused. But when the guy persisted in chatting her up, she began to look nervously around the bar. Then the Brit laid a paw on her knee, and she rose.

Morgan sighed to himself, turned, and headed to the table.

"Sorry I'm late," he said as he approached. "Held up."

Long-lost friends; the delayed date. Easiest roust.

She looked at him, surprised at first, then caught on.

"I was beginning to wonder."

The Brit was drunk, but not drunk enough to miss Morgan's bars. He took off like a fox chased by hounds.

They stood staring at each through the space vacated by the Brit.

"Thank you," she said finally.

He shrugged it off. "No problem. Take it as an apology. I was a bit abrupt the other day . . ."

"Please." She held a hand palm outward to him to stop his speech. "No work tonight, okay? It's still the weekend."

"Okay. But I thought journalists were never off duty."

"And I thought the military was ever vigilant."

They smiled at each other. Morgan allowed a sudden inspiration.

"May I buy you a drink?"

She smiled again and it made her nose squinch up at the tip. "I'd like that. Yes."

They talked for over an hour. It was Morgan and Kate. He obviously did not care for his given name, so she played coy with her last in return. But Morgan seemed in need of unburdening himself, Kate felt. None of the search for common friends for Morgan; none of the usual East Coast banter. Just right to the heart of the matter—the trial here and the meaning of it all. Victors' justice or the real thing?

She knew who he was, of course. Since their first meeting,

she had had time to think about it, to recall the name of Detective Morgan from the New York City Police Department. The Lombardi kidnapping: not many in New York who would not remember it.

But tonight she was creating a special bubble of time: nothing before and nothing outside of this table at the bar in the Grand Hotel. The sloppy drunk British soldier had been serendipity; the rest contrived. Questioning the staff this afternoon about the murder, she had discovered, quite by accident, Morgan's habit of a nightcap from the bartender. Had discovered, in fact, that the captain was staying at that very hotel. News to her. But the bat of an eyelash did seem to loosen men's tongues. And their wits. She was disgusted with herself for playing the coquette, but the longer she was in journalism the more she came to discover it was not about talent; not about the well-turned phrase or the deeper analysis. It was about who could get the story first.

So it was the dark-green Worth suit with a cream-colored silk blouse; her hair freshly washed and brushed to a silken sheen. Eye makeup, even, which for Kate was a stretch. And the passive female act. Not quite "poor-little-me"—she instinctively knew that a man like Morgan would not be attracted to that—but definitely a toned-down Kate was onstage tonight.

And it was working. Morgan left no interstice of silence unfilled with his opinions, from fears of *ex post facto* justice to building a postwar Germany free of militarism.

And despite herself, Kate began to like the man; his energy, his intelligence, his passion. He was not her type, actually. *What is my type, actually?* She had had suitors, but no real lovers. She always pictured the perfect man as a little more than six feet tall. Ruddy to light-complexioned. Morgan did not come close to fitting the bill on those counts. No taller than what? Five eight or nine? And dark, both his hair and skin. Not a bad-looking man at all, some women might find him quite dishy in fact, but not really her type.

If she were to do a profile on him, she would first focus on the physical attributes. Thin and angular with strong bones in the face, a prominent, slightly bent nose, dark hair, and hazel eyes with flecks of darker color near the iris. Well proportioned, handsome, in fact, in a bookish sort of way. But so obviously not regular military with his red-rimmed eyes and poorly shaven cheeks. Long hands, tapered fingers that expressed themselves when he talked, but she was sure he did not realize that.

The hour passed quickly by; neither touched the drinks in front of them. She was the one to look at her watch first. Always leave them wanting more, her father had advised. This in regards to good business dealing, but there were many applications to that homily, Kate began to discover.

He took her to the taxicab stand outside the hotel; there was one lonely cab waiting there. Then he waited for the cab to pull safely away, lingering on the sidewalk, watching her leave. Kate could see him in the side mirror of the old Mercedes.

As they pulled out of sight, she let out a sigh, and rolled her neck. But there was no tension there. She had enjoyed herself. It had all been a ploy to worm herself into Morgan's trust, but here *she* was going away and wanting more of Morgan.

Well done, Kate, she told herself. *Not quite the result you were looking for, though.*

November 19, 1945

Division of labor the next morning. Morgan was off to put to rest any lingering doubts they had about a black-market connection for the murders. He would check out the friends and background of the first three victims, go over the ground again, see if there were any traces not yet kicked over. A job for the American—not many of the former Allies going to open up for a German. But he'd seemed distracted to Beck, not really all there, his mind off somewhere his body would rather be, too.

Beck's part in the division of labor was Doktor Edmund Niedholer, leading specialist at the psychiatric sanitarium of Lauensee, near Nuremberg. Former leading specialist, that is. Lauensee had also been turned into a DP camp; the crazies let loose. *More victors' justice*, Beck figured. The Allies suspected any sort of institution run by the Nazis; thought they contained political prisoners. How wrong, Beck knew. That was a Soviet trick: Lock up dissidents as insane. You have to be insane not to be on Uncle Joe's side, right? But Hitler and company? Not for them. They simply gassed their enemies, or had them shot, or garroted. There'd been a thousand ways to die in the Reich.

Beck waited around the office at the Palace of Justice as long as he could in the morning, waiting for Imhofer to check in with a progress report. Finally, he had to leave a note on the outside of the locked office door telling the detective to meet later in the day.

Niedholer's home was in the southern suburbs. *So little damage here,* Beck thought, getting out of the jeep after he'd parked it on the pleasant street. *I should have listened to Helga: moved to the suburbs like she wanted. Gone into debt, what the hell.* But at the time it had seemed so supremely bourgeois.

I'm a cop, not a banker, he'd told her. She'd laughed and rumpled his hair. *Policemen are allowed to have lives, too,* she'd said. *And all of the nature for Lisabette to play in.*

It was put off for after the war.

Beck begrudged the citizens of these suburbs, their quiet, unbroken lives, while his had been turned upside down. Here the plane trees and the horse chestnuts were just dropping their gaily colored leaves onto the wide and placid boulevard, but in the center of the city, there was not a tree to be seen, not a bush or plant of any sort in sight. Not even a dandelion growing between the cobblestones. There was one color in Nuremberg proper: deathly gray. A gray sometimes punctuated with a deeper shade, almost charcoal.

Beck went to the massive door guarding the entrance to Niedholer's villa. He'd been there before, collaborating with the man on the Slasher. Looking for some insight into the bastard's motivation, psyche, soul—whatever. He'd been desperate. And Niedholer had not been sanguine about the chances of capturing that murderer.

"If a man wants to kill, he will kill," the doctor had told him at the time. "If he is willing to sacrifice his life in the commission of his crime, he most certainly will succeed. The only protection you can provide the public is his capture."

Which Beck knew bloody well already. So why go to Niedholer for yet another multiple murderer?

Because of the one bit of non-jargon sense the man had spoken those years earlier: "You must become your perpetrator, live in his skin, think his thoughts, breathe his air without flinching, without revulsion. 'Identifying with the criminal,' we call it, but not easy at all to achieve. To go beyond your assumptions of what is 'crazy,' or who is a 'lunatic,' you must trade places with your murderer. Not figuratively. Not metaphorically. You must become the murderer to catch the murderer."

It had made good sense at the time; better now. There were restraints then: his family for one. And instantly, Beck felt a glowing shame at the thought that his family could be classified as a constraint. But then he'd had a "normal" life to go home to at the end of the day; had a purpose and reality outside of trading places with someone who took pleasure in the rape and evisceration of young girls.

Now there was no such "constraint." No normal life to return to at the end of the day. No other reality to keep him from throwing himself into trading places.

He pulled the cord at the front door, heard the bell clanging inside. It took several minutes for someone to come to the door; it turned out to be Niedholer himself. No domestics for the Niedholers, it seemed. They had exchanged pleasantries on the phone when Beck had contacted him earlier this morning; now it was all business.

Niedholer led him down the hardwood-cobbled drive and out to the back grounds, sweeping up in a gentle rise to the roof of a summer house, which Beck could see far in the back. The grass was lush and high; no one had cut it in some time. Fruit trees were spaced at random intervals; one apple tree still held the final fruits of the year in its nearly denuded branches. Lilac bushes lined the perimeters: When he'd visited before the war, the lilacs had been in bloom, filling the yard and the house with their spicy fragrance.

They turned the corner of the villa to the entrance that opened to the garden, went up two flights of stairs to quarters on the second floor. Niedholer moved more slowly than before. He must be, what? More than seventy, Beck reckoned. He took the stairs with hands on knees for support. His bushy, dun-colored tweed suit had seen a lot of wear over the years: shiny at the seat, bagged at the knees, out at the elbows and cuffs where leather patched the heavy wear.

Niedholer made no comment on the two sets of rooms on the ground floor that appeared to be filled to bursting with women and children. Washing hung from the windows, white diaper pennons and pantaloon flags. Before, these rooms had been consulting offices. Beck suspected that DPs were living there now. Requisitioned or offered space?

Upstairs, Niedholer led him down a dark hallway past the kitchen and sitting room to his study, the same one they'd sat in six years before. It was filled to bursting with memorabilia: statuettes from Egypt; busts of Beethoven, Brahms, and Goethe; bronze friezes from Greece; walls hung with Persian carpeting and lined with bookshelves crammed with leather-bound and buckram-backed volumes standing upright, stuffed sideways above the upright ones, paper place-savers peeking out of the closed pages. More books on the floor, stacked in dizzying piles. Papers littered the huge mahogany desk Niedholer sat behind. A tiny man, his head barely showed over the mountain of documents that had found a home there.

They had hardly exchanged a word; Niedholer merely nodded his white-domed head at a leather chair on Beck's side of the desk, and Beck made himself comfortable in it. The old man looked at him, an eagle eyeing a likely mouse, with eyes the incredible blue of an Alpine lake. His nose was curved sharply like a raptor's; a wattle hung from his neck; age freckles dotted his forehead. He finally smiled with thin, lizardlike lips.

"What is it that you felt so urgent, Inspector? Not to do with our old friend, perhaps?"

Beck shook his head; this one was surely different, though he had given it a thought. How fitting to recommence his police work where he left it off.

"No, I think not. But we do have a bit of a problem. And I need first an assurance from you that what we say does not go beyond these walls."

The doctor puffed up like a rankled pigeon. "Would you like it in writing?"

Beck shrugged an apology. "It's from above."

Which made Niedholer smile in spite of himself; the irony of the phrase that ex-Nazis had been mouthing for months as an excuse for their wartime deeds.

"The Control Commission wants to keep these crimes quiet for the time being, not to upstage the trial. Political machinations, not my concern."

Niedholer nodded his tiny head. "I understand."

Beck joined his hands in a steeple over his lap, settled back in the chair, and explained, briefly, the circumstances surrounding the four murders.

"On November eighth, a Soviet soldier was killed near the Saint Johannis Hospital. As near as we can figure, he died at about ten p.m. A streetwalker found the body in the rubble. The victim's throat had been slashed with precision. One slash that opened the throat to the trachea. No secondary wounds, no tentative strokes."

Niedholer nodded, understanding the implication.

"The Soviet, Corporal Sasha Orlov, was in Supply; he had on him a large supply of penicillin, which subsequent tests show to be well out-of-date. The second victim, an American, Private Bill Todd, was killed three nights later, on the eleventh, in the Saint Johannis churchyard. Time of death is uncertain, but the local vicar himself discovered the body near midnight. At that time, the body was still warm. The victim's throat had also been slashed in much the same manner as the first victim. Also, a quantity of contraband goods were found in the soldier's knapsack."

Niedholer listened intently, squinting his eyes at Beck, tilting his head like an intelligent canine at times. Tiny swirls of silver gray hair showed in his ears, made widow's peaks on his eyebrows. But at this last statement, he interrupted.

"So why come to me, Inspector? It seems you have a black-market battle on your hands. I deal in aberrant behavior. These murders would appear to be simple business feuds."

"That's what the original investigators thought, as well. But there are several inconsistencies with that theory. The third victim, for example, Lieutenant Jean Grammond, a French law clerk, was murdered on the fourteenth, near the main train station. Thus far we have not found any black-market connections with this victim. Same modus operandi, however. A clean, almost surgical cut to the throat, according to our medical officer. And the killing once again took place in the rubble of a bombed-out building. Victim number four was killed on the seventeenth, but here we have a slight difference in MO. Killed in his room at the Grand Hotel, and there were trophies taken."

The doctor raised his hairy eyebrows at this.

"The little fingers were cut off," Beck explained. "Which indicates to me a sense of urgency on the part of the killer, a need for larger recognition. And this fourth victim was the first that was not an Allied soldier. Herr Viktor Krensky was a Polish nightclub owner. Thus far the only black-market connections with him is that he used it to purchase alcohol for his club."

"You mentioned several inconsistencies," Niedholer prompted.

Beck nodded. "There were also a series of notes left behind at the crime scenes. Calling cards with coded messages. Always in the victim's right hand. With victim number four, care had been taken so that the message was not obscured with the blood from the hand wounds."

Niedholer said, "I assume you have brought these 'calling cards' along with you?"

Beck nodded again, fishing the pages out of his overcoat pocket and handing them across the expanse of desk to the doctor. Niedholer took them in blue-veined hands, turning them front to back for a time before settling down to look at the text itself. Several minutes transpired, measured by the steady tock of a pendulum wall clock.

"I assume the underlined words gave you your coded messages?"

"That's right." Beck gave him a quick description of Morgan's decryption and the messages that appeared to be historical markers of the Third Reich.

Niedholer breathed in deeply as response. He had heard it all in his long career. Little surprised him.

"Well, I can tell you first off your perpetrator has execrable taste in literature."

"You know the sources?"

"Source," Niedholer corrected pedantically. "Our own dearly beloved Karl May, of course. His tales of the Wild West written from the confines of prison or from his Hamburg home. The fellow never got further west than Brussels, and his only training in writing was in forging checks—for which he served prison time. Yet he managed to spin dozens of tales of Shatterhand, a European adventurer in America, and Winnetou, his Indian sidekick. I assume you never read them as a boy, Inspector?"

Beck shook his head. "Never. Huck Finn in translation was more my style."

"I read him," Niedholer replied almost defensively. "But then literary fashions change. He was a favorite of Hitler's. Did you know that? The man had an entire library of May bound in calf at the Berghof." He made a small *tssk*-ing sound as people did these days when telling stories of Hitler.

Beck did not want to exchange crazy-Hitler stories today. "You say these are all from the same book or all from May?"

Niedholer looked back at the book pages. "I'm not a literary analyst, but I should think these are all from one of May's most popular novels, *Winnetou*. It glories in the noble savage who teaches the European greenhorn a thing or two."

Niedholer continued to examine the pages. "What do you make of the slashes at the bottom of each page?"

Beck glanced at the pages again as the doctor indicated the rust-brown markings.

"We weren't sure. Perhaps an attempted signature. Initials? They look similar on each."

"Yes, yes," Niedholer agreed. "Those are interesting. Instructive, moreover." The doctor fastened his liquid eyes on Beck: "I'd say your murderer strongly identifies with the noble savage concept. Might even see himself vindicating that precept in the face of the new conquerors. An irony there, of course, returning the noble savage ideal to the decadence of Europe."

"Wait." Beck sat up in his chair. "You're getting ahead of me. How do you come up with this identification? What are you seeing?"

"Why, the initial, of course. I thought you'd already made that surmise, Inspector. Those slashes at the bottom of the page make the letter *W*." He handed one of the pages back to Beck.

He looked at it and suddenly the letter came into sharp focus for him. How could they have missed it before?

"So it does."

"*W* for Winnetou, I assume," Niedholer said. "Ergo . . ."

"He's signing himself as the noble savage. He sees himself as Winnetou."

Beck paused, and then said, "So you agree?"

Niedholer understood the implications of the question.

"Oh, there is not doubt of it. You are dealing with a multiple or stranger murderer here. Some day, we shall find a better term for this sort of deranged individual who kills for no apparent rational reason and who picks his victims randomly."

Niedholer nodded at him happily as he spoke, as if talking about the latest theatrical offering at the old Crown Theater—now also a pile of rubble.

"And if I want to get into his skin . . ."

"Precisely, Inspector. You must begin to think like an Indian. To think like Herr May's Indian. To wonder what childhood trauma made our killer fixate on that novel. What form of possible abuse, fright, or terror coalesced with the reading of May to present such behavior? These would be instructive questions for you. There will be a certain profile to such a killer. Such defects begin early in life; they do not suddenly pop up in the middle of an otherwise normal adulthood. There will have been early transgressions. Perhaps a fire was set or pets were abused;

neighbors' cats went missing. Maybe even some violence done to another child with a sharp instrument, a razor or scalpel. In such cases, the perpetrator chooses his weapon early and does not deviate from such a selection."

Niedholer paused for a moment, looking again at the notes on the desk. He looked up at Beck once again: "And this does not come about simply because the child is bad. No. I forbade the use of that term in my clinic. We are all born as a clean slate; things are done to each of us that lead to the writing on that slate. There can be no cure without a recognition of the cause."

"But we are not talking of a cure, Doktor," Beck reminded him.

"Then think of such things as clues that will lead to the perpetrator's capture. Search for someone who has been damaged in childhood. All my research has shown me that such individuals are the products of some terrible childhood trauma. Some sort of abuse, be it physical or sexual. And usually administered by close relations. Look for the little boy dressed in girl's clothing as punishment, or the one overly protected and smothered by his mother's unwanted embraces, or who had his pants taken down by a drunken uncle. There would seem to be ritual involved, as well. Remember the Red Indian in this. The noble savage."

Niedholer suddenly looked upward, as if trying to remember something, trying to dredge up past experiences. There was silence for a moment.

"You make it sound as if we are looking for a sex maniac," Beck said. "But these killings aren't sex-related. There has been no genital mutilation. Nothing of that sort."

Niedholer fixed him with a penetrating look. "Killing in such a fashion, with a blade, is an *a priori* sexual deed, Inspector."

Beck took this in. Even if he did not completely agree with Niedholer's extreme point of view, it gave him a new direction to explore.

"So if we are talking about a profile . . ."

"Yes," Niedholer said. "I would say that you are looking for a male—that would seem to be your assumption anyway, no? Poison or a revolver is much more a woman's sort of weapon. Though there have been a fair number of female multiple murderers throughout history. There was the English cook Margaret Davey, whose favorite spice was poison. She was, I tremble to say, boiled alive for her crimes in mid-sixteenth century. And of course we have the noblewoman Countess Báthory of Hungary, who tortured hundreds of young women for her own sexual amusement. But mostly it's men, like Jack the Ripper, who fit the profile of multiple murderer."

Once again, the psychologist turned his gaze upward, as if striving to remember something.

"A male, then," Beck said by way of bringing Niedholer back to his profile.

"Indeed. You might look for someone who is a bit of a loner, somebody who has trouble with authority or self-control, or perhaps indulges in bizarre sex behavior or even self-destructive behavior."

Which sounded to Beck like about half the population of postwar Germany.

"And you may also be seeking someone of privilege. Someone who has means and opportunity to carry out such crimes unnoticed by others. Privacy is a luxury in today's Germany, Inspector." Niedholer nodded his head toward the floor, indicating the displaced persons occupying his bottom-floor apartments. "To commit these crimes, a killer would need to have the luxury of privacy to travel to and from the killings with no one asking him questions, and the privacy in which to clean up after such a bloody business."

"A broad profile."

Niedholer shrugged away the criticism. "You are traveling into the waters of investigation for which there are no charts. All I can tell you is that this one, like your last adversary, will continue his deadly task until you stop him. From what you tell me of method and technique, this is a practiced killer, methodical yet impassioned. He enjoys his work, so to speak. He will not simply go away as did the Slasher. There will be more victims. More and more."

He pointed to the passage from May, reading: " 'Not just one murder, but mass murder.' "

The words, spoken by Niedholer, were suddenly chilling.

"And your deduction about the fingers taken from the last victim, that they show urgency is absolutely correct. I think your killer desperately needs some recognition, some publicity. That's what all these clever crimes are about, after all. The encoded messages, the scheduling. There is an escalation here that is rather frightening. If your killer sticks to schedule, his next murder will take place tomorrow, correct?"

"That's what we have figured on, yes."

"And that the trial of Nazi war criminals also starts that day has, I assume, not escaped your attention."

There it is again, Beck thought. Morgan's fears about the trial somehow being connected to the murders.

"We are taking it into consideration, Doktor."

Morgan spent the morning waiting to talk with Colonel Maillot of French military security. A soggy Gitanes drooped from the man's down-turned mouth. His English was better than Morgan's French, but in whatever language you put it, Maillot was contemptuous of what he saw as the meager efforts of Morgan and his team to find this perpetrator.

Morgan listened to complaints ten minutes before being able to get a word in, and then discovered that Maillot had nothing he could use. The young man in question, Grammond, had a spotless war record, it seemed, fighting with the *Maquis* in the south of France. A law clerk, Sorbonne-trained, he'd come to Nuremberg to help with the French case. Kept to himself, did his work. No hobbies, immoral or other. Maillot nearly jumped out of his skin when Morgan mentioned the black market. Their dead Frenchman was a saint, it appeared.

Not much better luck with the Russians. The vodka-swilling Colonel Voschinsky was fond of *"Niet, niet."* No way were they going to have the memory of Comrade Soldier Orlov sullied with any linkages to the black market. Morgan had, at least, managed to avoid coffee with the French; with the Soviets, it was throw back several vodkas or no discussion at all. By the time he left the Soviet security headquarters on Bahmberg Allee at just past noon, his head was reeling from the effects of the booze and no lunch.

He had better luck at the American barracks, which had been the home of Private First Class Todd. There, he was just in time for the last dregs of lunch, but he was not complaining about GI chow. After gulping down the white and pink food—he did not want to ask too closely after its former incarnation—he went to the victim's bunk space and examined the footlocker. There were pictures of a sweetheart at home, a big girl who looked like she might know how to throw a steer for branding. In addition, there was a packet of letters from her, all of which contained the major theme of marriage once Todd got home. There was also a picture of the parents; the father looking rakish with a Stetson pushed to the side of his head, grinning around a toothpick as if he'd just told a joke, while the wife kept her mouth puckered and gave the camera lens a look of grave severity. *Life was no joking matter,* she seemed to be saying. Nothing here to indicate the kid was anything more than a 100-percent all-American soldier. But then how to explain the knapsack full of contraband found next to the body?

Todd's CO was Captain Woodruff, a quiet, bookish sort of fellow serving out his involuntary servitude for Uncle Sam. On the wall of his office was his CPA certification. Morgan imagined the captain carrying that plaque in his pack through the Battle of the Bulge. But Woodruff proved to have the only piece of valuable information of the entire day: the name of Todd's inseparable buddy the last several months, Private First Class Howard Baxter, latterly of the quartermaster's corps and now awaiting trial in the cells of the Palace of Justice. Woodruff was less forthcoming about the nature of the offense that landed Baxter in the stockade.

By early afternoon, Morgan had worked his way back to the cells at the Palace of Justice. The guard on duty took one look at Morgan's orders and nodded his head.

"Boy needs all the help he can get."

"What makes you say that?" Morgan folded the authorization letter from the Control Commission and put it back in the breast pocket of his tunic.

"Killed another soldier. Well, sort of a soldier, if you know what I mean."

Morgan had absolutely no idea what the man meant, but did not like the conspiratorial leer the guard cast his way.

Finally, though, once he was shown into the cells, he understood. Private First Class Howard Baxter was the hotheaded GI who had shot the Negro soldier in front of the Grand Hotel a week earlier. He sat on his bunk as Morgan entered, his eyes still blackened from his run-in with Morgan's knee, crusty cotton plugs up his broken and puffed-up nose.

Baxter recognized him as well. "Well, if it ain't the hero." He sounded like he had a bad head cold with the plugs up his nose. "Come to gloat, have you, hero?"

Morgan tried to place the accent. Bronx? Close enough. A wise guy, a tough guy. And like most of that sort, he was dumb and weak inside. Just had to take it to him hard enough to get him pissing in his boots.

Morgan stood over the young soldier; there was not even the luxury of a hardback chair in this cell.

"On your feet, soldier. There's an officer present."

The kid looked up at him with squinted eyes full of sudden rage.

"I don't see any officer. All I see is a sneaky kike bastard."

"You really do want this the hard way, don't you?"

Morgan grabbed him by the nose and the kid was on his feet in an instant, writhing in pain, but on his feet.

"Do I have your attention now, Private?"

The kid nodded, squeezing back tears. "Let go. Jesus, you're killing me."

Morgan let him go and wiped his hand on his twill pants. "Do we talk now?"

"About what?" The kid was fingering his nose, looking for the hurt part like a tongue searching out an infected molar.

"About your buddy Private First Class Todd, who got himself killed."

Surprise registered in the kid's eyes; Morgan could tell it was not feigned.

"What the hell you talking about? Toddy, killed?"

"There an echo in here?"

The kid kept touching his nose, then looking at his fingers to see if he was bleeding again.

"Hey, you really messed my nose up this time. Isn't there something about officers not being able to hit enlisted men?"

"What do I have to do to get your attention, Baxter? Do I need a pair of pliers here? I've got questions. You listen to them, you answer them. Understand?"

A look of cunning came over Baxter's weasel face. "And what do I get in return, *sir*?"

Morgan put his face into the soldier's now, so close he could smell the morning's coffee on the kid's breath.

"You don't get taken out of here this instant and summarily shot for insubordination and hindering prosecution. This is military justice, soldier. Never forget that. You're not out in the civilian world of 'make a deal.'"

The kid averted his eyes. His breathing came a bit faster. Morgan knew he had made his point.

"So okay. I'm listening," Baxter said.

"Your friend got himself killed the eleventh. That'd be the night after you ended up here. So it's news to you, right?"

"Right."

"You know what he was up to? Who he was meeting? Why the hell he had a pack full of contraband material—food, medicine, booze—with him at eleven o'clock in a German churchyard?"

"Shit. He got done there?" The kid suddenly slumped back down onto the bunk. Morgan let him be.

"I told him to be careful. Old Toddy, he was such a goddamn chump."

"You want to explain?"

Baxter shook his head, speaking to the floor. "Christ, Todd, he was like somebody out of a movie. You know, the girl back home in Wyoming, Montana, wherever. The ranch to go back to. One of those places they don't have a club for two hundred miles, where you got to go to the moon to place a bet. I'd die in that kind of place in under an hour. But old Todd, he loved it. Used to talk about how he was going to buy some land of his own and marry his little dreamboat and settle down and raise a bunch of heifers and little Todds. God."

He spoke as if this were the ugliest thought to come into his mind in years.

"And how was he going to finance this little dream of his?"

Baxter nodded, looking up at Morgan. "Yeah, well, he did errands, see. 'Redistribution of wealth,' he called it. Deliveries to certain people. I mean we got a starving populace out there, don't we? And there's plenty of stuff the army's got just goes to waste anyway. It's business."

"He worked for you?"

"Sort of. You could say that, in a way."

"Cut the crap, Baxter. The contraband's been traced back to the supplies at Fifteenth Regiment Quartermaster's Corps." Which was pure bluff, but the dope would never know, Morgan figured. "That's where you're assigned. So let's just move ahead here. I'm not after you for black-market activities. You've got yourself so deep in shit already, that's like hitting the cookie jar by comparison. So you supplied Todd with the stuff. You set up the meet. Who was he meeting?"

"That's the thing," Baxter said, his voice wavering slightly. "He wasn't supposed to be doing the meet. It was mine. I was going to be in that churchyard. But I ended up in here instead. So Toddy took over. That was a close one, huh?"

"The name, Baxter. Who were you meeting?"

Baxter shrugged. "German guy big in the market. Most

stuff passes through him. Maybe we could do a little deal here?"

Morgan reached for his nose again.

"Okay, okay. Guy called Rollo."

The name registered immediately with Morgan; he tried to do quick math to figure out when Rollo was imprisoned. After the Todd killing, he was pretty certain of that. Would have to check later.

"You ever do business with this Rollo before?"

"I mean, Rollo, for Christ sake. What kind of name is that?"

"How long were you doing business with him?"

"Not long. Couple of weeks. I like to establish my own distribution channels, if you know what I mean. My cousin Walt, he says that's the best way. Cut out the middlemen. Production and distribution under one roof."

"So what happened to your great plans?"

"Hey, you got to bend sometimes so you don't break. My cousin Walt's always saying that."

"Who was going to make you break?"

"Yeah, well, this Rollo guy had some pretty tough friends. They didn't like competitors, you know. Made that clear to me on a couple of occasions. I took the warning. I'm a businessman, so I decided to work with them for the time being. See what developed."

"These friends of Rollo's have any names?"

Baxter shook his head. "No. Young guys mostly, kids almost. But they had that look in the eye, you know? Like they could give a shit if you live or die."

Sort of like yourself, Morgan wanted to say, but didn't bother. It would be wasted on Baxter.

"You know, maybe they were after me. Set me up. Jesus, you get that Rollo. He's a real crook."

"I don't like the way Rollo's name keeps cropping up in this investigation." Morgan took a sip of beer from the frothy stein, then wiped foam from his upper lip with his forefinger.

The pre-dinner crowd was cheery and red-faced in Tegettner's Restaurant, one of those Nuremberg landmarks in the center of the city that magically escaped bomb damage when buildings to both sides of it had been reduced to piles of cement blocks and rubble. Inside, all was cozy and beery: the wainscoting on the walls was smudged a deep brown from generations of tobacco smoke; elk trophies stared out from high up on the walls under vaulted ceilings, looking somewhat askance at all the goings on as if it were all quite literally beneath them; the waiters wore tuxes—frayed at the cuffs and thin in the seat, but still tuxes. They bore their yeasty loads on silver trays—none of the buxom, dirndled girls of the Munich beer halls for Tegettner's. Beer was a ritual here; decorum was observed.

Beck sat across the large table from Morgan, nodding at his comment, but paying more attention to the large clock on the wall that told them it was already five thirty-three.

"He's a punctual man," Beck said. This was not a reply to Morgan's complaint, but a resumption of concerns he had voiced ten minutes earlier about Wieland Imhofer. There had been no sight of him all day. No notes left by Imhofer back at the office. The private who had driven him yesterday had reported dropping Imhofer off at a location near the Hauptmark in the afternoon. The detective had told the GI not to bother waiting. Maybe he had simply taken the day off and gone home to his farm to renew his supply of sandwiches. Beck was going to have to contact the man's wife soon, but wanted to put it off.

"Like I said," Morgan replied, "he'll be back once the cash runs low."

Morgan was sure that Imhofer was on the job for somebody else, double-dipping, and nothing Beck could say would make him think differently. *They seem so naïve, these Americans,* Beck thought, *but underneath it all is a grave suspicion of all motives, an abiding distrust in others.*

So Beck did not waste his breath. Instead, he downed his second chilled glass of Polish vodka. Morgan looked at the empty glass with faint disapproval, then took another sip from his first beer.

"Rollo was the guy our American victim was supposedly going to see." The American wiped at his foam mustache again. "Could he be our murderer?"

They had already been over this. Beck caught the Herr Ober's eye and pointed at his empty glass. A third drink was brought his way.

"Not unless he has powers from the grave," Beck said. "By the time our third and fourth victims were being killed, Rollo was already dead."

"Which means he has accomplices. Maybe whoever is engineering these murders wants us to think they are the work of one person."

Beck did not respond to this. Instead, he took the third vodka in one swallow, felt the cold liquor course with heat through his body. He caught Morgan's disdainful glance.

"Don't worry, Captain. I'll let you know when I start drinking for effect."

They were beating their gums because they had no one else to beat. Earlier this afternoon, meeting up again at the Palace of Justice, they'd decided to pay a visit to Colonel Adams. Beck's discussion with Niedholer had put him in Morgan's camp: Increasingly, he was beginning to believe these murders were connected to the trial. With the next victim scheduled for the next day, the very day the trial opened, those in charge of security needed to be apprised of the situation. Accordingly, they took their scant evidence—the decoded notes and clockwork schedule of killings—and made their way to Adams's office. And cooled their heels for an hour before being allowed in for a brief consultation.

Beck had taken an immediate dislike to the punctilious little man—he reminded him of Himmler without glasses. They showed their evidence, described the schedule the killer was keeping. Beck reported his meeting with Doktor Niedholer. Adams listened with half attention; he had a press conference in a few minutes. Kaltenbrunner, ex-head of Nazi security, had been rushed off to hospital, Adams explained. For a time, it had been feared that he had spinal meningitis and that all of the prisoners had been infected. After half a day of tense quarantine, it was found that it was "only" a cerebral hemorrhage.

"The scoundrel had a stroke," Adams told them, as if the Nazi had done such a thing merely to confound Adams. "And now we get word that the head Soviet prosecutor, General Rudenko, is still in Berlin. Come down with malaria, they say. I ask you, who gets malaria in Berlin?"

He looked at their amazed faces. "Look, gentlemen. What I am trying to say is, there is no force on Earth going to stop this trial. We have the weight of history behind us, rolling like a gigantic ball downhill. The momentum of righteousness is on our side, and nothing, not strokes, not a Russian's faked malaria, and surely not the schemes of some mad killer, is going to veer us off course. Let me give you some numbers here, gentlemen." Adams whisked a paper from his desk and read: "We have had almost a thousand men working on the restoration of this courtroom here since the summer. We have used more than five thousand gallons of paint, a quarter million bricks, a hundred thousand board feet of lumber, and more than a million feet of wire and cable." He thrust the paper back down on the desk like a prosecution attorney who had just made a damning point.

"Now I ask you, is some paltry killer going to stop the work of such a tribunal? We have twenty men in the dock who are charged with murders tallying in the millions. Rommel's niece has already been stirring up the press corps here, warning that the Bavarian Nazis are planning to blow up the court to keep the evidence we've gathered from becoming public. I am here to tell you that such considerations have been well taken care of." It was as if the colonel were practicing for his press conference, warming to his topic like a politician on the stump.

"There will be five M24 tanks surrounding the courtroom wing of this building, all of them mounted with seventy-five-millimeter guns. The hallways and roof will be filled with armed troops. MPs will be searching everyone going in and out of that courtroom. Even the judges are going to have to show an official pass. So thank you for the warning, gentlemen, but I think we have got things covered on that score. What I want you to do is to make sure that our killer does not hit the front pages of the newspapers back home. That he does not steal center stage. What we have here is perhaps the most important trial in the history of mankind. We're trying to establish the legitimacy of law in the field of war. If we are successful here, war may very well become a thing of the past. I am sure that I do not need to remind you that it is your job, gentlemen, to ensure the proper climate for such an august affair. To make sure that the rule of law maintains not only in the courtroom, but in the streets of this fair city."

Beck tried to contain his amusement; Morgan, on the other hand, was seemingly taking it all in with great seriousness, a solemn look on his face.

Colonel Adams checked his wristwatch one more time. "And now I must meet the men of the media," he said.

Five minutes, from entering to departure, Beck calculated. Outside in the corridor, Morgan was silent for a time.

"I need a beer," he said finally.

So now, after leaving a note on the door of their Palace of Justice office that specified where to find them in case of emergency, they were seated at Tegettner's. And running around in circles.

"You actually think this is about the black market?" Beck finally said. "After the other evidence we've accumulated. What's the purpose of the notes? Why all the complexity? I knew Rollo. Number one, he was not the violent type, and number two, he was not convoluted enough to come up with these coded messages."

"But number three," Morgan interrupted, "our friend Baxter said Rollo had some very nasty friends. So why don't we track down those fellows before we give the Rollo lead a pass?"

Beck was considering this proposal when Perlmann came

bustling into the restaurant, searching the tables with worried eyes. Beck waved to him.

"Inspector." Perlmann was out of breath when he got to their table. "You need to come with me," he said in German.

There was none of his usually relaxed manner, no Puccini today. Beck knew it was serious and did not like where his own thoughts were taking him. He was afraid to ask Perlmann where he needed to go.

"I'll meet you back at the office," he told a surprised Morgan as he placed a wad of dollars on the table.

"I'll go with you," Morgan offered.

Beck shook his head. Perlmann was already making his way out of the restaurant between the tightly packed tables.

Outside it was chilly; an icy rain had begun and people were scurrying along the darkening streets.

"He was found about an hour ago just under the Fleischbrücke," Perlmann said, lifting the collar on his brown leather coat against the cold. No need to say who. Perlmann knew Imhofer, knew the special relationship he and Beck had. Beck tried to keep his anger under control.

The old Kripo car was parked illegally outside the front of the restaurant; a red-faced doorman shouted at them as they got into the six-wheeler Mercedes, which had been blocking the entrance. *There was a time a man like that would not dare to make eye contact with a Kripo officer,* Beck thought. But again, such thoughts were only a game to keep his mind off the reality at hand.

"How did he die?"

Perlmann did not answer as he started the car and sped through the light traffic toward the Pegnitz River. No siren; no need of it with only some Jeeps on the road and the occasional bicycle. Beck gripped the armrest on his door in a tight hold, a man hanging on to a life buoy.

It took only a matter of minutes to reach the bridge just south of the Hauptmarkt. Beck could see a cluster of men along the riverbank; the frozen rain had turned to snow. The men were dressed in brown or black coats like Perlmann; at their feet along the concrete embankment, a tarp covered the body. It was a scene out of a painting, a winterscape by Brueghel with updated costumes.

Beck got out of the car and climbed down the narrow row of steps to the embankment. The three men turned to watch him approach. Two of them belonged to the ambulance waiting at the curb on the street above. The third was Manhof. There was no greeting between the two. Manhof made room for Beck to kneel by the body. He peeled back the tarp. Imhofer's face was bloated and gray as the sky; his mouth was gaping open. The stump of his tongue was clearly visible. The rest had been cut off. It was a signature of the homegrown criminal under- ground—a warning to others who were overly curious to watch their tongues or they too might lose them.

Beck flexed his jaw muscles. "Who found him?"

Perlmann answered: "An old guy was fishing and snagged him. Imhofer's body was caught on some docking cable along here." He indicated the edge of the embankment where fish- ing boats and small barges for the nearby market sometimes moored. "That was about four. By the looks of him, though, he's been in the water at least a day."

Beck nodded. Just after he was dropped off for his meeting yesterday, most likely. The meeting arranged with somebody in the local black market. The meeting that was somewhere near the Hauptmarkt.

Beck resolved that he wasn't going to talk with Frau Imhofer before he had her husband's murderer locked up for this crime or wrapped up in a body bag.

He felt a hand on his shoulder. Manhof was looking him straight in the eye as he turned.

"We've had our differences in the past," he told Beck. "I know how this must affect you. We'll get the man."

Beck said nothing. Manhof slowly withdrew his hand.

"And so you've come to me for help?" Major Hannigan was clearly enjoying this moment of vindication.

"We need some men for this evening," Morgan repeated, unwilling to give Hannigan the bone he desired.

Beck had no such scruples.

"Your assistance could prove invaluable in this operation," he said, stilling Morgan with a steely glance. Imhofer was his friend, his old colleague; he was not going to allow some private feud between the Americans to interfere with bringing his killers to justice.

Hannigan stuck out his lower lip in a satisfied smirk, looking, momentarily, not unlike the pictures of Mussolini that Beck had disparaged in the newspapers.

Hannigan gazed from Morgan to Beck and back again. His fingers did push-ups with each other at chest height as he sat back in his desk chair.

"Last time I loaned you boys some men, seems they were involved in a wild-goose chase. Your killer was busy in the Grand while they were freezing their tails off in the streets looking for a psycho. What do you have in store for them this time? An ice-skating party, maybe?"

He found himself enormously funny, chortling with a wet, thick laugh that let you know of his cigarette habit without seeing the pack of Lucky Strikes on the desktop.

Morgan's face turned red and he was about to unload on the Major, Beck could tell. He jumped in first.

"They'll be taking part in a raid on the headquarters of Werwolf activity in the city," Beck told him in a voice at once serious and confiding. "We'll need four or five of your best men. Men handy with weapons and not afraid to take a risk or two."

"Jesus Christ! So you boys are finally going to go to the source on this one. I was wondering when the hell you'd get around to that. Pretty obvious that it's Hitler holdouts responsible for these deaths."

"I'm surprised you didn't see to it yourself then, Major," Morgan blurted out. "While you were in charge of the case."

"I would've if you hadn't jumped my claim," Hannigan shot back.

Beck did not want this to get out of control. "Five men should do quite well," he said. "I trust you to find the best for us, Major. You seem a man who knows another man's worth."

It was almost midnight when their jeep roared out of the inner courtyard of the Palace of Justice, led by the massive troop transport that would break path, tearing down any piano wire strung across the streets at night. Morgan and Beck's jeep had a rear-mounted machine gun—just in case.

"I hope you're sure of this," Morgan said.

Beck stared straight ahead, not bothering to look at Morgan as he spoke.

"I'm sure. Aichinger was too piss-pants scared to lie."

The black market gnome from the hut by the Hauptmarkt. Aichinger had been Imhofer's lead to the Werwolves, and Beck had paid him a visit after Imhofer's body was discovered.

Morgan looked again at the set of Beck's jaw, the steely glint in his eye. Piss-pants scared, indeed. He could only imagine what had transpired in that miserable hut by the Hauptmarkt to make the gnome give up his sources.

Clear sailing down the Fürther Strasse, skirting what was left of the old city walls, and down Sandstrasse, into the tunnel running under the railroad tracks and out again into the Steinbühl district. Empty black streets; here and there, a fire pulsing in the ruins, a huddle of bodies seeking warmth. Morgan checked his Colt sidearm a final time; he'd issued Beck one, as well.

Soon Beck gestured to their driver, who, in turn, dimmed his lights at the transport in front. The vehicles pulled over, and a squad of five soldiers jumped out the back of the transport.

"Up the street," Beck said. "The cellar, fourth building on the right."

Morgan's eyes had adjusted to the dark, but that did not help. How to distinguish "buildings" in this state of collapse? He counted rectangular foundations, standing doorways, not much help.

Beck, unbidden, took the lead, and Morgan's detail formed

up in back, weapons at the ready. *They carry themselves like soldiers*, Morgan thought. *Find out soon enough if it's more than looks.*

"Someone needs to be standing when it's all over," he reminded the soldiers. "Or crawling. Aim low."

A nodding of heads, puffs of vaporized breath.

Morgan directed the jeep with the machine gun to pull up after them and seal off escape routes.

They moved off, following Beck. To Morgan's ears, they sounded like a battalion moving in the still night; the clap of boots on the pitted cobbled road, a nervous cough. Morgan thought he saw eyes in the ruins. Cat or human? He feared a set up. Simple little ambush. Still, he had to trust somebody. But Aichinger, the gnome?

"Over there," Beck whispered to him.

They picked their way through the rubble to the cellar door, a flat, hinged metal plate on the ground. Morgan nodded at the men—they'd gone over this earlier. No other way. Couldn't call out for surrender—the rats would likely scurry away in connecting underground tunnels. Toss a grenade as a warm-up? Hard to foresee the space down below, the resulting level of casualties. Plus there was no way to know if this was shared accommodation. Could be women and kids below.

"I'll take it from here, Beck," Morgan said.

The German looked at him, ready to argue, and then saw the resolve in Morgan's eyes and merely nodded.

A soldier leaned over to grip the door latch, balancing himself to pull it open quickly.

Morgan drew his Colt, eyed the rest of the soldiers, and then nodded to the one at the door. The soldier sucked in breath, heaved on the latch.

The metal slab did not move.

Another mighty tug at it and still no movement.

"Must be latched inside," the soldier said, looking at the others.

"Now what?" From Beck.

Morgan thought quickly. "We knock. It's the polite thing to do."

He leaned over the metal door, arm outstretched.

The shot came from his left; he automatically rolled to his right, finding cover behind a chunk of masonry. His men scattered in the ruins, taking up defensive positions firing in the direction of the first shot. The soldier at the door had not been so lucky, Morgan could see. He was down, holding his stomach. Firing came from in back of him now. Two positions at least, he registered, crawling for new cover as the dust and chip of ricochet flew past his head.

"Back up," he yelled through the shooting. "Get that jeep up here!"

His men were firing at will: no plan now, just instinct and reaction.

"Beck!"

No response for an instant. Then, "Over here."

He could see the helmets of some of his men behind rubble, hugging the ground. The angles of fire were all wrong.

"You see them?"

"Angels," Beck said.

Right. They had to be on high ground to get that firing angle. Morgan looked up into the dark and crumbling walls of buildings surrounding the field of fire. Another round pounded into the earth a few feet away. He thought he saw movement on the skeleton of a wall to his right. Tease him. He took off his helmet, held it at arm's length on the barrel of the Colt, keeping his eyes on the wall. Another shot, a hornet flying inches over the helmet. A silhouette in the frame of a window on what was left of the second floor. He cursed his useless pistol.

"Second floor, third window from the right," he called out. "You got him?"

A soldier answered: "Got him."

Another shot, then a burst of automatic fire. The silhouette toppled out of the window frame.

He could hear the jeep now, backing into position.

"High shots," he yelled out. "Spray the windows."

Yellow-golden tracer bullets poured out in the darkness, ripping into ruined walls. A yelp of pain, a groan. Morgan got to his feet, signaling his men to follow him as they spread deeper into the ruins under the covering fire of the machine gun.

Hunt and duck now, keeping each other in sight. No friendly-fire casualties. A scurrying and rustle ahead in the rubble; before Morgan could aim, the soldier at his right took the German down. A clean shot to the back—the German flew forward, arms splayed.

"We need one alive," Morgan called out. On the offensive now, they could pick their shots. Aichinger had told Beck it was a band of five—felt like more now in the middle of the action. More firing to his left. Morgan moved toward the shots, keeping low, feeling the bite in his thighs from his crouching shuffle.

Suddenly, the battle zone was filled with light; the truck had pulled up and turned on its headlights. Morgan and his men were caught in the beams like gray spectral marionettes on a stage. The crack of a shot, a GI down at his side.

Morgan squinted into the light. "Cut those beams!" Automatic fire pouring into the quadrant the shot had come from. "Lights out!"

The lights were finally extinguished, but all Morgan could see were dancing spots of illumination in front of him. It took him several moments to regain his night vision.

"Captain. Over here. We got them."

Morgan made his way toward the voice. He could see a couple of his men holding their weapons on two Germans, hands held high above their heads. The GIs stood almost a foot taller than the Germans, an odd tableau in the ruins. Four of them accounted for. He was about to call out "Good work" to his men when he heard the snick of metal on metal from behind a standing pillar to his right.

The barrel of a Panzerfaust, a primitive bazooka, was aimed straight at the backs of his men.

"In back of you!" He fired off two rounds at the barrel. His men whipped around, giving the two Germans they were covering a chance to go for concealed weapons. There was firing to his left, but Morgan was busy with the Panzerfaust. It swung his way, leveled at him for an instant, then he dove for cover. More shots in the darkness; the swat and slap of lead into flesh. Morgan on his belly in the clammy, dew-sodden rubble.

"He's down." Beck's voice.

Morgan let out air and got to his feet.

"You men all right over there?"

"Right. Two more Germans down here."

Damn. How far down?

It took ten more minutes to see how bad things were. Meanwhile, now that the firing had ceased, civilians were coming up out of the earth like corpses rising from the dead; the old and grizzled, young women so thin their eyes bulged in their faces. No men. The remains of Germany.

"Murderers," one of the women spat out. "Animals."

They gathered the bodies near the door to the cellar, broken open now. Nothing below ground but some stolen coal and a tattered copy of *Mein Kampf*.

In the illumination of the headlights and their flashlights, they could clearly see what a screw-up this had been. Five Germans laid out on the ground. And not one of them older than fourteen.

"Stupid kids," one of the soldiers said. "Playing at soldiers."

"They weren't playing," Morgan reminded him. But the two American casualties turned out to be a flesh wound to the hand, not a stomach shot, and one to the thigh.

The Germans gathered around, looking at the dead youths, squinting at the American conquerors.

"Get these rubberneckers out of here," Morgan finally told another of the soldiers.

Kids, he thought. *Just kids.*

"Not one of them worth the life of Imhofer," Beck muttered,

the pistol still smoking in his hand, blood spatter on his fresh white shirt.

Gunfire nearby drew her attention away from him.

Marcel Piquet also jumped at the sound of shots. He had seen no fighting during the war, called up only after the German occupation. But he had trained well and could tell from the sound what weapons were being used. Small-arms fire, a machine gun, carbines. The firing was only blocks away.

He'd served the Vichy government for a couple of years in a dusty hamlet miles from anywhere, where there were no fireworks, militarily or sexually. The only available females being an octogenarian chicken farmer and a milk cow or two. He was making up for lost time in Nuremberg.

Marcel Piquet was a survivor; when the Vichy regime fell in the fall of 1944, he'd traded in his uniform for a beret and trench coat and fabricated a legend for himself as a member of the Resistance in the South, soul survivor of his cell. Then, with the liberation, he'd taken up with de Gaulle's Free French forces and found himself an occupier in Germany.

Germany, land of opportunity and eager fraus and fräuleins.

He was making up not only for lost time sexually, but also economically. Things were going Marcel's way finally, with a city full of suits and bigwigs needing the kind of services and supplies he dealt in. And by the looks of this tall, smart-looking woman he was meeting, tonight was going to live up to the *réclame* he'd been fed about her.

Hell with the games, he thought, moving toward her as her eyes were averted toward the shooting. He was on her and tearing at her clothes before she had a chance to protest. They were down in the rubble rutting like animals, and Marcel was ecstatic. His hand was under her long skirt, feeling the slide of the silk stockings she wore, and that made him all the more eager, all the harder. His hands reached the elastic of her panties, and he tore at them, freeing his penis with his other hand, holding her down with his chest. He was into her and exulting at the feeling of control and absolute power. He only wished she would scream; that always made it better, more erotic. But she lay under him almost like a corpse.

He thrust deeply into her twice and then felt a stinging at his throat, saw her right hand finish its arc with a metal blade in it. His front was instantly warm. He looked down unbelieving, gasping. He was soaked in front; he felt a pulsing at his throat, blackness behind his eyes. His last thoughts were strangled by an erection that seemed to gain strength even as blood spurted from his jugular.

Marcel Piquet's hips made a final spasm as he died.

The killer struggled out from under the corpse, the man's penis making a sucking sound as it trailed out of her vagina. She felt that she might vomit, but controlled herself.

It had all gone horribly wrong. Just as the Frenchman was unbuckling his pants as requested, the shots rang out. Her demand to unbutton his pants was meant as a diversion, which before had always allowed her the opportunity to strike. This time, however, the killer herself became the victim, diverted, in turn, by the sounds of gunfire.

She must think quickly now. First the message, placed in the right hand. And the bloody swipe of the scalpel as with a fountain pen to leave the initial.

No time to worry about her appearance. Thank God that her long cloak had been open when he attacked her. Blood covered the front of her dress, but closing her cloak, she thought she could cover up any sign of the blood until she got home.

He had not ejaculated: no stickiness on the insides of her thighs. That was also something to be thankful for.

There were no signs of life in the ruins around them. That was why the meet was scheduled here. But she could not linger.

The man's penis was so small and defenseless now, a sagging white worm. She bent over, her scalpel at the ready, but a scuffling of rocks and debris nearby made her jerk toward the sound. She listened carefully. Could it be footsteps? She could not risk more cutting. She rapidly wiped the scalpel on the dead man's coat, then wrapped it in velvet, placed it in her pocket, and fled from the scene like a harried commuter chasing a departing train.

Behind her in the ruins, a small dog continued digging, following the scent of buried bones.

PART III

November 20, 1945

"Exactly what part of my command yesterday did you not understand, Captain Morgan? The part where I requested you to keep any bad news off the front pages or when I ordered you to keep deaths in the streets of Nuremberg from upstaging our trial?"

Morgan stood helmet in hands in front of Colonel Adams. He hadn't slept after the shootout; no stand-down, just coffee and the should've-could've routine. He didn't attempt to answer Adams. It wasn't really a question.

"But you're too smart for authorization, aren't you, Captain? You and all your OSS friends. Do you have the slightest idea of what it means to follow orders? This isn't your OSS cowboy and Indian games anymore, this is the army."

Adams was working himself up, but Morgan, his nerves shot, wished he would just get it over with.

"You know, you are making me sorry I requested you from Donovan. I thought you were a hotshot inspector who cleared cases, not another OSS wild man. What in God's name were you thinking? The trial starts in a matter of minutes, probably the single most important trial in the history of the world, and you decide to have a shoot-up the night before. You've got a great sense of timing, Captain."

The voice echoed off the wall in the large office. Out the window, Morgan could see dignitaries filing into the Palace of Justice, ready to start the proceedings. At least it seemed to disprove his fears that the killings had anything to do with the trial.

"Do you hear a word I'm saying, Captain? Is this sinking in at all? I won't have this type of insubordination—hell, I won't have any sort of insubordination. You've got the entire city at our throats, you realize that?"

"Sorry, sir," Morgan mumbled.

"What's that soldier?"

Morgan cleared his throat. "I said, sorry, sir."

"Oh, that's marvelous. Contrition. That and a pack of cigarettes will surely buy back the trust of all the Adolfs and Evas out there. Heavens above, Morgan, we're trying to win these people over. You comprehend that? They *were* our enemy. Past tense. That's what this trial is about, man. Hang the villains who misled the poor dumb Germans and get on with *realpolitik*. We need these folks."

Morgan did not like Adams, especially now, repeating the very arguments he had come up with halfway through the war. The working brief of the OSS was that the new enemy was going to be the Russians. That the Germans, neutralized, would provide a buffer between East and West. Christ, Adams and his by-the-book Military Intelligence G-2 friends would still be cozying up to Ivan if not for Morgan's assessment.

But he told himself to get it over with, to give Adams what he wanted.

"I see that, sir. New realities."

"You bet your sweet whatever on that, Captain. The new reality is that we'll need all the allies we can get to stop the Sovs in Europe. And to do that, we don't go shooting up a bunch of kids. Not in front of their parents and uncles and cousins and I don't know who all."

"Actually, there were no relatives present, sir."

That shot the redness up into Abram's thinning hair, brought him to his feet and sent a pudgy fist onto the top of his cherrywood baroque desk.

"I suddenly don't much like you, Captain. And I sense the feeling is mutual. General Donovan I respect. He was . . . is a genuine American, served his time in the military, saw the need for alternate forms of information gathering. But the OSS is gone now. Part of history. Donovan's disciples like you—you're not army. You're a law unto yourself. You're here because of Donovan, not because of your supposed accomplishments."

"I said I was sorry, sir. We were fired on. We returned fire. We engaged the enemy. In future, I will keep you fully informed."

Another fist to the desktop. "That's exactly what I mean. You will not just keep me informed, Captain. You will receive your operational orders from me. I am not simply part of the chain of command. I am the damn chain as far as you're concerned."

Morgan stood up straighter, blinking the exhaustion from his eyes. This was serious if Adams was swearing.

"Yes, sir."

The color began to leave Abram's scalp, receding to his nose. He sat at his desk again, making the springs groan in his leather chair. A glance at the file in front of him.

"Says here you lost one of your operatives. This some sort of revenge attack?"

"No, sir. We were seeking information on resistance cells."

"With a platoon of soldiers and mounted machine gun?"

"We had no idea what to expect, sir. The German resistance is a reality. They're killing GIs."

A flutter of Adams's eyes. A stubby finger poking at the file.

"This is what I need to see before you go off half-cocked, Captain. Understood?"

"Yes, sir."

"Anything else you need to appraise me of?"

"No, sir."

Adams let out air, a balloon come untied. "Dismissed, Captain. And find this killer, will you?"

Morgan needed to pass out for a few hours.

"Yes, sir."

Beck was waiting for him in the corridor amid a sea of WACs bustling up and down, arms filled with files, dossiers, death warrants.

"There's been another one," the former chief inspector said. "Not far from our action last night."

It took them fifteen minutes to get there. By that time, a pair of MPs had contaminated the scene, rifling through the dead man's pockets looking for ID, trampling any evidence that might have been left behind.

Morgan was too tired to be angry, though. He doubted their killer was going to leave anything behind. Neither Haskell nor Perlmann had come up with anything from the scene at the Grand Hotel. What could they expect from an outdoor crime scene so many hours old?

Similar MO as the other murders: the neck slashed from the front and a page torn from a Karl May novel, random words underlined, left in the victim's hands. *The timeline is off though*, thought Morgan. If the killer stuck to three-day intervals, the murder should have happened that night. Then he realized: Maybe he struck after midnight last night, in the early morning hours of the twentieth.

Morgan quickly saw something else that was different about this one. He and Beck stood along with two MPs staring at the shriveled penis poking out of the man's fly.

"Killed taking a piss?" the bigger MP said.

Morgan shook his head. He kneeled down, peering hard at the man's member. They'd need Haskell, need to do a swab, but the flaky matter he saw on the penis was dried vaginal fluid. He'd bet on it.

He stood up, feeling dizzy, but not because of sudden movement. His thoughts were spinning. He looked at Beck and the German nodded in silent agreement.

"Christ. It's a woman," Morgan said. "Our killer's a woman."

Chief Inspector Rainer Manhof had gotten word of the Werwolf shootout from a contact in the middle of the night. He had spent the hours until daylight tidying up that mess and thus learned of the killing of the French soldier only later that morning from Inspector Perlmann, who just returned from the scene and was in search of part of his kit that he'd forgotten.

"Haskell confirmed it," Perlmann said, savoring his bit of inside information.

"Confirmed what, Inspector?" Manhof was still peeved that one of his men had been seconded to Beck.

"That there were vaginal juices on the Frog's *Schwanz*. This great killer, the person who's got all of Nuremberg's underwear in knots, is a woman. Can you believe it?"

Manhof felt the blood leave his face; his breathing came hard.

"Inspector, you okay?"

He sucked air. "Yes, sure. I'm fine." Irritation in his voice. "How can they be sure? Maybe the Frenchman had sex beforehand. They're like animals."

"And just forgot to tuck his penis into his pants?" Perlmann grinned broadly. "I don't think so, and neither does Beck."

"Beck." Manhof almost spat the word out.

"He was a good cop in his day."

Things had gone very far in the rehabilitation of Beck, Manhof figured, if Perlmann felt safe enough to makes such a comment in his hearing.

"We don't want to keep you from your important duties, Detective," Manhof said with withering irony. "It seems Kripo is no longer enough for you."

Perlmann chose to ignore this, found the fingerprint dust, and was gone.

Manhof sat at his desk a few more moments, stunned. He had worked too long and hard for this all to go wrong now.

Beck. Beck again.

Manhof, the same age as Beck but longer on the force, had had to play second team to the chief inspector throughout the

1930s and part of the war years. Beck had all the advantages, attending the snooty Sebaldus Gymnasium and then Heidelberg University where he studied philosophy, and after that London for criminology. It all came so easily for Beck. While Manhof had spent his entire life, it seemed, trying to pick his way out of his working class roots: battling his way to the top of his *Volksschule* class, struggling as one of the few day boys in his gymnasium, writing papers for his idle aristocratic classmates at university to help pay his way through. He'd earned his law degree by sheer force of will and then had cast his lot with the criminal police, sure he could create a noteworthy career.

Manhof had to watch Beck take all the honors, see his faux patrician face in the newspapers when he broke the Feingold murder case. Like a bad mystery novel, that was, Manhof recalled. The butler did it, but Beck discovered that this butler was special: He was a long-lost cousin in disguise who stood to inherit the Feingold mercantile empire with the bludgeon deaths of the five family members. So, not a crazy killer on the loose as the tabloids had it, but a cunning plotter out after money. The promotion to chief inspector should have been his, Manhof's, but no, the flashy Beck had gotten it instead.

Manhof had his revenge later, though. First came the Slasher, who played Beck like an accordion—had him running in circles trying to preempt the next murder. Even threatened Beck's family. *That was fine justice for Beck*, Manhof thought.

But he got his real payback with the shoot-to-kill orders by the Gestapo. When Beck refused to institute those at Kripo, Manhof himself had been delegated to arrest the chief inspector. Yes, that had been a fine day.

Manhof had no problem instituting such an order. Unlike others in Germany, he did not have a pet Jew to protect. Let them all rot in Palestine. And the lovely bit—the great piece of irony—was Beck's rearrest after he was liberated in 1945. A word in the ear from Manhof to a an American de-Nazification official—an obvious Jew—that former Chief Inspector Beck of the Kripo had collaborated with the Gestapo in their Jew round-up programs.

That was art, pure art, and now Manhof found himself smiling. But this old grudge was not addressing the matter at hand.

Rainer Manhof was not going to let all his plans fall apart when he was so close. He thought he had finally rid himself of Beck, his barrier to advancement, and now, when everything was within grasp, to have this happen! He would not allow it to stop him. That was all there was to it. She had to be stopped.

He stood suddenly, got his hat and coat, and was out the door without a word to Hoffman, the deskman.

The baroness was at archery practice again. She loosed an arrow straight and true directly into the heart of the target a hundred yards distant.

"Remind me not to get in the way of your arrow, Baroness von Prandtauer."

She wheeled around, ripped out of her reverie by the familiar male voice.

Then she faced him.

"Chief Inspector Manhof. How nice to see you."

Behind him stood Falk, tall and skeletal, looking distressed.

"I said I should announce him first, Baroness, but—"

She waved the servant away. "It's all right, Falk. Kripo march to their own orders," she said. "Perhaps tea in the drawing room?"

Falk bowed low, then fled.

Manhof shook his head at the retreating servant. "Still with you, after all these years, I see. You should get rid of the man. He's always about."

"Where else would he go? My family was his profession. But let's not talk of servants." She put her arm through Manhof's, turning to the villa. "Tell me what brings you here, Chief Inspector."

Inside, seated in the robin's-egg blue drawing room, at the

Biedermeier table, and over tea, with Falk safely out of the room, Manhof skipped the preliminaries.

"When were you going to tell me about last night?"

Aichinger's body was found later that day. There had been no attempt to conceal the corpse under the rubble; his body had been propped up against a partly crumbling wall in Fleischgasse, not far from the Palace of Justice. Rubble youth had been using it as a target for a time, throwing rocks and chucks of masonry at the lifeless body, until a clergyman walking his schnauzer came upon them.

"What have we all come to?" he kept saying over and over to Beck, who had already taken his statement.

Beck simply repeated, "We thank you for your concern. This is a police matter now. You have done your duty as a citizen."

Suddenly, the elderly clergyman erupted.

"Does no one mourn for our country, for our lost youth? They have become utter barbarians. This, the land of Schiller and Beethoven. Worse than barbarians. Brutes. What did you do in the war, Inspector?"

The question caught Beck off guard. Finally, "I spent much of it in Flensburg, if you must know."

The clergyman sniffed at this, clenched his jaw, and stomped off, tugging his leashed dog along as it attempted to lift a leg on Aichinger's left shoe.

Morgan finished his searches in the surrounding rubble, his face a mask of disappointment.

"You didn't really expect to find anything, did you?" Beck said.

"Can't we get him bagged?"

"Haskell has had a busy day. He'll be here."

The young barbarians had done damage to the face, though it was still recognizable as the black market gnome Aichinger.

Worse was the damage done to the right frontal lobe; it was a mess of pink and shredded bone where the bullet had exited.

"Bullet to the back of the head," Morgan said. "I guess we don't need Haskell to tell us that. Or that it was an execution."

Beck averted his eyes from the dead man. Aichinger was dead because of the information Beck had gotten from him the day before. Clearly, they had not killed the entire Werwolf cell last night; the survivor, or survivors, would not have to think too hard to figure out who had informed on them. It obviously had not helped Aichinger's cause that Beck had threatened him with a gun to get the information.

No. Aichinger's fate was sealed once he'd uttered the address to Beck. *Stupid bastard should have gotten out of town*, Beck told himself.

"Don't blame yourself," Morgan said.

"Furthest thing from my mind," Beck replied. "I'm just sorry we missed one of them last night."

Back at the Palace of Justice, they set to decipher the message found on the dead French soldier. Morgan was employing the same four-one-two-three transposition he'd used for the earlier ciphers and rapidly had a legible message, once again in English:

"GO WEST YOUNG MAN."

Morgan continued to stare at the words. They made no sense to him. Beck, seated next to him, however, nodded his head at the message.

"More stations of the cross," he said.

"What Nazi holy day is this?" Morgan asked.

"The opening of the Western front in France. May 1940."

"And our fifth victim is French," Morgan added.

"Like Krensky, the Pole, and Case White, the invasion of Poland. It seems our killer is no longer choosing victims at random."

"Maybe," Morgan said. "I don't know if two out of five makes for a pattern or not. But one thing we do have is the schedule. Like clockwork, every three days."

Small things to be thankful for, Morgan noted. The world

had not come to an end because there was another killing on the twentieth, the day the war crimes trial started. They had managed to control the journalists thus far, but last night's shootout was surely going to prove too juicy, too big a story for some reporter on the make who would just say "screw it" to the news blackout.

What the hell, Morgan thought. *You cannot control the world.*

But you should be able to find one deranged female killer.

"Next killing scheduled for the twenty-third," Beck said, as if announcing a train departure. "Unless he starts to use symbolic dates again, like the first killing and the Munich Putsch."

"She," Morgan reminded him. "It has to be a woman."

Beck shook his head. "I have trouble accepting that. Poison, yes, or as Doktor Niedholer said, even a gun. But this frontal assault with what, a knife, a razor . . ."

"I understand," Morgan agreed. "It's nothing I've ever seen before, either, but there have been instances. Lizzie Borden back in the nineteenth century. A hatchet murder of her father and stepmother."

"Yes," Beck said, "but she was, as you remember, found innocent. Besides, those were crimes of passion, not coldly calculated multiple murders. But these victims seem to have no connection with one another. They're chosen at random, except for the last two, which afford a certain bizarre symbolism."

"Don't forget the possibility of a black-market connection to all this," Morgan said. "Or Werwolf. The deaths of Imhofer and Aichinger may well be directly connected to these other five murders."

"And Rollo," Beck muttered, low enough that Morgan did not hear.

"We need to check this latest victim for any black-market involvement."

"Maybe she's an accomplice," Beck said. "A decoy to get the victims defenseless."

"Two killers?" Morgan turned it over in his mind. "Could be. Or maybe she's a twisted prostitute who's getting even with her johns."

"Or a war widow seeking vengeance on the victors."

They were silent for a long moment. Too many possibilities. They needed another break, something to give them a shoe in with the investigation.

Before the killer struck again.

"We need to get this information out. Soldiers need to know, need to be on the lookout. No more making nice with the Helgas in the ruins."

"I beg your pardon?" Beck said. "The 'Helgas'? As in German women? Why not a foreign national? She obviously knows English. Why not a bloodthirsty American female journalist?"

"That's enough, Beck. I get the point. But we need to disseminate this new information to commanding officers."

"And lose the initiative? This piece of information is like gold to the investigation. When we put out decoy teams on the streets on the twenty-third, they know they are looking for a woman. But the killer doesn't know that."

"You sure? Someone savvy enough to elude us this long must understand that the last killing compromised her identity. Maybe she even wants to announce to us that she is a woman. A way of thumbing her nose at our efforts."

Beck, who had personal experience with such antics, could only sigh.

"So we notify all Allied commanding officers," he said. "And then pray."

He came to the bar for a nightcap, and she was there again. Toby served them, and three drinks later they had discovered a common liking for Mozart, the works of Thomas Mann, and collegiate football. The last was a guilty confession from Kate, with which Morgan quickly concurred.

"Not the brouhaha aspects," Kate said.

"No. Most definitely not the brouhaha," he mimicked.

She looked closely at him to see if he were making fun of her.

Morgan suddenly felt alive for the first time in months, years perhaps. Able to discuss something besides the narrow confines of his work, though he loved it. This night had been restorative for him, and he realized he did not want it to end.

"I need some air," he said. "Will you join me for a stroll?"

It was not exactly the smartest thing to do. Besides their own multiple murderer on the loose, there were bands of roving thugs in the ruins of the city, laying in wait for just such couples. Nuremberg after dark was largely a lawless heap of rubble. The Germans were left to fend for themselves from sunset to sunrise. It was not much better during the day, though at least there was more of a military presence then. But Morgan was armed, and he knew a safe destination close by and in a cleared area.

Once outside in the cold November night, it was eerie. She stayed close to him as they walked the lonely Königstrasse north. A scurrying in the ruins to their right caused her to grip his hand. He knew from experience the difference between human and rat sounds and was not worried, but he held on to her hand, squeezing it, reassuring her.

The church soon came into view; he did not know its name, did not know what took him inside it that first time over a month ago, but it had become his pilgrimage point in Nuremberg. Wordlessly, they entered the shrapnel-damaged carved stone doorway and came directly into the roofless choir. Gothic, the architecture made you automatically follow the soaring lines upward. Their eyes had long ago adjusted to the deep darkness, allowing them to make out shapes. A timid crescent moon shone through high cloud cover, casting a pale luminescence down through the open roof.

Kate gasped. "Is that—?"

He nodded. "They can't get it down. It's been stuck up there for months. Heavy machinery working here might damage what's left of the structure. They say they're bringing in a crane soon."

They both looked up at the German fighter plane suspended surreally in the high arches of the bombed-out church, like a child's model plane dangling from the ceiling. Numbers still remained on the fuselage: F-3103. An Iron Cross was painted on the underside of one wing.

"The pilot's still in there, isn't he?"

"They say so," Morgan said, averting his eyes from plane for a moment.

She shivered at the thought, drawing closer to him, taking comfort from his warmth.

"This is what you wanted to show me?"

"It touches me," he admitted, looking again upward. "Something about the futility of it all. The absurdity. I'm not really a religious man. To me, this is a wonderful piece of architecture. But that machine, whose only purpose is death and destruction, suspended here in this place of faith. Like it was defeated by the holiness here. The height of man's technology, his most durable metal, and what does it count against belief?"

He shook his head, looked from the plane to Kate. "Sorry, I can't really express it very well."

"You're doing fine." She looked at him, measuring him with her glance.

"Anyway, I come here sometimes. It's like a reminder."

She did not ask him of what, and he was thankful for that. And then a sudden shudder at the thought that he felt happy right now.

"Okay?" she asked, feeling his sudden change.

"Yes. Very."

It was not the most romantic place to share a first kiss, and the difficulty they had finding each others' lips past upturned collars and noses in the wrong places did not make for a movie moment, but the kiss itself, the warmth of it, the eagerness, the yearning, the pure simplicity of it, made Morgan smile.

It surprised them both, and brought them just as quickly back to reality, moving them apart from each other for an instant of reflection, neither wanting to admit what had actually happened.

November 21, 1945

The rapping at his door brought him out of deep and pleasant sleep. Morgan had not stirred in the night, wrapped around
Kate like a spoon.

"Morgan, you there?"

It was Beck's voice. Morgan wiped sleep from his eyes; Kate
stirred next to him.

"Time to go?" she mumbled.

"For me to go. You sleep." He pecked her cheek, got a
mouthful of hair. An old married couple.

What the hell was he doing sleeping with a journalist? The
light of day made last night's romance appear as what it really
was: idiocy.

She rolled over, facing him, tracing a finger along his jaw-
line. "You're having second thoughts . . ."

"Morgan?"

"Just a minute," he called out. Then, turning back to her, he
said, "No. No second thoughts."

"You're a terrible liar, Morgan," she said. "You don't have to
be afraid of me, you know. I don't bite. Remember?"

He looked at her for a moment longer, at the soft downy

skin at the base of her throat between the collarbones, at the freckles across the bridge of her nose, revealed once her makeup was off.

Honestly, this time: "No second thoughts. By the way, it's not Morgan. My friends call me Nate."

"Go," she said, pushing him off her as he began kissing her. "Your German is waiting."

Morgan wrapped the sheet around him and went to the door. Beck was about ready to knock once more.

"Sorry. Overslept."

Beck looked over his shoulder into the room. "I can see. The jeep's waiting. We're going to Imhofer's farm, in case you forgot." A knowing smile on Beck's face now.

"No, I didn't forget. Late night is all." And he closed the door.

The village of Adelshofen was about twenty miles outside of Nuremberg, far enough away to avoid the destruction of bombers and also distant enough that there were no displaced persons' camps or holding pens for suspected SS.

The pleasantly rolling hill country was dotted with small farms. Orchards were shedding their final leaves; muddy tracks led up lonely lanes off the narrow macadamized road they were traveling. Here and there, a chicken was frightened by the jeep, scurrying in a cackling feather-flurry out of the way. A cow chewed its cud placidly as they flew by.

Morgan felt himself relaxing for the first time in months: the effects of last night and of the bucolic countryside. He shut his mind down for the time being; there was no need to second-guess what had transpired with Kate last night. *Just let something happen for once*, he told himself. *Don't try to manage events or make them fit into your pattern.*

"Werwolf country out here," their driver shouted back at them over his shoulder. He was a young guy, barely twenty, if that. Morgan had been staring at the boil on the back of his neck just above the collar line for much of the journey. Jersey accent. He kept his helmet on. A Jersey boy who had an instinct for danger.

"Murdered the local mayor last week," he added.

Morgan exchanged glances with Beck—so much for that rustic relaxation.

The Imhofer farm was north of Adelshofen, up one of the muddy tracks, about a half mile off the main road.

"I'm surprised they have a phone out here," Morgan said to Beck.

The former chief inspector stared back at him. "I can't imagine they do."

"Then how'd you get in touch with the widow?"

"I didn't. But where else is she going to be?"

They had, however, managed to get word of her husband's death to her yesterday by messenger.

As they approached the old farmhouse, a woman stood in the road, a carbine held in her arms crossed at the chest. She continued to stare at them suspiciously until they drew close enough for her to get a good look at the occupants. Her frowning face broke into a wide smile that transfigured her looks from hag to Rubenesque Madonna.

"Beck," she shouted as the jeep came to a halt.

Beck jumped out first and was still deep in a one-armed embrace with the woman—her other hand still holding the rifle—when Morgan reached them.

"*Verdammt*, it's good to see you," she said as they broke the clutch.

Beck held her at arm's length by the shoulders. "I am so sorry, Traudl. He was a good man. One of a kind."

She sniffed, wiped at a sudden tear. "He was the best, my Wieland."

Morgan could follow their German but did not want to intrude.

She blew air out of chapped lips, a sigh that seemed to relax her whole body.

"The kids?"

"Oh, they're about. Feeding the pigs, bringing in the last of the apples."

"You expecting company?" Beck said, nodding at the rifle.

"You never know. Maybe they'll come to finish their work."

Beck did not bother to ask who "they" were.

Frau Imhofer eyed Morgan, then looked back at Beck with his suit of clothes, rumpled and a bit bloodstained from the shoot-out the other night, but still newish.

She ran her forefinger under the lapels of the jacket. "You're doing well for yourself again, I see."

"This is Captain Morgan," he said, deflecting the remark. "I'm working with him on the case."

Morgan greeted her, using his Swiss German. It seemed to work in Bavaria, as well. But she did not take the proffered hand.

They stood for an uncomfortable minute in silence.

"Let me talk with her alone, okay?" Beck said, drawing Morgan aside.

Morgan nodded. "I'll be down here."

No niceties of inviting the *Ami* inside for a cup of coffee. He went back to the jeep. The driver was wiping mud off the windscreen.

"Don't care too much for us around here, do they?" he said, not bothering to look up from his work.

"Can you blame them?"

The private turned to look at Morgan. "You don't mind me asking, sir, but you Jewish?"

"Should I wear a yellow star, Private?"

"You don't need to get that way with me, sir. You think I'm a good Jersey dago? Fuck no, sir, pardon my fucking French. I'm a Jew like you. A Jew car mechanic from Trenton. And I lost relatives in this mess. Can I blame them? Fuck yes, I can. Every last one of them."

He went back to cleaning the windscreen.

Morgan knew how he felt; truth told, he felt that way often enough. He did not want to experience sympathy, let alone empathy, for the Germans. They elected a madman as chancellor, let Hitler take over their country, scapegoat the Jews, rape the little countries surrounding Germany. They were flying high on nationalism, a feel-good drug. Then came the big war. The real war. The unwinnable war on two fronts. The drug of nationalism led them to the precipice and they all jumped.

Still, he couldn't help it. There was that feeling of sympathy when he saw the ruin of Nuremberg or witnessed the street urchins with bulging bellies. There had to be a break with the cycle of hatred somehow.

Morgan did not bother to say any of this to the private, however. Instead, he wandered off toward the outbuildings. He came on a pigsty just in back of the barn. Two tow-headed kids not more than eight were lugging pails full of slops for the three pigs snorting and blowing vapor bubbles inside the sty. They tossed in the scraps and then noticed Morgan. He raised a hand in peace, and one smiled. He moved toward them.

"You an *Ami*?" one of the boys asked. His brother, apparently a twin, tugged at his arm to go. But the boy who asked the question wouldn't budge.

"I am," Morgan said. "Good-looking pigs, there."

"Bacon soon," the brave brother said. "How come you speak German?"

"I lived in Switzerland during the war."

"But Switzerland wasn't fighting."

Morgan nodded at this. "That's why I was able to live there."

"So you didn't kill people in the war?"

Morgan had an instant image of the resistance man he'd killed, but put it as quickly out of his mind.

"No. I was doing other things."

"You were a spy, weren't you?" Now the other brother became very concerned.

"Come on, Hans. Mama said not to talk to them."

"It's okay," Morgan said. "I knew your dad a little bit."

"Was he a spy, too?"

"No, he was—"

"You kids get back inside. Now!" This from a much older youth, obviously a sibling by the looks of his blond hair and similar facial features.

Morgan winked at the brave brother as they moved away. The older brother approached, carrying a long pole with a scythelike tool wrapped to one end like a grappling hook for apple harvesting.

"You with Beck?" he said.

Morgan said he was, keeping his eye on the lethal-looking hook.

"Thought so," the kid said, setting his tool against the sty. "Nice jeep. We're trying to find an old one to pull the cart. Tractor's been broken down for months."

This older youth nodded at a tractor collecting weeds alongside a tool shed.

"Any idea what's wrong with it?" Morgan asked.

"I'm a farmer, not a mechanic. Willy, the local mechanic, he was killed at Stalingrad."

Morgan thought for a moment. "Hold on a second, okay?"

He went back to the jeep. The private was sitting behind the wheel now, reading last week's *Stars and Stripes*.

"Private, you're not going to like this request. Request, not order. But this family here, they lost their father. He was helping us out. German Werwolves killed him, cut his tongue out. He's got eight kids, a widow, and a farm that stands between them and starvation. He didn't fight in the war. In fact, he hid a Jewish family here on the farm. But he was most certainly German, just like his widow and kids."

"What's the request, Captain?"

"You said you're a mechanic. Know anything about tractors?"

"Anything's got an engine, Sy Steinberg can work on it."

"Good. You want to give this engine a try? They got a tractor dead in its tracks."

Private Steinberg eyed Morgan. "This some kind of test, Captain?"

"No test, no order. Just a request. People need a hand, maybe you could help."

Private Steinberg pursed his lips. "Hell, anything's better than reading week-old news."

Like any good mechanic, Private Steinberg had a small tool kit along with him in the jeep. They packed it back up to the tool shed where the older youth was now standing, joined by several other fair-haired siblings.

"This man knows engines. Maybe he can help."

"*Bitte*," the older son said eagerly.

Steinberg eyed the rusty tractor, set his tools down, rolled up his sleeves, and started examining the motor. The kids stood around him like he was a specialist called in to cure their earache, maintaining the same kind of hushed reverent silence they would for such a medical specialist.

Twenty minutes later, just as Beck and Frau Imhofer were returning from the house, Steinberg climbed into the tractor seat, pushed the ignition button, and the engine coughed and spluttered to life. The children roared their approval, and even Private Steinberg had to smile at his achievement.

Climbing down from the tractor, Steinberg received slaps on the back from several of the bigger children. The small, brave brother just stared at him.

"Where'd you learn how to do that?"

Steinberg looked at Morgan and he translated.

"Tell him I learned it from my dad. Just like they learned farming from theirs."

Frau Imhofer seemed to have lost some of her suspicion now, waving good-bye to them all as they turned the jeep around and left the farm.

"A regular goodwill ambassador, aren't you?" Beck said as they bounced down the pitted track.

"It was Private Steinberg here who saved the day. Good work, Private."

"Just an engine, sir." Steinberg kept his eyes on the track ahead.

"What did you learn?"

"She's scared. Guess she should be. I promised her a couple of guards for the time being. That's the bargain."

"Bargain?"

"Otherwise no information."

"You mean she told you something and you aren't giving it up unless I requisition a couple of soldiers?"

"Right. You've got it."

"I could throw you back behind bars."

"Yes, you could."

"Beck, you are a damn stubborn man."

"Deal?"

A curt nod of his head. "What did she tell you?"

"Wieland was on the track of Werwolves . . ."

"That's not news."

"Patience, Captain. *Ein bisschen Geduld.* Seems these certain Werwolves, they've got a powerful connection. Straight to Nuremberg Kripo."

"How high?"

"That she doesn't know. But it explains how they might be able to operate with relative impunity in Nuremberg. They've got a sympathizer on the inside."

"Which explains Imhofer's death," Morgan said. "He was getting too close to Werwolf cells; he had too much information. But this doesn't get us any closer to solving the multiple murders."

Beck sighed. "Maybe it does, Captain. Maybe there's a link between all these murders. And maybe we just caught our first break."

The wind swept across the empty Zeppelin Field, the former staging ground for the annual Nazi Party rallies, the *Parteitagen*, in Nuremberg, orchestrated by the architect Albert Speer. From 1933 to 1938, Hitler held huge, choreographed rallies in Nuremberg with a quarter million screaming loyalists hanging on his every word. They began in the warm days of September with the church bells ringing to greet Hitler's train at the station. Hobnailed boots made the narrow streets echo a *Volkssturm* beat as loyal Nazis from all over the far-flung Reich gathered in Nuremberg to troop out the Zeppelin Field and hear the words of their leader. Torches, and later Hollywood-style lighting, created a tower of lights in the Luitpold Arena, the tightly cordoned area of 92,000 square yard scarved out of the Zeppelin Field where the faithful gathered.

Today, GIs were photographing one another on the tribune stand above the remains of what had once been a huge black swastika emblazoned on the granite. Here, Hitler, Bormann, Göring, and other leaders of the Reich had spoken to the quarter million cheering and frantic loyal Germans gathered below.

But the GIs were oblivious to the importance of this sacred place, too busy playing tourist, mimicking the Nazi salute for one another, and generally giggling like schoolgirls.

The new masters of creation, thought Manhof ruefully. He had gone to all but one of the rallies.

The Americans were also too busy to notice or care about the two Germans standing a mere hundred yards distant: Chief Inspector Manhof and the hulking youth next to him.

"Why don't we kill them," the kid said, his hand moving to the revolver he was obviously carrying in his coat pocket. The greatcoat was tattered, his boots falling apart, secured only by strips of leather cannibalized from the overhead hand straps of the few trams running the streets of Nuremberg. He smelled as if he might have last bathed at the fall of Berlin.

"We don't kill them now," Manhof said as if talking to a toddler, "because we do not want to tip our hand. What if one escapes? Then where is our plan?"

The youth, Klaus Ohlendorf, considered this; Manhof could almost hear the gears turning. But Ohlendorf had his uses: He was quite efficient as a killer, having been trained quickly in the art in the closing days of the war, when even children of twelve were expected to take up arms or risk being strung up by the SS.

Thus far, he had been entrusted with dispatching both the snooping private investigator, Imhofer, and that fool from the black market, Aichinger.

Yes, Klaus Ohlendorf most definitely had his uses; calculation and planning were not among those, however.

"I suppose so," Ohlendorf allowed. "We'll have our revenge soon enough, right?"

"Be assured. But business now. Do you know the man?"

"I've heard of him."

"I repeat, do you know him by sight? Could you recognize him?"

Ohlendorf spit green phlegm onto the cobbles.

"I take that as a negative." Manhof reached into his pocket and pulled out a picture.

"He a convict? I thought he was a traitor working with the *Ami*'s."

"He's both. And you know where to find him. He is about to undo all that we have planned. Do you understand? He must be eliminated."

"Destroyed," Ohlendorf muttered.

"And you cannot be taken into custody, not questioned."

"I would never tell."

"Not even when they crush your testicles with a nutcracker? Cut off one finger at a time and force you to eat them? Don't say never. The *Ami*'s are barbarians."

"Animals."

"You don't get taken alive. Understood?"

"What am I supposed to do?"

From another pocket, Manhof picked out a capsule similar to the one he'd put into Rollo's food.

"You chew on this. Bite down once and it is over. You'll be a German hero. Your name will live forever."

"My mother will know?"

"Oh yes, I will tell her personally."

"Forever?"

"They'll write songs about you."

It was near dark when Morgan and Beck got back to the Palace of Justice. They rode in the jeep around to the back to the motor pool with Steinberg. The front of the building was a security nightmare with the court just out for its second day of session.

They were getting out of the jeep when shuffling steps from in back of them made them turn quickly. Morgan's hand went to the automatic at his hip, but he saw it was an old lady.

"Inspector Beck," she said.

"Who's asking?" Beck said, stretching his long legs out of the jeep.

"A woman who has information. A woman who knows something I bet you'd like to know about your killer."

Morgan was ready to send the woman on her way. It had been a long day, and he wasn't in the mood for dramatics.

"Why are you coming to me with this information?" Beck said.

"Thought you might want to make up for the Slasher."

"What's she talking about, Beck?"

"Maybe we should have a talk, *gnädige Frau*. Do you drink coffee?"

"In another lifetime."

"Beck?"

"Let's go to the office, Captain. I'll explain later."

Upstairs, Beck busied himself with the electric plate, getting the water ready. He used the last of the coffee in the press. Soon the office was filled with its rich aroma.

The woman, Bertha Krauss, cupped her chapped hands around the cup, breathing in the vapors, and thought she was in heaven. She would pay for this later, she knew, with bowels in a twist, but for now she greedily sipped the coffee, holding it in her mouth to relish the taste.

"Now, what do you have to share with us?"

She eyed Beck. "Not so much share as sell, Inspector."

"Well, then, what are you selling?"

She smiled, partly at the taste of the real coffee and partly at Beck's obvious interest.

"I have a bowel complaint, you see."

"We are not really interested in your intestinal tract," Morgan said in his precise Swiss German.

"He speaks! Well, I only mention it to say why I was up in the middle of the night when that poor soldier was killed."

Now Morgan's attention was also won over. "What soldier?"

A blink from Beck let him know he should back off, let the former chief inspector conduct the interview.

"The soldiers told me the next day it was a Frenchman. The *first* Frenchman," she added with a smirk to let them know how well informed she was.

"And you saw something?" Beck prodded.

"Oh yes. I was about to do my business when I saw the soldier die. I hid in the rubble as the killer passed by. And I saw something shiny in the night."

"And you did not tell the soldiers investigating the scene?"

"No. I was afraid that the killer might come back for me."

"And you no longer fear that?"

"I fear poverty and starvation more. Now, what are you willing to pay?"

Beck made no threats; he knew the psychology of such informers. Say you're going to lock them up and you lose them. If she was willing to risk the killer coming back for her just to get some money, nothing Beck could say would frighten her.

"Twenty dollars." He looked at Morgan to make sure the captain had some money on him; Morgan nodded.

"I was thinking more in the area of a hundred."

"We don't have that kind of money lying around," Morgan interjected.

"But we can get it," Beck quickly added. "If it's worth it."

"My daughter's child has a terrible cough. He never gains any weight."

"We can help him. We have doctors," Beck said.

Morgan noted the sudden use of "we."

"Give her the cash you have," he said to Morgan. "A sign of goodwill."

Morgan counted out forty-two dollars from his wallet and handed it over to the lady, who immediately rubbed it between her fingers.

"You'll get the rest when we get this information. What was shiny in the night?"

She shot them a grin that showed several missing teeth. "A medal. The cross. An Iron Cross."

"The killer was wearing an Iron Cross?"

She nodded.

"You're sure about that?"

"The moon came out just as he was passing me. I could see the silver outlines of it glinting in the moonlight. It's a sight I'll never forget."

"Where was it?" Morgan asked.

"On the killer, of course."

Beck shot him a questioning look, but Morgan continued.

"No, I mean where on the killer. Was it on the chest, on the side, around the neck?"

She thought hard, taking another sip of the coffee.

"The neck."

"You're sure of that?"

"Yes. And now you mention it, there was some glinting above the cross, too. Some shinier metal, I couldn't make it out."

"We will get you your money," Morgan said. "And tell us where you live. There will be a medic team there tomorrow."

"It's good information, isn't it?" she said.

"Yes," Morgan said, looking at Beck. "Very good."

"I should have asked for more."

"One more thing," Morgan said. "You said the killer was a man. You could see the medal as 'he' was passing you."

She nodded, uninterested now.

"You're sure it was a man?"

Bertha Krauss squinted at him, a look of suspicion on her face. "You calling me a liar?"

"What was the killer wearing?" Beck said, interrupting Morgan.

She shrugged. "Wearing? Clothes, of course. A great coat or a cloak. Long, very long. And he wasn't a big man. Like he might have stolen it from someone larger."

"A hat?"

"Like a hood, I think. From the cloak."

"That is excellent," Beck said. "You have earned your money."

She smiled at them through her broken teeth.

Beck and Morgan exchanged glances. They were both thinking the same thing: *The small figure in the great coat could easily have been a woman.*

And so, they got another break. After they tracked down more money from the bursar's office, they sent Bertha Krauss on her way. Alone in the office, Beck looked at Morgan.

"Good questions, Captain."

"Good training at OSS."

"The Knight's Cross of the Iron Cross, then," Beck said. "It looks similar to the Iron Cross but is worn at the neck."

"Are you a betting man, Beck?"

"Not really."

"Too bad, because I would offer you odds that the bit of shiny metal above—"

"Is the Knight's Cross with Oak Leaves."

Morgan shot a forefinger pistol at him. "Exactly. And that narrows things down a bit. If it were just an Iron Cross, we'd be looking for several million recipients during the war. Just a Knight's Cross, and the number is in the thousands. But with Oak Leaves?"

Morgan paused dramatically.

"Please, Captain, the suspense is killing me."

"Fewer than a thousand were awarded."

"And it's narrowed down further," Beck said. "Ours is worn by a woman."

"Which means she either earned it herself or is the widow of war hero."

Beck nodded at this. "We can forget the first category. There were only a couple of female winners of the Iron Cross, none for the Knight's Cross."

"And we assume the recipient is from the Nuremberg area."

"Not necessarily," Beck reasoned. "Maybe she has come here, where the trials are being held, to make her symbolic statement."

"But where does she stay? In some cellar? There's not a room to be had with the trials here."

Beck remembered something Doktor Niedholer had told him—something that seemed insignificant at the time, but now, paired with the information of the Knight's Cross, helped fill out a profile.

"Someone of privilege," he muttered. "Not a crazed prostitute."

"What's that?"

"When he was profiling our killer, Doktor Niedholer said to expect someone of privilege. Someone who would be able to commit these crimes unnoticed by others. Someone who could travel to and from the scene of the crime, who could clean up afterward with no questions asked. There has to be blood spray involved in these killings, no matter how careful she is. She took trophies in one murder. That means she has privacy wherever she is living, and Niedholer was right. Privacy is a luxury in today's Germany."

"Which means the suburbs," Morgan said. "Most freestanding buildings in the center are destroyed or occupied by foreigners—defense and prosecution teams, military, witnesses for the trials."

"A widow, in the suburbs, of some standing and privilege, whose husband was a war hero. And someone who had a childhood sexual trauma, a history of torturing animals." Beck knew he was forgetting something. It had been niggling and nagging at him for several days. Now suddenly, it was quite clear.

"That's it. The code. She writes code. Is it a complex one?"

"Not very. But not something the usual citizen comes up with, either."

"This well-to-do widow of a war hero knows about codes and killing. Where did she learn these things? We need to keep asking ourselves that."

"The focus right now is on the Knight's Cross," Morgan said. "The Nazis kept detailed records of all their activities. They're still being sorted through in Berlin."

"And we've got two days before she strikes again," Beck added.

Morgan looked up from the notes he was taking.

"What did she mean about the Slasher? That's the second time someone's mentioned that."

"I thought you knew everything about me, Captain Morgan."

"Obviously, I don't. I've been patient. Is there anything I need to know?"

Beck sighed, eying Morgan, and knew it was time to share. He gave him an overview of the Nuremberg Slasher and how he, Beck, the European expert on such matters, was unable to stop a multiple murderer in his own backyard.

"You don't think he—she—is back at work, do you?"

"No," Beck shook his head. "Different MO totally."

"But that one got away from you, you say. Made you look a bit like a fool. Is that going to be a problem on this case, make it too personal?"

"Murder is always personal for me, Captain Morgan."

"You really are too modest, Miss Wallace."

"Kate. Please."

They were seated again in the drawing room at the tiny rosewood table with its inlaid wood of pinkish hue sharing a pot of coffee.

The baroness smiled winningly. "It is a custom we Europeans find hard to adopt," she said. "Your American instant first-name basis. Here, it takes years for us to assume an informal *per du* basis. Colleagues may work alongside one another for decades and still refer to one another with surnames and be on the formal *Sie* standing. One night at a wine tavern may obliterate such social lines, but I guarantee you, the next day at work it is once again Herr Schmidt and Herr Klein."

Kate felt a gentle reproof at her assumed intimacy, but in ways she was beginning to feel a friendship, even a kinship with Baroness von Prandtauer. She respected her for her family's sacrifice; she admired her for her good looks, her social ease, and her taste in clothes.

"But if you insist," the baroness said. "Kate." She patted the younger woman's hand across the table. "And you should call me Sissy. Short for Elisabeth."

Kate beamed at this, as if an understanding house prefect at one of the expensive private schools she had attended were befriending her. And there had been a number of such schools as Kate Wallace rebelled over the years at being sent away from the family home following her mother's early death.

"And I still say you are too modest. I have read your articles. They are very good. You are a journalist. How lucky to have such a calling. To be in and of the world. Women of my station, of my generation, were not so fortunate."

"You make yourself sound like a dinosaur, Sissy. But you're still a young, beautiful woman. You can build a career if you want. The new Germany will be different, you'll see. Democratic. Women will have a place."

Baroness von Prandtauer smiled warmly at the American.

It was at that moment that she decided she would eventually kill Kate Wallace. She would take great pleasure in the feel of the scalpel digging through the soft, pink flesh of Kate's throat.

The *new* Germany. Not if Baroness von Prandtauer had anything to say about it.

"I really must get back to my article," Kate said, checking

her watch. But she had no intention of working the night away; to the contrary, she was hoping to fuck the night away again with Captain Morgan. She felt herself blushing at the mental use of the word. Yet that is what it was. You could hardly say "make love the night away" or "sexual intercourse the night away." She longed to feel Morgan, Nate, once again wrapped around her, inside her.

The baroness interrupted these pleasant thoughts. "Have you discovered anything about those terrible murders I mentioned last time we had tea? My friends tell me there have been more. Five in all. The city is living in fear."

Kate felt a sudden shame. She had approached Nate in the first place to learn about these murders. But their relationship had quickly moved in a different direction. She wondered for the first time if he was not merely handling her, manipulating her to keep her away from the story of the murders.

"There was mention of a killing at the Grand Hotel," Kate said. "But there seems to be a media blackout on it. None of the journalists are covering it. The trial is the focus."

"Well, it seems a strange way to conduct journalism, doesn't it? To avoid such a dramatic story in favor of the boring comments that one hears coming from the Palace of Justice. Very little drama there, I am afraid. After all, the verdict is preordained."

"Not necessarily," Kate said. "Of course, the Soviets would rather just take the defendants out and shoot them, but the American judges are going to make sure this remains a fair trial. Those in the dock are innocent until proven guilty. I found it amazing what Justice Jackson said yesterday on the opening day of the proceedings. He made it very clear that while the new law prohibiting crimes against humanity is first applied to Germany, that it will also apply in the future to those nations who now sit in judgment."

"Fine rhetoric," the baroness said.

"It's true, though. This trial really does mean a new day in international law. No more aggressive war, no more targeting civilians."

"We shall see, Kate. The future is a long time. But it is good that you are involved in what you do. One would hope, however, for some exposure of these other crimes taking place day to day in Nuremberg."

Kate nodded. "You're right. I'll try to look into them. Really."

"I am sure you will." The baroness smiled again. "I am sorry to keep you."

"No, not at all. Thanks so much for the coffee and chat," Kate said, standing and extending her hand to the baroness. Kate was surprised to be embraced by the older woman instead.

"To be young again," the baroness said as she released Kate. "I suspect a young man might be waiting."

Now Kate was blushing.

"Yes, see? No need for excuses with me, Kate. We are friends, right?"

Kate nodded, allowing the baroness to maneuver her toward the door. She paused a moment at a heavy oak side-table placed against the wall. Above it on the wall was a gallery of photographs in silver frames. Kate immediately focused on one of an elderly military man in uniform covered with decorations and medals. His face with thin and sharp, hair combed back severely. He wore a monocle in one eye.

The baroness noted her focus. "My husband," she said. "That was taken not long before the end. He was very proud of his achievements."

"You must miss him very much."

"I think of him daily," the baroness said.

And this was absolutely true, but not for the reasons this American would think. His death was deserved; he had betrayed the Fatherland. It was a death demanded, foretold.

"If there were only more like you and your husband," Kate said.

"Yes, quite," the baroness said. "Who is this lucky man?"

Kate prevaricated for an instant and then decided she would not mind confiding.

"He's an American."

"*Quelle surprise!*"

"All right. An American captain. He was formerly with the OSS."

"Ah, the spy agency."

"How did you know?"

"My husband was with the Abwehr. There is little about spies I do not know."

"But they've disbanded it now. He's here for security."

"Does this young man have a name?"

Kate nodded. "Morgan. Captain Nate Morgan."

"A strong-sounding name," the baroness said, trying hard to cover her real surprise this time. The name Manhof had mentioned the other day; one of those investigating the multiple murders.

The baroness filed this bit of information away. It would come in handy later.

"Be safe," she said to Kate. "It is a dangerous world out there."

November 22, 1945

Beck got an early start. Morgan was not in the office at eight thirty as planned, and the former chief inspector was damned if he was going to drag the lovesick man out of his room at the Grand again. Let Morgan enjoy himself with his new friend. He assumed it was that journalist that had come badgering them with questions about multiple murders in Nuremberg. Beck hoped Morgan knew what he was doing; his experience with journalists led him to believe that they would do anything to get a story. Pillow talk was one of the easiest sources for leaks.

But he put it out of his mind. Morgan was trained in espionage; he wouldn't be so stupid.

Beck had work to do. Last night, they had sent word to army investigators in Berlin to begin a search for files on Knight's Cross recipients. No telling how long that would take. Meanwhile, he had a hunch he wanted to verify. He knew little about victim number six, Corporal Marcel Piquet, other than his rank and nationality.

These were multiple murders, to be sure. But Beck wanted to be certain that there was no consistent motive involved—that they actually were "stranger murders." Time for a chat with the French superiors and colleagues of Corporal Marcel Piquet.

He took the back stairs down to the motor pool. Private Steinberg was there as arranged, a jeep already requisitioned for his use.

"No captain today?" Private Steinberg said.

"Previous engagement," Beck said. "You know the way to French HQ?"

Steinberg did not answer, looking instead over Beck's shoulder to the exterior of the garage.

"Someone's lost," he said.

Beck swung around to see a large youth in a tattered greatcoat approaching.

"Off-limits here," Beck said in German.

The youth kept coming.

"You have a hearing problem?"

"Inspector," Private Steinberg called from in back of him. "His right hand."

Too late, Beck saw the youth pull a Walther P38 out of the coat pocket, firing as he approached.

Beck dove to the ground next to a metal barrel of oil waste, fumbling for his Colt. Shots came from behind him now, too; the *ping* of ricochets echoed in the garage. The kid kept moving and firing, ejecting one clip and slapping another in. Eight more bullets, Beck automatically registered.

A bullet tore at the cement next to Beck's face, stone chips cutting his cheek. The Colt was in his hand now, and he pulled off two quick rounds, feeling the recoil through his shoulder.

He rolled, fired again, found cover under a jeep, and fired now at the legs covered in the greatcoat, at the worn boots tied together. A groan and the youth went to his knee. Beck fired twice more and the kid was down.

He scooted out of under the jeep, sprinted to the wounded assailant, and kicked the gun out of his hand. He looked down at the face—it was twisted into a grimace of pain and hatred. His right hand dug into his coat pocket again.

There was one bullet left in Colt's magazine.

"Don't do it," Beck said. "I'll take your head off."

Two shots fired from in back of him did just that, leaving pink pulp where once there had been a face.

Beck turned to the shooter. Manhof held his Sauer 38H out in a triangle from his body.

"He was going for another weapon," Manhof said.

Beck leaned over and dug into the pocket. No gun, just a tiny capsule.

Manhof shrugged. "Looked like he was going for a gun. No need to thank me, though," he said, and walked off.

Beck quickly took in the scene: Drivers and mechanics were now poking their heads up from behind vehicles and iron barrels, anywhere they could find cover when the shooting started. The stink of cordite filled the place.

In front of Beck's requisitioned jeep, Private Steinberg lay in a pool of blood, a carbine at his side.

"Haskell says the capsule held cyanide," Beck told Morgan later in the day when they met up in their office.

"So he planned to die, if taken alive." Morgan looked skeptical.

"He died because Manhof executed him. Two shots to the head. The kid was down. I had him covered."

"So what are you saying?"

"I don't like how Manhof keeps turning up. At Imhofer's body, now at this shooting."

"He is in charge of Kripo. It's his job to investigate murders. And this morning he had a jeep scheduled, just like you."

"Just like us," Beck reminded him.

"Right. I should have been here this morning."

If he had been, Private Steinberg might very well be alive, Morgan knew. The ripple effect of life. He'd stayed in bed an extra fifteen minutes with Kate Wallace, and Sy Steinberg, mechanic from New Jersey, who was much better with a wrench than a carbine, died.

"You in love?"

"Please."

"Remember: She's a journalist."

Morgan made no reply. But he knew Beck was right. And last night, she'd wanted to talk a bit more than he had been comfortable with.

He changed the subject. "I know you and Manhof have this history, this professional competition."

"It's much more than competition."

"But we want to keep him on our side."

"You sure he is?"

"This is exactly what I mean, Beck."

"And this is what I mean, Captain Morgan. We have eight murders on our hands, five from our multiple murderer plus the deaths of Rollo, Imhofer, and Aichinger."

"But Rollo took his own life," Morgan interjected.

"While in custody. And after he told me he had some big information to sell. Nice coincidence. But I'm rethinking that, too. Rethinking what Wieland Imhofer told us about Rollo, that he died because he knew too much. That capsule we found this morning? The SS gave them to operatives working behind the lines in case of capture. Gestapo used them during the war to get rid of annoyances. I checked at the prison. The log there says Chief Inspector Manhof was the last person to see Rollo alive. He visited the cell at about dinnertime, signed his name on the manifest. I think if we dig up Rollo's corpse, we're going to find his cyanide capsule still in place in his hollowed-out tooth."

Beck eyed Morgan. Not suicide then, but murder while in custody.

"Go on," the captain said.

"So I've been doing more thinking about motive."

"Because of your visit to the French sector today?"

"Very much because of that. What is the one thing that links almost all of these murders?" But he did not wait for an answer: "Four of the five killed by our woman have links to the black market."

"That's what the French told you about Piquet?"

"That's what his German mistress told me. It seems Corporal Marcel Piquet had big plans for himself in postwar Germany. He was short on specifics, but he always carried a big roll of cash and was not shy about spreading it around."

"Gambling?"

"Not with that kind of consistency. Even a gambler has to lose sometime. But according to his girlfriend, he was never short on cash. And he had access to luxury goods others could not find: chocolates, cognac, silk stockings, real coffee."

"Black market," Morgan agreed.

"And we know Rollo was running it, along with Aichinger. And Imhofer used the tip from Aichinger to track down the Werwolf band."

"But how are they connected to the black market?"

"Muscle," Beck quickly said. "Let's say someone is trying to take over the Nuremberg black market, getting rid of the competition. He's going to need backup, somebody to do his dirty work."

"And so he uses this band for his own purposes, maybe even tells them they're doing it for the Fatherland."

"Right," Beck said. "Convincing them that they're getting the money for the cause, to rebuild the Reich. Who knows, maybe that is what really was happening."

"They don't want the inquisitive Imhofer spoiling their plans."

Another nod from Beck.

"Number nine fits the pattern, too, then," Morgan said.

Beck looked at him, puzzled.

"The kid who tried to kill you this morning. That makes nine. He could be Werwolf. The last part of the gang."

Beck considered this for a moment. "And remember what Traudl Imhofer told me. Wieland had information linking the Werwolf to Nuremberg Kripo."

"Wait, you're going back to Manhof, I assume. But why all the artifice? I mean if this is all about a power grab for the local black market, why not just do it? Kill the competition outright. Why make it look like a multiple murderer at work?"

"A diversion," Beck replied. "A red herring. Something to make us run around in circles thinking that the sky is falling. Remember, the third victim had nothing to do with the black market."

"Another diversion," Morgan said. "To keep us from seeing the big picture."

"Right. And that would keep us from looking for logical suspects among those who might be trying to gain control of Nuremberg's black market."

"But that doesn't explain our multiple killer. What makes her tick? Or is she the brains of it all . . . just making it look like someone insane at work?"

"No. I think somebody else is playing the *Magister Ludi* here, with all of us. Even this kid today. He was prepared to be the brave soldier and end it all before we could question him about who put him up to killing me."

"So if you've got your money on Manhof, why doesn't he just let the kid do his business? Why risk being present at the scene or calling attention to himself by shooting the kid?"

"He needed to be sure. The kid had probably outlived his usefulness. If he'd killed me first, then Manhof is the hero who takes him down. If, as happened, the kid failed, Manhof wanted to make absolutely sure the kid did not talk. Having the pill found on the body was a kind of insurance for him. Who's going to suspect him if the kid already had a way to avoid questioning?"

Morgan thought about this for a time.

"I would not want to live inside your mind, Beck. Still, I think it's time we had a little talk with Manhof."

He didn't like the way Beck had looked at him this morning. Not one bit.

Chief Inspector Manhof was beginning to think it was time to cut his losses. He had gained most of what he had planned. His major competition in the black market was now dead. Those who could trace his links to the Werwolves were also dead, including that fool Imhofer and the drooling idiot Klaus Ohlendorf. His own role in the day-to-day operations of the market were shielded by an intricate web of cutouts, none of whom knew his true identity. And it would stay that way as long as he was in charge at Kripo and directing investigations away from the black market. After all, there were much more important investigations to pursue, such as a madman stalking the streets of Nuremberg.

It was time to end that little diversion, he thought with regret. A pity, really, for what he had planned for the baroness was quite elegant. Something to put the capstone on his career.

"Anything from the canteen, Chief Inspector?" This from Hoffman, the deskman. By the looks of his waistline, he could afford to miss a few meals.

"No, nothing, Sergeant. Have a good lunch."

Hoffman looked a bit surprised at Manhof's friendly reply.

Once the officer was gone, Manhof returned to the matter at hand.

The murder of Baroness Elisabeth von Prandtauer.

She had well and truly outlived her usefulness, and she was the only one who could directly tie him to the murders.

The plan was to have her kill herself, and as many of the public and others in the court as could be achieved, by a small bomb. The baroness, the wife of a good German, would, he assured her, be treated with deference when she attended the trial. Manhof had convinced her she would be carrying an incendiary device that she should leave in her chair after excusing herself for a bathroom break. In truth, it would be a timed explosive deadly enough to kill her and all those around her in the visitors' gallery if she made it that far, or anyone around her when her bag was being inspected.

Manhof thought proudly of his lovely plan. Quite baroque in its way, but fitted with precision clockwork.

He had recruited the baroness to commit the series of murders knowing she was quite competent in such matters. Manhof had first met her when investigating the suicide death of her husband, General von Prandtauer, following the failed attempt on Hitler's life in 1944. He and other traitors at the Abwehr had been part of the plot; the general had been lucky enough to avoid capture and slow death by garroting. Or so Manhof had thought initially.

The baroness had watched him closely the day in late July 1944, when he examined the general's body. Strange way for a military man to end it, Manhof had thought. A revolver bullet to the temple, perhaps, but to cut one's own throat with a razor? It gave Manhof a slight shiver of nausea to look at the gaping wound.

"You are thinking it odd for him die so, aren't you?" the baroness suddenly asked.

Manhof looked at her more closely now, at the eyes that had shed no tears, the hands that rubbed together incessantly.

"Perhaps."

"It was."

"How do you mean?"

"My husband had an abject fear of blood. That was why he chose the Abwehr. Not a real soldier at all. Not like my brother. My brother sacrificed his life for this country. He was a true hero. My husband was a traitor. He deserved such a death."

"Baroness, just what are you trying to tell me?"

"I killed him. I would do it again. Him and every other defeatist that would make my brother's sacrifice meaningless."

"You did this?" Manhof had looked again at the savage cut at the man's neck, exposing the esophagus. "Perhaps it is only the strain of the moment."

"Do I need to show you my weapon? One of my father's scalpels. He was a surgeon, you see. Quite famous in his day. He gave both me and my brother one of his scalpels when he retired. We were only adolescents at the time, but I have prized it all these years."

"Shall we make it our little secret, Baroness?"

Manhof had convinced her to keep quiet about the murder; he had covered her tracks, made sure the medicos declared the death a suicide.

And he had owned her since then. Sexually, yes; but that only infrequently. Truth be told, she frightened Manhof with some of the painful games she wanted him to play. But more importantly, he had owned the baroness's loyalty. Manhof had instinctively known that it would be to his benefit to have such a person on his side. In the summer of 1944, he could see that Germany was losing the war; Baroness von Prandtauer might very well be considered the widow of a resistance hero by the Allied victors. Manhof could use a protector.

And then, after the final cataclysm and the occupation, came his brilliant plan to gain control of the black market and to use the baroness as his programmed killer. By that time, he knew her well enough to trust that she could do it. He merely pointed her in the direction of likely victims whom she believed were vital witnesses in the upcoming trials. She had been the one to concoct the ornate messages left behind; her husband's espionage and code training at work there.

And it was all intended—so Baroness von Prandtauer believed—to culminate in a sort of *Götterdämmerung* at the trial itself, when her incendiary device would go off. Meanwhile, with security forces on high alert in the streets of Nuremberg searching for the mad killer, Manhof and his men would take the court hostage, demanding that Göring be set free, put on a plane for Spain.

All purest fabrication, of course; the stuff of absurd novels. But the baroness had been taken in. It would be her sacrifice for her dead brother.

Manhof did not like to think what kind of relationship those two had had.

Instead, the baroness would be blown to bits along with many others at the court. Manhof had no intention of lifting a finger to save the egregious Göring. No, he would be too busy getting to the bottom of this latest atrocity.

Chief Inspector Manhof, despite all odds, would soon uncover that the explosive device had come into the court with Baroness von Prandtauer, and then, investigating yet further, he would find evidence at her villa that she was indeed the notorious multiple murderer terrorizing Nuremberg. The little fingers taken from the Pole, Krensky, would prove that to all. It had taken some convincing on Manhof's part to have the baroness perform that bit of carnage, though he thought she secretly relished the ghoulish chore.

This investigative coup would make Manhof's career.

That is why, earlier, when the baroness had allowed the French soldier to have intercourse with her, and thereby alerted Beck and his American captain to the fact that their murderer was a female, Manhof had allowed the plan to go forward even with increased risk. In the end, he had reckoned, it would help his cause if others already knew the killer to be a woman. It would make his revelations about Baroness von Prandtauer easier to fathom.

But now, she was too much of a liability. Beck would be poking and prodding into his affairs, he felt it in his bones. The baroness had to die, and sooner rather than later. No *Götterdämmerung* at the trial unfortunately. Loose ends needed tying up.

Or cauterizing.

November 23, 1945

"You're making a habit of these visits, Inspector Manhof."

He disliked the silly pretensions of the baroness, calling this dark and stuffy room where they were seated the drawing room in the English style.

"It is Falk's day off, no?"

She nodded. "You seem to know quite a lot about my daily schedule."

"It is my job to know such things. I wanted to deliver the information for tonight personally. This is a very important witness for the prosecution. He can place Göring at the Sobibor camp. It would be damning testimony against the field marshal."

"Then we must ensure that this witness does not have his day in court."

She raised her cup of tea to him in salute. Manhof also disliked the baroness's insistence on tea with lemon. He was a coffee drinker; tea was for those who had no stomach for life. But he sipped it anyway, to please her, to keep her lulled and pacified.

Yes, tonight would be a most important victim, he told himself, puckering his lips at the bitterness of the lemon. Tonight, it would be the baroness herself who would be the victim. They would keep to the three-day schedule to the very end. How fitting. No black-market-competitor-cum-prosecution-witness would be waiting for the baroness tonight in the rubble; instead, death would be awaiting her arrival. Manhof himself would see to it, surviving an attack by the crazed woman. His story was prepared: he bravely put himself in harm's way, knowing that the murders occurred in three-day intervals. He walked the barren streets of the city—bait to catch the killer. And he succeeded, but was sadly unable to take the killer alive.

Oh, yes. Manhof had the story all prepared; his team knew he would be out on the streets tonight as a decoy. He would still be a hero in this revised scenario, still be the one to crack the case and get rid of the last bit of damning evidence against him in the process.

"Well, are you going to tell me or not?" the baroness asked.

Manhof ventured a second sip of the tea. Important to keep her at ease—not to arouse her suspicion.

She smiled at him and suddenly he felt a shortness in breath as if he had been running. He sucked air but could not seem to get enough oxygen. The cup in his hand toppled to the floor, but he could barely hear it crashing.

"Is something wrong, Chief Inspector?"

Her smile, the victorious look of it, was the last thing he saw as he slipped into blackness and a coma leading to death.

His face still bore the twisted rictus of amazement it had when he realized he had drunk tea laced with his favorite poison.

So much more ladylike this way. The baroness laughed at her little joke. A lady's way to kill, with poison and not a blade.

Poor Rainer. He was always such an obvious man. She had been expecting him to intercede with her holy mission ever since their angry altercation following the Frenchman's death. But it was the supposed incendiary device he gave her for use at the trial that finally tipped his hand. As a poor little woman—a killing woman, but woman, nonetheless—she was not to know about such things. But she did. She was the widow of General von Prandtauer; she could recognize an explosive device when she saw one.

The vapid American reporter had supplied the rest of the information needed. Last night over coffee and cake, the American told her the gossip she had gleaned from her lover, the infamous Captain Morgan: the fact that a number of the victims had connections to the black market.

The baroness instantly saw what Manhof had been up to: using her to do his dirty work, eliminating the competition, most likely. Not witnesses against the brave Germans in the dock.

And then she would be sacrificed and silenced at the trial.

So *durchsichtig*, so obvious. Poor Rainer. Hardly a contest for her.

Not like her brother, Gerhard. There was a real man, a real adversary. She recalled with a hot sexual flush their little games at night, their mother dead and father tucked in his study with his medical books. The lovely scalpels he had prized them with. Gerhard was the inventive one. He would read to her from the works of Karl May and then initiate her into the games of Winnetou, the brave warrior who showed no pain.

Brave warriors never show pain, Gerhard would say in that splendid voice of his. *Brave warriors are silent about their pain.*

Now she just needed to dispose of Chief Inspector Manhof's body before any of the nosy boarders discovered him and before Falk's return. And she knew the perfect place for him.

Colonel Adams made a pirouette, spinning around from the window to face Morgan.

"You find something amusing, Captain?"

"Not at all," Morgan said, wiping the smile from his face. But Adams had, for a moment, looked like a tiny, very pissed-off ballerina.

"That is good, because there is nothing humorous about the

fact of our allies are now complaining to the Control Commission about the lack of headway we're making in this case. The Russians, in particular, are anxious to take over the investigation. Can you tell me, Captain, why it is we can beat the daylights out of Hitler and his SS thugs, and then be stymied by one puny woman in the streets of Nuremberg?"

"Inspector Beck is working on a new theory. She may not be working on her own."

"Wonderful. Marvelous. Perhaps you can both theorize the killer or killers into prison."

His voice rose to a crescendo as he spoke—an angry martinet.

"You know what the date is, I assume, Captain?"

"Yes, I am aware, sir. We will have patrols out tonight as we did last night, just in case."

Morgan had been among the patrols; he was still suffering from lack of sleep.

Adams shook his head, disgusted. He moved to his desk, lifted a newspaper, and tossed it in front of Morgan.

"I suppose you have seen that? The blood is in the water. They'll be no stopping the press now."

Morgan looked at the paper. It was a copy of the European edition of *The New Leader.* Morgan saw the article Adams was referring to at once—on the top right-hand turn column above the fold of the front page. The headline screamed out at him in three-line, forty-point type: CARNAGE ON THE STREETS OF NUREMBERG!

The byline was Pierpoint Phipson, but the information contained in the article was the outline that Morgan had stupidly shared with Kate the other night. The number of killings, the three-day intervals, coded messages, suspicions of black market or Werwolf involvement. And the final insult, the article even named him, Morgan, as the lead investigator in the case. The article did not mention that the killer was assumed to be a woman; that was one piece of information Morgan had kept from her.

Christ, what a fool he had been. She had been playing him just to get a story. This Phipson character was probably in it with her; she couldn't use her byline or risk losing her goose with its golden eggs of information: Captain Nathan ("call me Nate") Morgan.

"Fuck her," he said aloud, newspaper still in hand.

"I beg your pardon, Captain. There's no need for profanity."

"Sorry, sir. I'll pull the press pass of this Phipson. The rest of the press corps has agreed to avoid rumor mongering."

"Seems this chap is dealing with more than rumors, Captain. You folks have a security breach?"

"No, sir."

"That German you have working for you. Can you trust him?"

"Absolutely."

"Then find out how this reporter got his information. If there is such a breach, I want it mortared over PDQ, understood?"

"Yes, sir." He would mortar it, alright. Tight as a cask of Amontillado.

"You stole my notes." Kate was livid.

After seeing the article in this morning's *New Leader*, she rushed to the pressroom at the Palace of Justice. Henry Brandt and Pierpoint Phipson were in their usual places; a small congratulatory crowd had gathered around the latter.

"Welcome to work, Miss Wallace," Phipson said by way of response.

"It's unethical. Those notes were not meant for publication. Not now, at any rate."

"What notes would those be?" Phipson spoke with an irritating mid-Atlantic accent, as if he had been educated in England.

"You are a cad, Phipson."

"Oh my. We *are* reaching for expletives."

The other reporters laughed.

"All right, how about this? A fucking cad."

There was a brief moment of silence. Brandt touched her arm consolingly.

"Fair game, I am afraid," Phipson said. "Notes left for all to see."

She had been an idiot to put down the basics of Morgan's revelations. He had told her them in the strictest confidence. But she had to record them; she knew there would come a time, after he had broken the case, that she could be the first to background it with such information. But Kate had never intended to break Morgan's trust, never intended them for publication now.

"Is that the journalist's credo, then?" she said. "If so, you don't bend over in the communal shower. Drop your soap, you leave it lying, right?"

"Now she stoops to *crudités*," Phipson punned, but the other journalists were no longer finding the altercation humorous.

Brandt turned to his colleague. "You mean that story was pilfered from Miss Wallace? You admit it."

"Admit it? Of course, I do," Phipson said, beaming. "All in a day's work. The journalist's job is to gather and disseminate information. From whatever source."

The others groaned at this cynical comment, members of an outraged Greek chorus.

"Did you vet the information?" Brandt demanded.

"I assume Miss Wallace took care of that." Phipson glanced her way. "Right, Miss Wallace? During those loving *tête-à-têtes* at the bar of the Grand Hotel?"

She did not say another word, merely scooped her notebook from her workspace, and stormed out of the pressroom.

"Maybe she has an explanation," Beck said. But he doubted it.

"Let's just forget it. We've got to organize the patrols for tonight."

She appeared at the door then; Beck could see the anxiousness in her face.

"I'm sorry," she said, not waiting to be invited in. "I never meant for anyone else to see the notes."

Morgan looked through her with cold distaste.

"Listen to me, Nate. I'm not your enemy. I would never betray you. Phipson saw my notebook. I promise you."

Morgan remained silent; the muscles worked in his jaw.

"Perhaps another time, Miss Wallace," Beck finally said, rising and taking her arm.

She shook herself free. "Don't patronize me. And don't nudge me out. I can leave under my own steam." She looked imploringly at Morgan. "Christ, say something, Nate. Don't let it end like this. We have something special."

"I believe you have all the information you will get from me, Miss Wallace," Morgan finally said in a monotone. "Now, if you don't mind, we have official business here. Should I get an MP to see you out?"

"I tell you it was an honest mistake. You can't believe that I was just playing you. Can you?"

She looked long and hard at him. Finally, she shook her head. "You're a cold bastard. No wonder you're alone. The perfect spy, looking for betrayal from anyone you know. Just so you know, you were right about me. I did intend to play you at first, to get behind your defenses and get my story. But after our first night talking together, I knew I could never do that. Knew that I honestly feel . . . felt something for you."

Morgan continued to gaze at her as if at an exotic bit of fauna.

"I'm wasting my breath, aren't I?"

Beck did not want to be witnessing this anymore. He busied himself with troop deployment schedules for tonight, arranged quadrant by quadrant.

"Good-bye, Miss Wallace," Morgan said flatly.

A dead body is a bag of blood, the baroness knew. The daughter of a famous surgeon knows many facts that she might not care to initially, but ultimately she was grateful to her papa for sharing his knowledge with her. It made her feel an equal to her clever brother, Gerhard.

Diastolic pressure continues for a brief time after death, so that if she cut into Manhof's jugular now, she would get a bit of blood spurt. However, she did not want the Villa von Prandtauer to be the crime scene. No. She had another place in mind for that.

It was no coincidence the baroness received Manhof in the drawing room, for its French doors behind the damask curtains allowed easy access. She made sure that her guests were all out for the day, and then fetched a wheelbarrow from the garden shed next to the garage. Once in the drawing room, she tipped the wheelbarrow down and scooted Manhof's lower body in. Righting the barrow, she was able to lift the torso in as well. This she covered with a tarp from the shed.

She wheeled the barrow out to the shed, looking the part of a serious gardener. In the shed, she trussed Manhof's feet with a stout rope, threw one end over one of the exposed timbers in the roof, attached this to a winch, and then turned the handle, suspending the body like meat in a butcher's shop.

After a half an hour or so, the muscles in a corpse relax and the blood vessels expand. Without the heart to pump, no blood would come out. Thus, the baroness needed to use gravity to establish her crime scene. Blood simply flows to the lowest part of the body after death.

Gravity, simple gravity, she thought as she locked the shed door behind her.

November 24, 1945

"He said he was going to play decoy last night," Perlmann said. "But nobody really believed him."

Beck looked down at the body, its head lolling over a chipped step on the tribune stand. The Zeppelin Field was empty today except for the Kripo team and the American soldiers. An old lady looking for wood had found the body this morning; she stood shivering next to Morgan. Beck doubted they would have the same luck with her as they had with Bertha Kraus, the witness to the killing of the first Frenchman.

Which made him think: *When the hell was Berlin going to get them the information on Knight's Cross recipients? After half of Nuremberg had been slaughtered?*

A large amount of blood was pooled under Manhof's head on the step below. It was hardening into a rusty brown pool. *So much blood for such a small man*, Beck thought.

And so much for his theories about Manhof. Beck felt nothing other than disappointment. He had wanted Manhof to be the one. Wanted it too much, perhaps. Had his hatred for the man clouded his rational judgment? It was possible.

"There's something strange here, Beck," Perlmann said.

Beck refocused. "Strange how?"

Perlmann shook his head. "That's a lot of blood."

"Yes. His neck has been slashed. That happens."

"I'm not a medical man, but that wound looks pretty severe."

Beck was beginning to lose his patience, but finally understood what Perlmann was getting at.

He kneeled down to get a better look at the wound. The carotid had been severed clear through, the gash digging deep into the esophagus. A wound like that would result in a quick death. When the heart stops beating, the blood stops spurting.

Beck looked again at the pool of blood. No spray nearby—no spatter on the other steps by the body, either.

Morgan came up the steps, having finished with the old lady.

"Find anything here?" he said.

Beck rose, wiping at the dust on his knee. "A lot of blood for such a severe wound."

"Maybe he bled out afterward"—Morgan gestured to the body—"his head is the low part. Gravity."

"Maybe," Beck allowed. "But where's the initial spurt then? The pooled blood is too tidy. And too much."

"Is this more of the Beck and Manhof duel?"

"No." Beck was fervent about that. "I think we need an autopsy here."

Morgan put his gloves on, leaned over and using thumb and forefinger carefully took the book page out of Manhof's right hand. Habit at work—just in case of fingerprints on the note. But there wouldn't be any, just as with the others. And even if there were, they had no database of prints. No crime records left after the carpet bombing of Nuremberg. Criminology in these circumstances was not science but pure deduction.

"Shorter message this time by the looks of the underlined words."

"It doesn't fit," Beck said. "Manhof is German. The other victims were all Allied soldiers, the victors. Where's the symbolism?"

They discovered the answer to that question an hour later

after returning to the Palace of Justice and working out the code.

"VALKYRIE," Morgan said.

"Let me see." Beck was tense as he examined the decoding process.

"Right," he said.

"So the death makes a crazy kind of sense," Morgan said, understanding the significance of the coded word.

"If Manhof were one of the conspirators, that is."

Valkyrie, the code name for the July 20, 1944 plot to assassinate Hitler by members of the Wehrmacht and German security services. After the failure of the bomb set by Colonel Claus von Stauffenberg at Hitler's Eastern Front military headquarters, the Wolf's Lair, Hitler wreaked terrible vengeance, killing five thousand real and supposed plotters.

"Maybe he was one that got away," Morgan said, thinking out loud. "But how does our killer know that?"

"Maybe she doesn't," Beck said. "We're dealing in symbolism here, right? It's not as if the other victims were personally involved in the invasion of Poland or *Kristallnacht*. They're stand-ins. The placement of Manhof's body on the tribune steps of the Zeppelin Field fits that profile. Pure theater: Traitor to the Reich dies where the Nazi propaganda machine was at its strongest."

"So just any German would do?" Morgan said. "Manhof was a decoy last night, according to Perlmann. Just bad luck?"

"Or maybe he was a traitor in another way."

By early evening, they had the report from Haskell: Based on the stage of rigor mortis, postmortem lividity, and body temperature, the pathologist estimated Manhof died sometime the previous morning or afternoon. Surely not later than six in the evening. The report also indicated significant traces of potassium cyanide in the body.

"So you were right," Morgan said to Beck.

"About the staged killing, yes," Beck said. "Not necessarily about Manhof's involvement in all this. But it raises doubts."

"We need to trace Manhof's movements yesterday."

"I'm already on that," Beck said. "The other Kripo officers say he left the office at about ten. Manhof was the secretive type; he didn't share his destination with the desk officer. He did requisition a jeep, but he drove himself."

"That was the jeep found at the scene?"

Beck nodded.

"You get the odometer reading?"

"Shows it was driven about fifty miles."

"Outside of Nuremberg, then. Which could mean the DP camps, prisoner of war camps. Any number of destinations."

"Nothing public, though. I mean, Manhof must have been strung up like a carcass most of the day to ensure blood to the head and set up of the phony crime scene."

"Which, in turn, means that our killer is playing games with us," Morgan said.

"Maybe," Beck allowed. "Something to check on anyway."

They exchanged glances, both having the same thought.

Beck was finally the one to say it. "But it can't be the Imhofer farm. We've got a pair of soldiers there."

Morgan decided to sleep on it; he was beat. Two days with only a few hours of sleep.

Beck, it appeared, was made of stronger stuff. He stayed on at the office, looking through the first batches of Teletype just in from Berlin.

"They're including them all," he groaned as Morgan left. "Even the Iron Cross recipients. This could take weeks to plow through."

Earlier, the baroness had lingered in bed, the sacred Saturday. Falk was accustomed to her sleeping in on that day, no questions asked.

Now evening, she was playing the hostess at dinner. Colonel

Jensen had returned and taken up lodgings once again in the maid's room under the eaves. And the British translator, Beth, sat at another table with the pompous young red-haired American lawyer, William-never-Bill. *The mousy translator is obviously in love*, the baroness thought, but doubted the girl's sentiments were reciprocated.

The baroness was gracious to them all.

Colonel Jensen had brought back several bottles of Boodles British Gin with him from London; he made a great show of presenting one to her.

"It's Churchill's favorite, they say."

"I hope I am not depriving him, then."

"Oh, I daresay there's enough of this stuff to go round, even in times of scarcity." He surveyed the room. "Speaking of which, seems our Miss Wallace is rather scarce tonight."

"She *has* been busy now that the trial is under way."

"All work and no play. Not good for a young woman."

The baroness had a sudden urge to bring the quart bottle of gin down over his stupid grinning face, to ruin that perfect smile and orthodontics.

Instead, she said, "I believe she has a young man."

"Might it be the young man mentioned in yesterday's *New Leader*? I seem to recall seeing them together."

"I'm not aware of the story you're talking about."

Colonel Jensen quickly outlined Phipson's article for the Baroness. "Causing quite a buzz at headquarters, as you can imagine. We pulled his press pass, of course, but now that the story is out, it will be difficult to contain. One wonders if Miss Wallace was privy to such information."

"I am sure I do not know, Colonel." She was trying to keep the elation she was feeling inside from showing on her face. Finally. The world would hear of her accomplishments. "And why would you want, as you say, to contain this news?"

He smiled at her in a condescending manner. "Well, we needn't go into that. Complicated matter. And the trial should be the news focus."

"I see." Again, she avoided the temptation to thwack him over the head with his bottle of gin.

She left the colonel's table and quickly greeted the other two guests, hardly listening to what they were saying, thinking instead of the newspaper article and her work the night before. Her husband may have been a disloyal swine, but he would have been proud of her achievement still.

After securing Manhof's body in the shed, she had driven his vehicle—an American jeep—to the rear of the estate, parking it on a service road near the gardening shed in an area where none of the servants prowled. All was in order by the time Falk had returned from his reluctantly taken day off. She had to force the man away from the villa once a week just so that she could have some peace. He was always about, always lurking in a corridor. The faithful retainer taken to absurd extremes. He had been with her family since she was a child, since her mother had died. She could not simply let him go; that would never do. The proprieties had to be kept.

But it made it more difficult for her, working around his snooping eyes.

She had pleaded a headache and an early night. Waiting until the house became deathly quiet, she sneaked out the back stairs, clothed in one of her husband's gardening outfits, her hair piled under a fedora. Again using the wheelbarrow, she deposited Manhof's body into the waiting jeep, along with an old bicycle, covering both with a tarpaulin.

Then, for the next several hours, she had driven around and around the suburbs of Nuremberg.

This was a stroke of genius, she thought. One assumed the mileage was tracked on such vehicles; the investigators discovering the jeep tomorrow would scratch their heads wondering where Manhof had been all day, unable to trace the vehicle back to the Villa von Prandtauer.

Finally, still undetected by foot patrols of soldiers, she had driven to the Zeppelin Field in back of the tribune. The really hard part had been dragging the corpse to the steps, but she had found unknown reserves of strength and energy to accomplish the task. It had been a real joy to feel the scalpel slice through the flaccid skin at Manhof's neck. The moon came out from behind a cloud momentarily to allow her to see that her preparations had not been in vain: Blood oozed out of the wound, pooling on the step beneath the head.

After that, she had pedaled the bicycle back to the suburb of Greilauer, crept back up to her bedroom by four in the morning, and then slept like a baby until just before noon.

"Baroness? Don't you think so, too?"

The interrogative tone brought her out of her reverie.

"Sorry, just planning tomorrow's menu. Think what?"

The redheaded attorney, William Stanton, looked at her closely. "That they all should hang. Make an example of each and every one. They showed no mercy, neither should we."

"Absolutely," she said.

It was at that moment she decided she would carry through with the original plan.

Kate had stopped crying three hours ago; her tears were all used up. She had now moved on from sadness to pure anger. Who the hell did Nate Morgan think he was to dismiss her? She was the daughter of Bertram Wallace, *Senator* Bertram Wallace of the great state of Pennsylvania. Her father could buy and sell Morgan ten times over.

She knew at that moment that things were pretty bad if she was invoking her father. She only did that in moments of desperation, as when Colonel Jensen groped her on the flight to Nuremberg.

God, am I that desperate? That helpless?

No, she decided. *I am neither desperate nor helpless.*

She knew how she could get back at Captain Nate Morgan, formerly of the OSS. She would crack the case that was stumping him. She would win the laurels that he wanted for himself.

She would like to see his face then.

She took another swig of the schnapps she had bought earlier in the day from the *Stube* near the Palace of Justice. It tasted of fire, but was made from plums. A bit of distilled alchemy.

Exactly what *she* intended to do: Build a career for herself out of the ruins of this stupid love affair. Alchemy or phoenix from the flames?

Crap, she thought. *Now I'm mixing my allusions. Illusions. None left.*

Kate Wallace was beginning to feel very dizzy.

November 25, 1945

The sound of church bells grew louder and louder until her head felt it would split. Waking, she realized the sound was an insistent rapping at her door.

Kate rolled over to look at her clock and pain severe enough to make her groan shot through her head.

The baroness's voice sounded from the other side of the door: "Miss Wallace? Are you quite all right? Kate?"

Her eyes focused slowly on the alarm clock: nine forty-two. She couldn't remember the day of the week for a moment.

Another round of rapping. "Kate? Are you there?"

"Just a sec," Kate said, getting out of bed. She looked down, discovering she had not even gotten into pajamas last night, and wrapped her nakedness with a silk robe. Every step she took made her head hurt more.

She opened the door to a very anxious-looking baroness.

"I am sorry to bother you. But I was afraid something might be amiss. We haven't seen much of you lately."

The baroness glanced into the room, to the near-empty bottle of schnapps, the mess of clothes spread about chairs and the floor.

"Kate?"

The baroness's concern broke through Kate's defenses. Tears came again as she let herself be enfolded in the baroness's strong arms.

"Oh, Sissy. I am so unhappy. I didn't write the story. But he won't believe me. He just looks at me . . . looks through me as if I am invisible."

"It's all right," the baroness said, moving her into the room and closing the door in back of them. "Sissy is here to take care of you. Don't worry. Things will be fine."

She maneuvered Kate back to the bed and tucked her in.

"I'll get you some coffee."

Kate grabbed her hand. "Thank you. You are a true friend."

The call came at ten that morning. Beck was at the Palace of Justice going over the Teletype files from Berlin, searching for the Knight's Cross in the haystack of Iron Cross citations.

The voice on the other end was businesslike; the matron imparted her information as if reporting a minor weather front.

"There was no pain," she said. "She passed peacefully. We tried your hotel—"

"I've been at work all morning."

It was as if he had to make excuses. The information was slowly sinking in.

"No matter. It happened in the night. Her heart was frail."

He sat numb at the desk for several moments after hanging up the receiver. Morgan came back from the cafeteria, two cups of coffee in hand.

"You okay, Beck?"

The inspector looked up from the phone. He could still remember the day they got their first phone in the flat. His mother was skeptical of it at first, fearful of getting a shock as she cranked it. His father teased her, pinching her lightly when she touched it and she jumped, screaming like a child.

"Beck?"

He focused on Morgan now, at the cups of coffee in his hands.

"It's my mother. She died."

Morgan went with him. Beck didn't want company, but the American would not listen. He drove and Beck looked at the ruins of his city under the first coating of snow for the year. The pure whiteness hid the evil below, the sadness and loss all around. Rubble kids were out throwing snowballs, finding happiness wherever they could. One of them lobbed a snowball at the passing jeep.

In the suburbs, the snow was thicker on the ground. It crunched underfoot as they walked along the sidewalk to the sanatorium.

"I'll wait here," Morgan said at the entrance to the building.

Beck did not argue. He found the matron who solemnly ushered him down the long hall to the room he had secured for his mother by working with the Americans. Well worth it to make the last days of her life more comfortable. In the room, the curtains were drawn; a tiny lump huddled beneath the covers. Once the matron left, he threw open the curtains letting in bright light reflected off the snow in the wide expanse of parkland in back of the sanatorium.

It was moments like this that had made his position at Kripo so difficult: He could not bear to look at dead bodies. He forced his eyes to her face, waxen-looking now, unreal. He traced his forefinger along a cold cheek.

So trite, but she did look at peace. The peace she had been seeking ever since his father—her adored husband—died four years before. Her heart had broken, had been ruined, on that day; it simply stopped beating today.

"Join him," he said aloud. "Be happy together again."

But he would not cry. Why not? Why hold it in?

Suddenly, the last words his mother had spoken to him came back. Just last week after he had gotten a decent suit of clothing.

Why do you never talk of your poor wife and child? It will poison you to keep it bottled inside.

He thought of them often enough. Helga, whom he had loved with a sort of steady passion that made thought of ever having another wife seem absurd. Not only a betrayal, but an impossibility. And Lisabette, the tiny betrayal with her name. Her brief and lovely life stolen from him.

The senselessness of it: The war was already lost when the bombers stuck on the night of January 2, 1945. By that time, the *Ardennenoffensive*, or Battle of the Bulge as the Americans insisted on calling it, was lost, the last Nazi offensive; Americans had landed on the beaches of Normandy the previous summer and were pressing on Germany from the west. To the east, the Russians were advancing. Poland had fallen in the summer of 1944. The war was over, but still the bombers came, more than five hundred British Lancasters. Within an hour, they had destroyed ninety percent of the center of the city, killing eighteen hundred residents, displacing a hundred thousand more.

He took comfort in numbers for a moment, going through the litany of destruction like a statistician instead of a grieving son, father, and widower.

The numbers did not protect him. He knew what he needed to do, must do.

He took his mother's hands from beneath the covers and folded them together over her chest. Then he willed himself to bend over her still body and kiss her forehead.

"Good-bye, Mother," he said from the door. "Thank you."

He stopped to deliver orders to the matron for a burial service—she would have a proper funeral even though thousands still lay rotting under the ruins. She was not one of them, not a number.

Neither were Helga or Lisabette.

Morgan was waiting on the steps, clapping his arms around him to stay warm. Snow flurries had begun falling again.

"You needn't come with me."

"It's all right. Nice day for a drive. Where we headed?"

"I'll direct you."

The narrow alleyways behind the train station had nearly been obliterated; there was a plot of ground without street signs. But finally, Beck was able to navigate them to 23 Breite Gasse, where his apartment house once stood. The house number hanging from the lintel of the front door was all that remained of the facade. Other houses to each side were in the process of clearing; the removal workers had not yet reached there.

Morgan remained behind once more as Beck swung his long legs out of the jeep and made for the destroyed building. It had been a low, three-story building, baroque with cramped rooms and little daylight, but Beck had always relished returning there after his shift, the smell of roasting pork from the oven, Lisabette at the table working on her latest art project. Home.

Their apartment had been at the rear, second floor. He picked his way through the rubble and the charred window frames. Anything resembling a fuel source had long since been scavenged. When he first returned to Nuremberg from Flensburg prison, he had stopped at the ruined facade, unable to go further. What was there to salvage? Wife and daughter both blown apart and then incinerated.

But now he was determined to find some memento from that former life, something to remind him of the lost ones. He reached what appeared to be the rear of the building, still a pile of rubble, and he began digging at the broken mortar, the shards of glass. He felt his fingers cut several times, but could not stop himself from digging deeper and deeper in the pile. There had to be something, some reminder of his old life.

He was down on hands and knees, tears pouring down his cheeks. He heard a moaning and realized it was coming from him. Holding it in all this time, and now it was coming out, coming out. His vision blurred with the tears, his sobs came more slowly. It was like a fever crisis, breaking and healing at once.

And then he felt metal with his left hand. He concentrated on the spot, throwing away chips of mortar and brick, uncovering the corner of what appeared to be a metal box that survived the flames.

A flash of remembrance. But no, it couldn't be. Their third anniversary, Helga had presented him with a finely tooled metal shaving kit. Much too fine to contain mere shaving materials.

He dug more vigorously, trying to contain his emotions. It couldn't be. But soon he let himself believe that it was so. The very metal shaving box from his third anniversary. Into it, he had put small items from his daily life. Inconsequential objects to others, but for him small treasures. He cleared the dust and grime from it and recognized clearly the arabesque design etched into the lid. He hugged it to his chest, hearing the objects inside rattle as he did so. He looked up into the falling snow and said a silent thank you.

"You okay, Beck?"

Morgan was standing a few yards away.

"I heard noises . . . sorry."

"No, don't be." He swept his arm over the ruins. "Our home. My Helga and Lisabette."

Saying their names out loud was a release, a relief.

He wiped at the tears. "I found this. It was an anniversary gift."

Morgan did not know what to say. Before, these ruins had been someone else's problem. The Germans had started the war, had bombed London first; this is what happens in war. But this was Beck's loss—Beck's family destroyed. All Morgan could feel was shame.

"I'm so sorry," he finally said.

Beck continued to hug the box, nodding his head.

"Perhaps there's something else we can find?"

"No," Beck said softly. "This will do." He got up, remembering the lock of Lisabette's baby hair he had placed in the box; a broken Mont Blanc pen, Helga's favorite. The detritus of their lives together. Treasures. He would open it in private—save it for a time when he was badly in need of such emotional sustenance. Like when you are a kid and you keep the best part of the pastry for later.

November 26, 1945

The look in the victim's eyes was worth it all: surprise, shock, horror, betrayal.

How the human eye could convey that bevy of emotions was a wonder, she thought as the dying body collapsed to the rubble-strewn floor. Blood was everywhere, staining her husband's field tunic, freckling his medals. She closed the cloak over the uniform, took the two book pages out of her pocket, and placed one in each hand of the helpless body, bleeding out on the stone floor.

She looked high overhead, marveling again at what she saw suspended overhead—like a puppet theater.

A final rasping breath at her feet reminded her of one more task. She leaned over, searching through the pockets of the victim's overcoat, careful not to get blood on her hands or cloak. She felt a folded piece of paper in the inside pocket, removed it, opened it, and quickly read the message.

The baroness nodded, then jammed the note into her own cloak pocket.

November 27, 1945

Their driver pulled into the Königstrasse, familiar territory for Morgan, not far from the Grand Hotel. Was the killer returning to old haunts now? Had they ever been able to discern a pattern to the location of crime scenes?

Before he could answer his own question, Beck shouted for the driver to stop.

"This is it," Beck said, hopping out. "Sankt Anna. Mother of Virgin Mary."

Morgan sat for a moment, stunned: It was the bombed-out church where he and Kate had first kissed.

"Inside?" he said incredulously.

"She's very inventive, our killer."

They picked their way through the rubble of the fallen roof; Morgan let his eyes wander up to the damaged arches where the German fighter plane still dangled.

"You know this place?" Beck said.

Morgan nodded. "I've visited it before."

Perlmann stood over the body, shaking his head. He was accompanied by a pair of MPs. The three of them parted as Beck and Morgan approached.

Morgan felt another jolt as he surveyed the body from a distance.

"A woman."

"You might have told me on the phone," Beck said to Perlmann, who shrugged the suggestion away.

"Maybe it's not ours," Morgan said, afraid to look at the face. Too many coincidences here.

"Oh, it's yours all right," Perlmann drawled in his Nuremberg German. "All the signs."

"Perlmann's right," Beck said as he took a deep breath and stepped back a pace from the body.

Morgan finally forced himself to step closer and look at the face of the dead woman.

No, not her after all. The tenseness left his body; a barely audible sigh escaped his lips.

Morgan knelt over the body, examining the wound to the neck. It *was* the work of their killer.

"Two this time," Beck said from in back of him.

Morgan now looked at the victim's hands; there was a page from a book in each.

"Getting clever, isn't she?" Perlmann said.

Morgan searched the woman's coat pockets for identification. He didn't need a passport to tell him that she was not German; her coat, her perm, everything about her said foreigner here for the trial. He found a passport in a small purse that lay under the body.

"British," he said, but no one responded. "Elizabeth Garrison, twenty-eight, formerly of Brighton."

In the back of the passport was a special pass for the trial.

"Translator. Shit." Morgan was thinking of Adams. This would surely set him off. He might even strip Morgan of the investigation.

Maybe I should be, Morgan thought. *We've been running around in circles with this, getting nowhere.*

Meanwhile, Beck was examining the two book pages. "From Karl May again. There's mention of Shatterhand and Winnetou. One good thing, though."

"What's that?" Morgan said, standing and stretching his back.

"Looks like she's using a simple initial-letter code."

"Let me see." Morgan took one of the sheets, following the underlined words. Beck was right.

"Dresden," he said, putting the first letters together in his head.

"She's talking to us in this one," Beck said, handing the other page to Morgan, who quickly deciphered the message. "I serve a higher court."

"Nothing down in Hades but bones." Morgan looked to the direction of Perlmann's voice; the bottom half of the detective's torso was underground, only his shoulders and head showed above the flagstone floor. Morgan had not noticed him go underground.

"Catacombs," Beck explained. "We might have gotten lucky and had a witness again."

"No sign of squatters, either," Perlmann said. "Piles of bones tend to keep even the displaced away."

Morgan turned his attention again to the coded messages, and now Perlmann climbed the rest of the stairs out of the catacombs, shut the metal trapdoor by the altar, and came over to peer over Morgan's shoulders at the pages.

Beck looked overhead at the fighter plane now, then down at the corpse of the British translator.

"It's all theater," he said. "Symbolism and theater."

Morgan nodded; he knew what Beck was getting at.

"We're no longer looking at the holy days of the Nazi state, but at the crimes of the victors," Beck began. "She says it here," he pointed at one of the pages. "She serves a higher court. Higher than the one at the Palace of Justice."

"What mumbo jumbo is this?" Perlmann said.

"It's retribution for Dresden," Beck said. "For the fire bombing. The British and your pilots," he nodded at Morgan, "dropped more than three thousand tons of high explosives and incendiaries on the city in the middle of last February. Thirty-five thousand civilians killed, twelve square miles of the city destroyed in the ensuing firestorm."

Morgan felt a chafing at Beck's mention of *your pilots*, but let it go. This was not the time or place to discuss the morality of such area bombing, of the London Blitz, or of who did what to whom first. Beck was right; their killer was moving on to new themes.

"Bomber Harris," Morgan said. "The mastermind of the raids was British. That's why the British victim."

Beck looked overhead again. "And this time, the roles are reversed, she's saying. The German plane overhead, the dead British civilian below."

Perlmann had obviously had enough of psychology and history. He started scouring the crime scene for any trace of the killer.

"There's another thing we should focus on," Beck offered. "She's diverged from her pattern in several regards."

"The female victim," Morgan said.

"Right. And then there's the symbolic motive. It's seemed to have changed. From canonizing the high points of the Reich to punishing the victors." Beck paused.

"You said several regards."

"The second note. It's a clue. She is trying to help us, tell us that she finds us poor competition." *Just as with the Slasher before the war*, he thought. "This second note is significant. It's like she wants to level the playing field, make it a more competitive match."

"Or raise the stakes, heighten the pleasure of the kill."

They both looked upward at the suspended plane for an instant, and then Beck began going through the small handbag: a tube of lipstick, a ration card, and a blue billet card with a name and address.

"I'll take the lodgings," he said. "There might be something in her room." But Beck did not say it with great hope. "Or maybe one of the other lodgers knows what would take a young woman out alone into a bombed-out church in Nuremberg."

Morgan would just as soon accompany Beck, but he had to face the music with Adams instead.

"Let's hope somebody knows something at the lodgings," he said.

He rapped on the door a second time before someone came. It was a large, thick, heavy door—a representative door, the property management people would say—and it opened slowly, like the lid of a sarcophagus.

What greeted him on the other side of it might well have made good contents for the crypt: He was a tall, gaunt man, dressed in black with a face as gray as his tie. His thinning hair was combed slick back in an oily shine like the reflection off of wet tarmac.

"May I help you?" Not so much a question as a veiled threat.

"I've come to see Frau Prandtauer," Beck said.

"Baroness von Prandtauer," the man corrected. "Is she expecting you?"

Beck fetched his credentials out of his breast pocket.

The servant peered down his long nose at them, sniffing with disdain. Beck could hardly blame the man; it had the appearance of an identity card some imaginative adolescent might come up with given sufficient card stock and access to ink. Nothing like the metal disk he once carried as a Kripo chief inspector. Ironically enough, with the murder of Manhof, he was getting that position back again, but for some reason he could not fathom, it had to go through the Allied Control Commission, who would issue his new identity card, first.

Until then, he carried a toy card that made butlers wince.

"Herr Beck," the butler read. "With the Allied Control Commission."

"Inspector Beck." His turn for correcting. "I am liaisoning from Kripo with the Americans. Now, may I see your employer?" He could not bring himself to use the woman's title. Never could stand the phony nobility.

"I shall announce you," the cadaver said, and closed the door in Beck's face before he could protest.

Beck was about to use the brass knocker again when the door swung open quite energetically this time, revealing a handsome woman in a brown tweed dress and green cardigan, stout walking shoes on her feet. Small wrinkles showed at her gray-green eyes as she smiled at him.

"Inspector Beck?" She thrust out her right hand at him, giving him a firm handshake. "I do apologize for Falk. He's the protective sort, you understand."

"Well, these days one can hardly blame him." He disliked such small talk, but found the baroness brought it out in him. *The baroness.*

"But please, come in, come in. How may I help you?"

She was late thirties, perhaps early forties, Beck assessed. Well preserved.

"And you must forgive my dress. I was just headed to the range."

She spoke brusquely, officiously, *in medias res*, as if everyone must know her schedule.

"You shoot?" he said, following her through the large entry hall to a smaller room at the back.

"Bow and arrow," she said, turning back to him momentarily, then opening the door to a room with heavily draped windows, oak furniture that seemed to lurk in the corners, and a parquet floor covered in wine red rugs. In the dim light, he could barely make out the color of the walls, a subtle robin's-egg blue. Over a sturdy sideboard, one wall was covered with photographs.

She sat at a tiny rosewood table and gestured to the chair across from her.

"Now, please, what brings you to our villa?"

Just then the servant, Falk, entered, tea tray in hand. Setting it down on the table between them, he then made a great show of backing out of the room, as if he were a retainer to the emperor and could not show his backside.

The baroness poured out two cups; Beck waited for Falk to be gone before proceeding.

"You have a British guest staying here, I believe. Elizabeth Garrison."

The baroness squinted at this. "Elizabeth? No . . . Oh, you mean Beth. The young translator. Sorry. She uses a shortened version of her name, it appears. I hadn't realized the coincidence."

"Coincidence?" Beck said.

"My own Christian name is also Elisabeth."

Beck did not reply to this, but placed the identity card on the table and slid it across to the baroness.

"Yes," she said. "That is Beth. Did she lose her card?"

"I am afraid I have some bad news. She is dead."

The baroness clapped her hands to her mouth. "My God," she muttered. "How? When? I was just talking with her last evening at dinner."

"Did she mention plans to go out last night? That she was meeting someone?"

Beck observed the baroness closely as she shook her head. "No, just talk of the trial and how demanding it is to do simultaneous translations. Dear young Beth. But what happened to her?"

Again Beck ignored the question. "Did she have friends here? A confidante, perhaps?"

"I really don't know. I mean, she usually took her meals with Mr. Stanton. William Stanton, that is. He is an American lawyer. I believe he is working in some capacity for the prosecution. They would talk together at meals. I am a private person, Inspector. And I respect the privacy of others as well."

"Is Mr. Stanton in his room?"

"No, I believe I saw him go out several hours ago. I assume he is at the trial or the Palace of Justice."

Beck nodded. "Perhaps I could see her room." He stood, smoothing his slacks as he did so. The tea sat untouched.

The baroness remained seated. "Inspector, you have studiously ignored my requests about what happened to poor Beth. I believe I deserve some sort of explanation."

"Actually, you don't," Beck said. "She died. And now I need to see her room."

Her hands were resting on the fragile table, and at his comment she flexed them together until the knuckles turned white. Beck thought the baroness was not the sort of person you wanted for an enemy, but so be it. It was not his job to please people.

Any trace of warmth on her part vanished. She got up and silently led him out to the hall again and to a flight of stairs going up. As they climbed to the first landing, another person was descending out of the gloom.

Beck was amazed to see her. "Miss Wallace," he said as she was passing.

She turned, not recognizing him at first, then reddening when she did.

"Oh, hello."

"Beck," he offered. "Inspector Beck."

"Right. Yes, we met briefly." She looked at a loss for words. She also had a sad air about her, like a person who has lost somebody close to them.

"Poor Beth is dead, he says," the baroness blurted out. "But he refuses to tell me anything about it."

"The British woman? How terrible," Kate said. "She was here just last evening. What happened?"

"We are investigating the death," Beck said.

"You see," the baroness chided. "Prevarications. That is all we get."

"You didn't happen to speak with her last evening, did you, Miss Wallace?"

"No. No, I didn't. We didn't really talk much at all. A polite hello at meals, that's all."

"So you could not direct us to any friends of hers, colleagues?"

"None, other than William-never-Bill."

"Pardon?"

"Mr. Stanton," the Baroness explained. "He is rather particular about the use of his given name."

Beck noticed the conspiratorial look that Miss Wallace and the baroness exchanged and assumed theirs was more than a purely formal connection of landlady and lodger. But the American turned to him again with a smile that was genuine. It seemed for a moment that she wanted to say something but thought better of it.

"I wish I could be of more help to you all."

"Yes. Well, nice to see you again, Miss Wallace," Beck said and then proceeded up the stairs. "Which landing?" he asked the baroness.

His ears were still ringing. Adams had, in fact, arranged a little ambush for Morgan at today's meeting. Sitting in on the execution had been Colonel Yuri Voschinsky, the red-faced Soviet security chief; Major Hannigan, smiling like a man in the catbird seat; Brigadier Charles Nelson, of the British forces in Nuremberg, with his bristling mustache; and Colonel Maillot, of French military security, the razor-thin Gaul who lit each new Gitanes off the dying embers of the old one. They had all been gathered by Adams to let Morgan know what a shitty job he had been doing. Nelson and Maillot were especially petulant; after all, their nationals had been victims of the killer.

"It won't do, it really won't," Nelson spluttered in his plummy accent. "You chaps must control this situation. One thing having soldiers put in harm's way, but now our women must live in fear, as well. A translator, for God sake. Where's the sense in it? I know her father, by the way. Good man, decent fellow. Had a good war. And now this: His daughter butchered in Nuremberg."

Morgan listened contritely through this harangue, but when Maillot started up with his fractured English, Morgan tuned out.

Instead of asking how they might help in the investigation,

each of the Allied security chiefs took this as an opportunity to exercise power, to try to make Morgan squirm, to point fingers and pass the blame.

"You really do need to take the yarmulke off and get on the stick, Captain," Hannigan said as the meeting was concluding.

At which point, Adams had wisely moved between the two men.

The upshot of it was Morgan had a week left. If he did not catch the killer by then, it was back to MI for him.

Fine by me, he thought.

Morgan had given little thought to what he was going to do after the war. He'd been a good cop in New York. He supposed he could go back to that. But if this current position were any indication, he was no longer taking great pleasure in investigative work. He missed the field, missed Switzerland and Dulles. Even missed Wild Bill Donovan, for all his bluster and mad schemes. But in the postwar world, it didn't seem there was going to be place for espionage and agents. Not in the civilian world, at any rate.

So a move back to MI did not seem that bad to him at the moment.

Back in his office, he began going through a new set of documents from Berlin. Despite his repeated instructions, Berlin continued to send lists of every Iron Cross recipient in the former greater Reich. Even with Inspector Perlmann helping out with these lists, the job seemed neverending. The Kripo man was busily going through another batch of recipients in his own tiny office.

So many heroes, you would think the Nazis would have won the war.

"Can we talk?"

He looked up from the files. Kate stood in the open doorway, looking as beautiful as he remembered. He had to check his emotions, force himself to remember her betrayal.

"Not much to talk about."

"What happened to Beth, the British translator?"

"Where'd you hear about that?"

"Your colleague Inspector Beck was at the villa."

Morgan stared at her blankly.

"The Villa von Prandtauer. Where I'm lodging. Beth was lodged there, too."

He remembered his irrational fears that morning upon seeing that the victim was a woman, fearing that it was Kate. Not so irrational after all, it seemed.

"This does not get in the newspapers. The only reason you're still credentialed is because of your father's influence. Otherwise, you'd have been on that plane out of Nuremberg along with Phipson."

"You are an incredible dolt, do you know that? I can't believe I ever thought I loved you."

The word, once spoken, brought stillness to the office. She turned red in the face at the admission.

"More maneuvering?"

"Screw you, Morgan. I'm concerned, is all. Beck would not say how she died. She wasn't a friend, but she lived under the same roof."

"So you're just curious?"

"So I am just concerned. As in compassion for a fellow human being."

He was about to make a curt remark but paused. She'd used him, why not return the favor?

"Can I trust you?"

"That's not the way to begin a reconciliation," she said. "Whatever you think, I did not betray you."

"Okay," Morgan said, going over the options. He needed to smoke out the killer, get under her skin somehow and force her to act stupidly. To make her lash out rather than continue her calculated mayhem.

"We've profiled the killer. There are only a handful of people who know this . . . it's a woman. We think it is a deranged prostitute at work, a woman who has suffered personally at the hands of our soldiers."

Kate absorbed this. "And Beth?"

"The English translator?"

A quick calculation: Kate would not be here if Beck had given the specifics of the English woman's death.

"Not one of the victim's. She was run down by a truck. We're trying to figure out why she was out last night, but it wasn't our killer at work."

He felt comfortable lying. It was part of the skill set learned during the war. Planting stories in the legitimate press. No self-respecting journalist could help himself with such information.

Morgan hoped to be reading it in the front pages of tomorrow's papers.

The alternative was to trust Kate with the truth, to ask her to plant a phony story. But, in fact, he did not trust her.

Beck finally tracked down William Stanton at the Palace of Justice, in the American defense research section. He was not at the trial itself, but instead worked behind the scenes combing through the boxes of evidence gathered from around the former Reich. Labeling atrocity photos, cross-filing eyewitness accounts for future trials. It seemed the Allies were going to be making an industry of these trials; there was enough evidence left behind by the Nazis themselves—obsessive collators of their misdeeds—to seed several more years of proceedings against lower-level SS.

Stanton's shock at the news of Miss Garrison's death was real, Beck could see. He was the sort of chipper, buoyant American to whom nothing bad had or could have happened. His face turned pale at the news, as if a bit of his secure world had been chipped away.

Theirs had been a platonic relationship, on his side anyway, he explained. His fiancée was awaiting him in Baltimore. No, he had no idea what would take Miss Garrison out last night. She had broached the possibility of a shared drink sometime at the Grand, but Stanton had, of course, demurred. He had made an early night of it last night.

Beck had a sixth sense about such things; nothing to be learned here other than the fact that Miss Garrison may have had a crush on this unpromising young American.

It had been an early start that morning—so early, in fact, that Beck had gone off without his gun. After the shoot-out at the motor pool, he did not think it was a good idea to go about unarmed; he decided to go back to his lodgings quickly before conferring with Morgan.

His requisitioned jeep was still on duty; he was at the hotel in ten minutes. The Hotel Terminus was run-down enough in the best of times; now it had the stature of a flophouse. Voss, the night clerk, was snoring behind the main desk as Beck entered the shabby lobby. A potted palm, long dead, drooped in one corner like a bad stage-prop from the movies. The stairs were unlit; his room was on the third floor, just large enough for a narrow bed and chipped wardrobe. But he was lucky to have it, lucky not to be living rough in the ruins of the city like thousands of others.

He'd kept busy since yesterday, trying not to think of his mother's death. The funeral was scheduled for tomorrow.

We've all got to die. She'd lived her life; she was with her beloved husband now.

But he didn't really believe any of it. There was a hollowness in him when he thought of her.

His gun was in a drawer in the wardrobe. The metal shaving box was next to it.

Maybe it was time now. He could use the comfort of his wife and child.

He strapped on the gun, then took the box out lovingly, carefully, as if holding a fragile bit of Murano glass. He sat on the bed and slowly opened the lid. Inside, as remembered, was a lock of his daughter's hair, stored in a small, round, glass coin collector case. The broken Mont Blanc from his wife was there, as well. At the bottom, he could see the white outlines of an envelope. He tried to remember what that might be but couldn't. He gently moved the other contents aside and removed the letter: It was addressed to him and dated February 12, 1938.

A flash of memory made his throat go dry, his breathing speed up.

He knew what it was. Opening the flap, he pulled the letter out and unfolded it. The words had been cut from newspapers and magazines. There had been no prints to discern. The message was clear: *I know where you live. I know you have a daughter.*

The words still chilled him, as they had done years ago.

A personal message from the Slasher—a warning. A threat.

He had kept that letter like a talisman, a symbol of his own inability to solve the crime.

He would not let that happen again. Ever.

Back at the Palace of Justice, Beck told Morgan he needed the rest of the day to make arrangements for his mother's burial.

"May I come?"

"You never met her."

"But I know you. Is it okay?"

A curt nod. "Okay. Fine. It's scheduled for tomorrow in the late afternoon. At the Saint Rochus Cemetery on Rothenburger Strasse. That's—"

"I know where it is. Just outside the old southwest walls."

"Encyclopedic mind."

"It's my job."

Beck nodded. "Three thirty."

"I'll be there."

"Seems sort of a precious act in the midst of all this."

"What? Giving your mother a proper burial?"

"There are thousands rotting under the rubble. Nuremberg is one huge cemetery."

Morgan said nothing.

"But she'd like it," Beck said. "Next to her husband, my father." He shrugged.

"Sometimes I wish I believed," Morgan said. "It makes times like these easier."

"The nice white lie of religion." He remembered something. "You know, I saw your friend this morning, Miss Wallace."

"Right. She mentioned that."

"So you're seeing her again."

"She made an appearance here."

"I have a feeling about the woman. I don't think she set you up. There was something about her today—a sadness."

"Matchmaker now, are you?"

"Life is long, Morgan. You don't want to live it alone." He grabbed his coat before the captain could reply. "Till tomorrow."

On his way down the stairs, he realized there was something about this morning that was nagging in the back of his mind. Something he had seen but not really paid attention to. It would come to him if he stopped trying to force it.

The last of the light. Days were drawing in. As a child, she had railed against this time of year: the short days, the trees denuded. Now she loved it, the bleakness, the dying light.

"Just off, Baroness," Falk called out from the straw-backed target twenty yards distant. He tugged mightily with his thin arm to dislodge the arrow, his entire body shaking with the effort.

She fitted another arrow onto the string, then pulled it back slowly. The muscles in her right arm flexed as she did so, bending the bow further inward, transferring the muscle energy to the bow itself, endowing it with life. Falk was standing too close to the target—too bad. He was the one who insisted on accompanying her today. Protective as an old maid.

The bow curved further inward, and she steadied it now, adjusting the elevation and siting down the arrow. Then the slow release of the bowstring that turned into a whiplash of force, transferring the energy collected in the bow to the arrow.

It flew high and true. Once it was released, the arrow held little interest for the baroness; she was thinking instead of the silly British girl and how easily she had been duped.

"Bull's-eye, Baroness," Falk cried out, but she paid him no attention, busy fitting another arrow on the bowstring.

The note from William Stanton had done the trick, as she knew it would. Requesting a discrete *tête-à-tête* at a certain church in the city. "Oh, and do bring this message with you, please. We don't want our little assignation becoming the stuff of gossip."

Typed officiously as such a note might be by the redheaded American lawyer. But most definitely not from him. The baroness had made sure that William Stanton was out for the day before slipping the note under the British girl's door.

And the silly little bitch had played right into her hands, arriving a full five minutes early at Sankt Anna, the bombed out church where—Kate Wallace had informed her—she and her American captain had first kissed.

She really must thank her American *friend* for providing such a symbolic crime scene.

Thursday, at the trial. That would be her thanksgiving to Kate Wallace and all the other Americans and victors. Her own private *Götterdämmerung*. And a final symbolic gift, as well, for Thursday was the beginning of Hanukkah.

So easy, really, she thought, her mind going back to the killing on Monday. Another arrow flew into the twilight.

She knew that the police and military were now looking for a female killer, so she simply disguised herself as a man, pulling her hair into a tight bun and wearing one of her husband's old hunting hats accompanied by a long cloak. Underneath, she had put on his dress uniform.

Oh, the look of horror in the British girl's eyes when she had opened the cloak to reveal her uniform and scalpel at the ready.

A frisson of delight coursed through her at the thought.

"Too bad, Baroness," came Falk's voice out of the growing darkness. "Just missed."

She had a momentary desire to send an arrow straight for Falk, but at the last instant moved her aim a pinch to the left.

Nothing rash—nothing hasty now to spoil the rest of the plan.

The jeep bounced over the rutted streets, and Morgan shook his head.

Not another one, he thought. *Not now.*

Something wasn't right. For one, it was the wrong day.

Their killer had been methodical, every three days from the first killing on November 8. And it was too early, only nine thirty-two, Morgan could see by the green glow of the luminous dial on his Bulova.

They were there in five more minutes, the eerie orange light of flares illuminating the scene. A figure wrapped in a cloak sat huddled on a broken chunk of masonry, two beefy Military Police standing sentinel nearby. As Morgan drew closer, he could make out blood splatter on the ground next to the cloaked figure. Was there something familiar about the way she was sitting? *She*, because they had called it in as a female perpetrator. Otherwise, the cloak gave her a sexless appearance. Could be a man, could be a woman.

"Captain," one of the MPs saluted at Morgan approached.

"What we got here, Lieutenant?" he said to the rosy-cheeked MP.

"Sir, me and my partner here, Lieutenant Grimes, we saw this lady leading a soldier off the main road into this ruined building. We heard from our sarge about these murders, so, you know, we were suspicious."

Morgan scanned the scene, looking for a body.

"And?"

"Well, we stuck around for a few minutes. We heard some shouts and came running. The lady here was busy with this."

He pulled a bloodied handkerchief out of his jacket pocket

and unwrapped it to reveal a straight razor, its blade still wet with blood.

"We disarmed the lady," the youthful MP continued.

"The victim?"

"We got the ambulance here. They packed him off to the hospital. Mostly cuts to his hands and some to his, well, you know, his privates."

The woman looked up now, glaring at the razor. Morgan could not make out her features in the light.

"He tried to hurt me," she spit out in Nuremberger German so thick that Morgan barely caught it.

"You wait," he barked back at her. Then to the lieutenant, "Did he make a statement?"

"No, nothing. Just kept babbling about his privates."

"Called it his johnson," Lieutenant Grimes added.

"You get a name?"

The MPs glanced at one another then looked downward.

"Lieutenant? A name?"

"Negative on that one, sir. Sorry. It was all a bit crazy, blood everywhere and then the meat wagon came."

Morgan turned his attention to the woman, not bothering to dismiss the other two.

"You have a name?"

She fixed him with a look of contempt mixed with fear. "Dagmar."

"That's a start. Family name?"

"Schwanz," she said, smirking at him.

"Cute. Family name? Don't make me ask again."

"Hoffmann."

"So, Dagmar Hoffmann, stand up."

No, Morgan decided. Something definitely not right about this. Not a fit for their profile at all.

She mumbled something incoherent.

"Now," he shouted, making the MPs jump, too.

She did so.

"Open your coat."

"Why—"

"Just open it."

Underneath she had on an aged and tattered evening dress, silk stockings with patches, but no medal.

"You ever married, Dagmar? And don't lie. I can check." A fabrication, but she would not know.

She flexed a jaw muscle. "Not so you'd notice."

"What do you do for a living, Dagmar?"

"What's it look like."

He restrained himself from slapping her. He wanted to badly. "Just answer the question."

"I fuck GIs. Understand?"

"But you didn't fuck this one. You tried to kill him."

"Like I told you. He wanted to hurt me. I don't take it in the arse for anyone."

"He wanted anal intercourse, is that what you're saying?"

"He was trying to rape me."

"Good luck with that story."

"Pig."

Morgan stared back at her with cold contempt.

"Okay," she said. "Dagmar gives a man a good time. But she doesn't do perverted acts. She doesn't let her body be abused. You ask anybody on the street."

"I'll do that. Meanwhile, you'll be staying with us."

Then to the MP: "Lieutenant. She goes to the women's wing at the prison. She's got a name. Don't mislay her."

"Right, Captain."

"It was self-defense. I was protecting myself from that animal."

"I believe you, Dagmar. Okay. But I need to do some follow-up."

"How am I supposed to earn a living in jail?"

"Be inventive."

It's what I get for lying to Kate, he thought as he left the scene for his jeep. *Here's my murderous whore.*

Later that evening, after the dinner hour, she went to Kate's room. The American had not come down to eat. Still feeling the pangs of love, the stupid little cow. Her and her Jew lover. They made her sick. But she still had need of Kate Wallace.

She had the pass to the spectator gallery at the trial secured; Colonel Jensen had seen to it. Now to get Kate to accompany her. Then, at the trial on Thursday, she would set the purse-size bomb Manhof had given her, excuse herself to go to the ladies' room, and then kill herself and as many spectators and witnesses as she could—Kate Wallace among them.

That would be a statement they could not keep out of the papers. That would show the proud victors what the Germans thought of their kangaroo court.

But she needed Kate Wallace for this plan to work—needed an American in tow so that she could get into the spectators' box without being too thoroughly searched.

The baroness finally reached the door, and Kate opened it on the second knock.

"Let's share some gossip," she said, brushing past the American and into the room. Without being asked, she sat in one of the Biedermeier chairs at the table. "Poor young Beth. Such a terrible thing."

The baroness was not expecting the reaction she got. Suddenly, Kate opened to her once again, as she would to an older sister, telling the baroness of her visit to Captain Morgan that afternoon, of his assurances that Beth had not been one of the victims of the murderer on the loose in Nuremberg. And then, like a naughty girl, sharing another secret after making the baroness promise first not to tell anyone.

When she heard the words—that the Americans were looking for a deranged prostitute as the person responsible for the killings—she felt a cold horror. She could not control her emotions.

"Sissy, are you all right? Your face is suddenly so pale."

"You know, I might be coming down with something. I haven't been feeling right all day."

It was all she could do to get out of the room without being sick.

A prostitute!

In the hall, she breathed deeply several times and then headed for her room.

She realized that she had not invited the American to the trial on Thursday and turned around. Then she stopped.

Anger wrapped her like a cold friend. No. She would not go to the trial after all. Instead, she would hold her own trial at a higher court. She would show the two Americans that it was not a deranged prostitute at work, but a proud German woman. It would be the last thing they would ever discover.

November 28, 1945

There had been another snowfall. The southern suburbs where Doktor Edmund Niedholer lived were powdered white, the snow muffling the sound of bicycles and pedestrians.

The funeral arrangements had all been taken care of and Beck, with a few hours to himself, decided to play a hunch that morning, realizing that when he first spoke with the psychologist, they had assumed their perpetrator was a man. Now that they knew it was a woman, perhaps Niedholer could offer different advice.

In his study, Niedholer listened patiently to Beck's explanation of their investigations to date, including the decoding of messages from the Karl May novels.

"You should have told me before," the doctor said, opening a drawer of his desk and skimming through files until he found something, pulled out a manila folder, and set it on the desk between them.

Beck could read the name upside down: "Thalweg, Elisabeth."

Niedholer sat silently for a moment.

"What?" Beck said.

"Doktor Heinrich Thalweg was one of our foremost surgeons," Niedholer said, folding his hands on the desk in front of him. The knuckles were turning white, Beck could see.

"He brought his young daughter to me for help in 1925. She presented with sleep disorder and mood swings. Worse, she had been killing animals in their neighborhood. It started with their own parakeet, but she soon graduated to a neighbor's cat, then a dog, a dachshund. The necks of the animals had been slashed."

"But—"

"Wait," Niedholer said firmly. "There is more. I gave the girl a physical examination and discovered small mutilations of her body, localized around the genital region. The young girl had obviously been abused and quite regularly. But she would say nothing of her abuser. Only . . ." He picked through the file until he found what he was looking for. "Yes. Here it is. Only that 'brave Indians do not tell.' "

He read further in his notes. "It appears that Karl May was her favorite author."

Niedholer was silent for a moment, then sighed. "This was serious, I knew at the time. Not just that she was being abused, but that she was already displaying such antisocial behavior. In fact, she was quite proud of her accomplishments killing those animals; she had dreams at the time of one day being famous for such skill, she told me."

Beck could no longer keep quiet. "What became of her?"

"The cuts were consistent with those made by a surgeon's scalpel. At first, I could not believe it. But it had to be so. I broached the subject with Doktor Thalweg, and he was horrified at my suggestion. He immediately took his daughter out of therapy."

"Had he abused his own daughter? Then why would he bring her to you, knowing you would discover it?"

"Perhaps he wanted to be stopped. Perhaps it was not him at all. I was unable to follow up on the case, though I never forgot it. It came to mind when you visited me about your killer, but at that time it seemed so clear that we were looking for a male. Yet now . . ."

"How do I find her?"

"As I say, I have had no contact in over two decades. Doktor Thalweg, I know, was a widower at the time. I heard that he died before the war. There were so many cases, you see. I could not follow up on all of them."

"Nobody's accusing you, Doktor Niedholer. Is there an address in her file?"

Niedholer sighed, opening the file again and searching through the pages. "This is from 1925. Who knows if it is still valid?"

He passed the patient form to Beck: 169 Johannes Strasse.

"This is near the Saint Johannis Hospital, isn't it?"

Niedholer nodded. "Doktor Thalweg was a resident there. Why?"

"That's where the killings started. The young Soviet soldier was murdered near the hospital. His throat cut with what must have been a scalpel, the forensics say."

Niedholer stood, a look of urgency on his face. "Find her. It must be her."

Morgan finished with the last of the morning papers, even checking the wire services; there was no story about the Nuremberg killings, no tales of a mad prostitute wreaking vengeance on the conquering allies.

He felt an uncommon emotion: guilt. He thought he had purged that facility forever during his years in the OSS. But there it was again, like an old friend.

What was it Beck had said last night? That Kate had not been the one to set him up. What if it were true? What if her explanation was the fact and not a convenient fiction? That would mean that he had thrown her over for nothing. That he had destroyed a possibility for happiness out of a sheer need to believe the worst in everyone. That his OSS training was still ordering his life, making him believe that everyone would betray him, eventually.

Maybe there was still a chance. Like Beck said, life was long. Maybe it was time to start trusting again.

It took Beck an hour to ascertain that 169 Johannes Strasse was a pile of rubble. The neighboring house, 171, one of the old half-timbered buildings for which the city had at one time been so famous, was still standing. Its inhabitant, Frau Wagner, remembered the Thalwegs well, though according to her, they had already sold the house before the war; in fact, not long after the father had died.

They were seated in Frau Wagner's front room. The doors to all the other rooms in the house were secured; Beck had the feeling she was living in this one room, trying to stay warm. She offered him reheated and most probably resteeped tea. A woman of about sixty, she was stuck in the role of coquette, which she must have been playing most of her life. He had to listen to her woes first: the death of her husband on the Eastern Front—"He was too old to go, of course, but the old fool had to join up"—the loss of her family money, a miserable case of shingles.

But finally, she made it worth it: "The son was an artist, you know."

"No, I didn't," Beck said. "Didn't know there was a son."

"Oh yes. Gerhard. Quite the handsome one, too. Had some success as a painter. I believe he had a studio near the castle. His sister, though. She was something. My cat went missing. I still swear it was her at work. A strange little girl. Pity the man who married her."

"Did she marry then?"

Frau Wagner shrugged, then gave him a winsome look. "I believe so, but don't know to whom. Memory serves right, it was some rather important military man or other. Were you in the military, Inspector Beck?"

Frau Wagner's telephone book was from 1942, the last time it was published. Gerhard Thalweg had had a phone at the time and an address to go with it: 23 Schildgasse, apartment 10. As the good Frau said, near the old castle. If he survived the war, perhaps brother Gerhard would know the whereabouts of his sister.

Luck of the draw, Beck figured, once he had made it back to the center of the city. The buildings on both sides and across the street from 23 Schildgasse were piles of rubble, but this one stood, a low baroque house with a street door blown off its hinges.

He entered, orientated himself, and started up the stairs. In back of him, a white-haired pensioner appeared out of a lower apartment.

"Hey, you," the man called out.

Beck turned to see a double-barreled shotgun pointed directly at his chest.

"I know how to use it," the old man said with a savage hiss. "So just go back down the stairs the way you came."

"I'm Kripo," Beck said calmly.

"And I'm Hermann Göring. Like I said," he jerked the shotgun to his left, "back down the stairs."

Beck did not like arguing with buckshot; he did as the man said, but as he moved to go past the old man, the pensioner had to adjust his gun to let him by and Beck saw his opening. He thrust upward against the barrel with his right elbow and moved in under it to land a blow to the man's solar plexus. An explosion of air from the man's mouth and the shotgun clattered to the flagstone landing. Beck quickly picked the gun up, broke it open, and discovered there were no shells in the barrels.

"You're the watchman, are you?"

The old man held his stomach, grimacing at Beck.

Beck pulled out his identity card and thrust it in his face.

The old man squinted at it. "You really are Kripo."

"That's what I said."

"I try to keep squatters out. That's not against the law, is it?

My wife is sick. We can't have half of Nuremberg camping out here. Somebody complain?"

"I'm not here about you. I'm looking for the studio of Gerhard Thalweg."

The man's expression brightened. "The artist. Fine young man. Died in Russia."

"*Scheiss,*" Beck muttered.

"No reason for foul language. A relative of yours?"

Beck shook his head.

"I've done my job all these years, even after hearing he was killed in action. Figured a relative would show up one day to claim the belongings. The young man made me his caretaker before he left. Wanted me to protect his prized canvasses. Paid me handsomely, too. No, you cannot say that Maxim Kralik does not do his duty."

"You have a key?"

The old man nodded.

Beck thrust his hand out to him. Kralik drew back.

"Police business," Beck said, using the pitiless voice of authority. Kralik responded to this, pulling out a large brass key and setting it on Beck's open palm.

"You'll not interfere with any of his property."

"Wouldn't think of it," Beck said, already on his way up the stairs.

"Return the key once you're done," Kralik called after him. "Apartment ten."

It took Beck several minutes to work the lock. Whatever the old man had said about doing his job, it appeared that job did not include entering the studio. The lock had not been turned in years. Finally, he heard the satisfying click of gears, and the door opened into darkness. He did not even bother feeling the walls for a light switch; there would be no electricity in this house. He made his way blindly across the room where he could barely discern curtains. He pulled them aside to discover the windows had been covered in dark oilcloth for blackout purposes. He peeled the cloth off the panes and bright light flooded the room. He could now see that sheets covered the furniture; canvasses were stacked against the walls, also covered in sheets. Dust lay thick everywhere; only his faltering footsteps across the room showed in the thick patina on the floor.

It was like walking into a mausoleum. He had no idea when Gerhard Thalweg had been called up, but it had probably been early in the war. His studio must have been standing unused for five years at least. He pulled a sheet off one stack of canvasses to reveal bucolic landscapes and frivolous urban scenes at cafés and wine gardens. Beck seemed to recall the style now; Gerhard Thalweg had been, if not a fashionable painter, then a popular one in the 1930s. Beck picked through the paintings; they went against the grain of the modern expressionist art of that time. No danger of Gerhard Thalweg's art being condemned as decadent by the Nazis. There was something too sweetly saccharine about the scenes to please Beck's taste—an artificial quality, a striving to please the consumer. He replaced the sheet.

He was looking for a desk, something with drawers where Thalweg might keep an address book, letters, anything to point to the whereabouts and married name of his sister, Elisabeth.

A bedroom was located off the main studio; he tore off the blackout cloth there as well and finally found a desk under another dusty sheet. Its drawers had been emptied; however, one of them was locked. He tried to force it, but could not. Before the war, he would have carried jimmies, a set of plain keys, all sorts of tools that might help him now. But that was before the war.

It was the bottom box on the left side of the desk. Beck got down on hands and knees and jabbed his fist up into the thin boxwood of the bottom of the drawer splintering it. He tore the wood apart and the contents of the drawer spilled onto the ground.

The purple velvet wrapper cushioned the drop to the floor so that there was not a clattering sound. Unwrapping the velvet, he saw there would have been such a racket, for inside was a gleaming steel scalpel.

Then he went over the studio more professionally, looking for other hiding spots, examining clothing in wardrobes. He found the next horde in a false backing of the wardrobe in the studio. There were a series of oil paintings on small wooden panels depicting what appeared to be torture scenes: a young girl with feathers in her hair, tied down with leather tongs at her wrists and ankles, suffering various indignities. An arm holding what appeared to be the scalpel he had just found was mutilating her pelvis. One painting had an inscription: *Brave Indians do not flinch from the pain.*

He thought he recognized the young girl in the paintings. He had seen her somewhere recently, he was sure.

She had come down with a bad cold. No trial for her today. She was in bed feeling sorry for herself, her throat raw and head throbbing.

Kate could hear activity in the house: the creaking of the stairs, doors opening and closing, water running in the pipes. By mid-morning, such sounds had ceased. The others, William Stanton and Colonel Jensen, had already gone about their business at the Palace of Justice. She could imagine the knowing looks her colleagues would exchange when they noticed her empty place in the press gallery.

Last night, after the baroness had left, Kate sat at her typewriter and began tapping out a story. The amazing thing was, however, that it was not a newspaper story at all, but a short story about a young, female American journalist who meets the love of her life at the Nuremberg trials.

Well, all right. Memoir, perhaps. She had fleshed out the scene of her first connection to Morgan at the bombed-out church—Sankt Anna she had subsequently learned—and the sudden closeness she felt to him in that bizarre atmosphere.

That page still sat in the typewriter carriage, for she had not wanted to finish it last night, wanted it to linger, wanted to capture the words and emotions of that moment exactly as they had been.

She gazed over to the typewriter, but knew she was in no shape to continue with that now. Then she dozed on and off throughout the morning, dreaming alternately of Morgan and of the baroness.

By early afternoon, she had had enough of being sick. She went to the bathroom down the hall and took a hot bath. She would suffer a reprimand from Falk later, surely, for this was not her bath day and Falk would reiterate in his broken English that fuel was dear. Not merely expensive, *dear.*

It would be worth a lecture, though, Kate thought as she dried off, suddenly feeling much better. Her stomach growled, and she realized she had not eaten since last evening. She was, in fact, hungry. A good sign.

She was busy drying her hair with her towel and did not hear the bathroom door opening, was not aware there was anyone else in the room until she saw the reflection in the mirror.

She spun around, clutching the towel automatically to her nakedness.

"Baroness . . . Sissy, you startled me—"

"Shut your mouth, you little fool." The baroness's face was twisted in an expression of hate like a snarling animal. She drew a Luger out of her tweed jacket.

"We have work ahead of us. Do as you are told and you might live."

The minister pulled out his gold watch from under his thick surplice, once again checking the time. The wind picked up, blowing snow across and into the freshly dug grave. Two bearers stood shivering at graveside, ready to lower the casket containing Frau Beck.

No ashes, Beck had told Morgan. There had been too many ashes in Germany the last years, he had explained. His mother would return to the earth slowly.

So where was Beck? Morgan now looked at his Bulova: three fifty-five. He was worried about Beck; you don't forget your own mother's funeral.

The minister was hatless and his wispy hair fluttered in the breeze. His cheeks were scarlet from the cold.

"We really must begin, Captain Morgan."

"Another few minutes," Morgan said. *"Bitte."*

He spent the afternoon tracking down one false lead after another.

Kralik, the caretaker for the Thalweg's apartment, had no knowledge of a sister. He did, however, have the address of the painter's art agent.

"A Jew, I think, but he had connections so he probably survived."

Beck wanted to put his fist into the man's face.

Beck had played musical chairs for hours, going from one lead to the next. Herr König's gallery was no more; it and its contents had been incinerated during the American bombing raids on the city eleven months ago. Herr König, however, he managed to track down via neighbors. It astounded Beck the resilience of the people, their pure stubbornness. Their homes were reduced to rubble, but they insisted on remaining in their old neighborhoods, finding shelter where they could, in lean-tos constructed with waste material; in cellars; even in the catacombs of bombed-out churches. König was, in fact, taking refuge in the catacombs of the Spitalkirche, according to a crone wrapped in layers of ragged sweaters and woolen skirts who was the *de facto* assemblyman of her neighborhood. But König, once Beck tracked him down, had little to tell him about Thalweg, nor did he know of a sister. He was busily packing his few belongings, for church officials had discovered that their catacomb was being occupied and were sealing it. Consecrated ground was being defiled by the homeless of Nuremberg, it seemed.

König did, however, have the names of several other painters who knew the secretive Thalweg: "Not a very forthcoming young man," König said. "But his canvasses sold well to the nouveau riche and lower echelon Nazis."

Beck spent the rest of the afternoon on a wild-goose chase looking for the other painters of whom König had told him.

It was now five o'clock, and he had discovered that two of the painters were dead; the third, very much alive, wanted to pummel Beck for bringing up the name of his archrival. And no, he did not know of any damned sister.

It was then Beck remembered his mother's funeral.

Kate had no idea of time; she was bitterly cold, that was one thing she did know. The baroness had left perhaps an hour ago, wordlessly, and afterward Kate struggled with the ropes, but each time she tugged at them they seemed to tighten. The baroness—*Sissy*, she thought, ruefully—had secured her well; soon she simply lay on the damp clammy earth and tried to control her panic. All about her were the bones of dead people. She had seen the chamber illuminated before the baroness left. A tourist to these catacombs, she would have found them intriguing. A prisoner here, she was terrified. Deep breaths did the trick for a time, slowing her heartbeat, focusing her mind on the physical.

She tried to piece together what was happening. Before leaving the villa, the baroness had forced her, at gunpoint, to place the call. She had tried to resist, but then the baroness took out a scalpel and threatened to puncture her eyeball. Kate did not know how she was able to control her voice on the call, but she had, speaking to Morgan in a sprightly manner as if it were all a lark, making an assignation with him for later tonight. She hated herself for the insouciant tone she was able to conjure up, for betraying Morgan in the most callous manner. She felt a sudden knot in her throat; her breathing came more quickly.

Focus, she commanded herself. She had to keep her mind working, analyzing, not rioting into panic.

Get it down like a journalist would, she commanded herself. *Put the facts together; see the larger picture*. But what this all pointed to did not bring any analytical comfort to Kate.

There had been no explanation from the woman, merely the command that she place the call to Morgan, and then she was

in some time. Kate had tried to keep track of time, to know how
far they traveled from the villa, but it was no good. She lost
count as the car rattled over uneven roadway, as she began to
choke on the exhaust fumes leaking into the trunk. Then they
stopped and the trunk opened. It was already dark, early sunset
this time of year. The baroness had found a quiet side street; no
pedestrians were around.

"Say one word and you die. Scream for help and I will blow
your head off."

She took of the ropes and gag until they were inside once
again, and then escorted Kate down to the catacombs.

No, there was little comfort in analysis, for what this all
added up to was that the baroness, the widow of the "good German" General von Prandtauer, was a ruthless killer using her as
a pawn to lure Morgan into a trap.

What this meant was that the baroness was most likely the
mad killer terrorizing all of Nuremberg, and now she intended
to take the life of a prime victim, the very man who was hunting her.

Whatever it was the baroness had planned for her, Kate
knew one thing: She would no longer be a simple victim. No
longer be filled with panic. She would plan. She would find a
way out of this.

Morgan sat at his desk at the Palace of Justice wondering what
the hell had happened to Inspector Beck. He had checked at
the tiny Kripo office; Perlmann had been there, busily going
through military awards lists. No, he'd told Morgan. No sign
of Beck.

Something had made him forget his own mother's funeral.
What? Morgan didn't like this one bit. Beck's one-armed detective, Wieland Imhofer, came to mind. He went missing, too, and
later turned up in the Pegnitz River.

He looked at the note on his desk: "Meet Kate." Doodled as he took her message before leaving for the funeral. An odd request, but then he had not been able to turn her down. He did want to see her. But with Beck gone missing . . .

He lifted the receiver, asked for an outside line from the WAC operator and also for a local number. If Kate called him, then there must be a phone where she was staying. He got a line and listened to the chirrup of ring tone for a full minute before giving up. Too late, he figured. She was already on her way. He would have to meet her, let her know something important had come up, and then set a search for Beck.

Exhaustion finally won out; she fell asleep for a time, she knew not how long. Her mind was fuzzy, she felt as if she were a child again, at her Pennsylvania home with her cat, Tabby, on her bed, nuzzling her in the early morning, gently waking her to be fed. This time, however, the nuzzling was not a dream. There was fur against her face, and now it was not soft and cuddly, but sharp and probing.

She let out a muffled scream, rolling and twisting her body, and the rat scurried off a few paces. Her vision had adjusted to the darkness, and she could see the glowing eyes of several more rats behind the brave leader. It stretched its neck, lifting its snout as if smelling her. A lump of fear formed in Kate's throat, quickly forgotten when she felt a nibbling at the back of her leg. Rolling in that direction she saw more rats, sniffing, circling. Her entire body began to tremble, to shake uncontrollably.

For minutes, she continued to roll this way and that, thrusting her head at an attack, kicking her lower body. One rat got close enough to her to draw blood on her cheek. The liquid felt warm on her skin in the chill air. She flailed about, hands and feet secured in ever-tightening slipknots. Breathing was difficult with the gag; she began to feel light-headed from the exertion.

She couldn't pass out. That would mean a horrible death. Deep breaths were impossible, for she had to keep her body in perpetual motion or the rats would attack. Light-headedness turned to dizziness. Her eyes would not focus, only her blind will kept her flailing at the ever-more-emboldened rodents. Tiny teeth sunk into the back of her thigh, biting right through her clothes. She rolled quickly in that direction and trapped the animal, then pushed her body down on it, feeling a satisfying crunch under her. The rat lay limply beneath her, no longer fighting.

She struggled to a sitting position, scooting backward until her shoulder hit a stack of bones in back of her. She had seen this mound of bones, at least six feet in height, when the baroness had her flashlight on. It looked precariously built and now with her shoulder against it, she could feel it move slightly. But it afforded her some protection against rats coming in back of her. She would have to sit quietly so as not to bring the stack of bones tumbling on top of her.

And then she had an idea.

No one was in the office by the time Beck got back. He had to get in touch with Morgan, to let him know about his discoveries. He felt guilt at missing his mother's funeral, but was sure she would understand. Triage. The war had taught them all about that concept.

Where the hell was Morgan when he needed him? He checked the captain's desk and immediately saw the scribbled note: "Meet Kate."

Wonderful. But where?

"So you're back."

Beck whirled around at the sound of the voice. Perlmann stood in the doorway, a piece of paper in hand.

"Your captain was looking for you. I think he misses you. Could it be love?"

"Bugger off, Perlmann. Where did he go, do you know?"

"True love, indeed. No, I do not know the whereabouts of our *Ami* friend. But I do have some information."

Beck nodded for him to continue.

"These lists from Berlin—"

"I know. There are thousands of names."

"I think I might have found something."

He entered the office and held out the paper in his hand to Beck.

Morgan grabbed a quick bite to eat first. The beef had more gristle than meat, but he figured he was still doing better with calorie intake than most in Nuremberg. The problem was that the GI dishing out the slop at the Palace of Justice canteen made it seem like he was doing Morgan a favor.

A carrot lurked somewhere in the stew, a turnip, a few potatoes. Hot enough to scald the roof of his mouth.

After eating, he checked out a jeep from the car pool and headed down Fürther Strasse to the Altstadt. His was one of the few vehicles on the road and he made good time in the evening darkness. Snow flurries began as he parked his vehicle and made his way on foot along the deserted Königstrasse. An old Mercedes was parked in a side street; strange to see a civilian vehicle out. But he had other things to occupy his mind as he made his way toward the church.

Beck did not bother to knock, but barged in with Perlmann at his back. He nodded for the detective to check upstairs while he headed for the sitting room and morning room. There was no one about. But in the morning room, he went to the display of photos over the sideboard and looked again more closely at the picture of the military man. That was what had been nagging him, what he had seen and not really observed: the pictures on this wall when he interviewed the baroness the day before. Now, looking more closely at General von Prandtauer, the "good" German, he could see the medal at the man's neck—just as Perlmann had discovered on the Berlin list. "Awarded for extreme bravery and duty to country, this twelfth day of February, 1943, to General von Prandtauer, the Knight's Cross with Oak Leaves. *Heil Hitler!*"

Frau Wagner, the one-time neighbor of the Thalwegs' thought that their daughter, Elisabeth, had married a military man. Yesterday, in this very room, discussing the dead English girl, Baroness von Prandtauer had made of point of telling him her Christian name was Elisabeth, just like that of the slain translator.

It all fit. Elisabeth Thalweg was Baroness von Prandtauer. And now, looking at her younger self as photographed in wedding pictures, Beck was certain this was the young girl portrayed in the hideous paintings of Gerhard Thalweg. The abuse of the young Elisabeth had not come at the hands of the father, but rather at those of her brother. And the codes used on the book pages left behind at the murders she had obviously learned from her spymaster husband, of the Abwehr.

He put his hand out to take the picture off the wall.

"Please leave that alone."

Beck swung around to see Falk standing in the doorway to the drawing room.

"Put it down, Falk."

In the man's hand was a massive ash-wood bow, its arrow neatly lodged in the bowstring. Falk's right arm was trembling with the effort to keep the string pulled back.

"You should not have come here. You and all those like you bringing down my master and now my mistress."

"You know what your mistress has done, Falk? Do you realize the crimes she's committed?"

"For Germany."

"She's a multiple murderer, Falk. A sick woman."

Falk let out an animal scream of protest, his arm shaking now badly with the strain of holding the arrow in place. Beck knew he would have to act quickly; the man was devoted enough to do anything for his mistress. This close, it would be hard for even Falk to miss him with an arrow, but he knew he would have to risk it, dive to the ground, and roll.

Then Falk's head jerked forward violently, the arrow flew

harmlessly out of the bow, and the old servant crumpled to the floor, unconscious.

Perlmann stood in back of him, a chamber pot in hand. "It was all I could find," he said sheepishly.

Ten minutes later, after trussing Falk with the servant bell rope, they ascertained that the house was empty. The boarders must be in town; there was a Control Commission soiree at the Grand Hotel—free eats and drinks would bring all the foreigners out of their rooms tonight, Beck figured.

He found what he assumed was Kate Wallace's room; a typewriter stood on the Biedermeier table, an unfinished story still in the carriage.

He remembered Morgan's note: "Meet Kate." Bells sounded in his head. He began searching the room.

"What are we looking for?" Perlmann asked.

"I'll know when I find it."

"The master of haiku," Perlmann muttered.

Half hidden by a drooping coverlet, Beck found a purse. Inside were the usual: a metal case containing face powder and a mirror, a change purse with U.S. dollars and Allied-issued German marks, a note pad, and several pencils. And at the bottom of it, a celluloid identity card.

He showed the identity card to Perlmann.

"Who goes out at night without their ID?"

"Exactly," Beck said. "I think we've got a problem."

Meet Kate, the note said, but where? Where?

Perlmann glanced at the paper in the typewriter carriage.

"My English isn't so good, but this sounds more like a love story than a news article."

Beck went to the table and quickly skimmed the note. He stopped at the words "Sankt Anna." He read further. A first kiss, a special place.

And the scene of the murder of the English translator. He thought quickly; two notes at that murder. A new MO. The first note giving the symbolism: *Dresden.* As if the murder of the English translator had been in revenge for the fire bombing of that city. The second note had said, *I serve a higher court.*

The baroness was becoming judge and jury now, usurping what was going on at the war crime's trial at the Palace of Justice. She was talking to her hunters, giving them clues, egging them on.

A higher court.

"We've got to get back into the old city," he said to Perlmann. "Now."

The church was quiet as he entered.

"Kate?" he called out.

Maybe she was running late.

The metal was cold against his head. He knew instinctively it was the barrel of a gun.

"Raise your hands very slowly, Captain Morgan."

His mind raced; a female voice, British accent over the German. Educated. Upper class.

The metal dug sharply into the base of his skull. "Do as I say."

He put his arms up, still processing, just as his OSS trainers had taught him to do. Looking for clues, inroads, weaknesses. Keeping the panic at bay.

She marched him over toward the altar, stopping at the metal trapdoor in the floor to the catacombs.

"Open it," she commanded.

"What is it you want?"

Another jab of the barrel against his scalp, this time with enough savage force to make him lose his balance.

"Open the trapdoor."

He bent over, trying to get a look at her between his legs as he lifted the heavy metal trapdoor. Fetid air from below engulfed him. He stood up, suddenly attempting to turn on his attacker. The barrel rested against his temple; he caught a half vision of the woman, though dressed as she was in a long cloak and her hair covered by a fedora, he would not know her sex other than by the sound of her voice.

"Down the stairs," she commanded.

"There are others on their way. I have backup."

"I don't think so, Captain Morgan."

He heard what seemed to be the muffled grunts of an animal from below.

"Where is Miss Wallace?"

"Down the stairs." Her voice had the sharp edge of a knife to it.

He began descending a flight of stone stairs; a flashlight came on in back of him lighting the way. The amber pool of light lit only the stairs and his eyes slowly adjusted to the penumbra of the surrounding catacombs. Reaching the bottom step, he peered into the darkness, hearing a scuffing noise and more of the moaning sounds.

Suddenly, the flashlight played ahead of him and he could see Kate, trussed and gagged, sitting on the floor. Blood flowed from a wound on her face. Around her numerous rats lay motionless. Red beady eyes of others glowed menacingly on the fringes of the orb of light. He could see Kate's eyes, the pleading in them, the sadness.

Then, the back of his head exploded in pain, white points of light jumped in front of his eyes, and he fell to the stone floor.

They were stopped by the Güterbahnhof, where a contingent of MPs were checking every vehicle.

"The horn, Perlmann. Give them the horn."

He did so and one of the MPs looking through the back of a truck turned his powerful light on their car, shooting his middle digit at them. Then he strode over to the driver's side.

"You boys in a hurry?"

Beck handed his identity card to the man who took it in fingers the size of wursts. The MP sniffed at it.

"You make this at kindergarten?"

Beck was not in the mood for *Ami* humor.

"You might contact your Major Hannigan and find out. Or tomorrow you'll find yourself cleaning latrines at a DP camp."

The man sucked on thick lips, considering this.

"We're looking for black-market activity. You can ask him yourself."

Then turning back to the truck in front, he called out, "Major . . . Kraut here says you know him."

The major stepped around the front of the truck to be illuminated in Beck's headlights.

"That so?"

He strode to the car, a thickset bantam rooster carrying a quirt, a Colt six-shooter strapped to his right thigh—a bad imitation of Patton.

Wonderful, Beck thought. He had last seen the man the night of the raid on the Werwolf cell, after discovering Imhofer's body. What was that? Nine, ten days ago? It seemed an eternity.

As the barrel-chested major approached, Beck remembered how he had dealt with the man at that meeting.

"I don't know no Krauts," Hannigan spluttered as he reached the car, looking in at Perlmann. "Don't intend to, neither."

Then he shined a light over to the passenger seat where Beck was sitting.

"Oh, it's you. Morgan's Kraut."

"That's right, sir."

"You got a problem?"

"We are in rather a hurry, Major."

"Are we then? *Rather* a hurry."

The MP laughed at the toney accent Hannigan gave the word. Beck thought he could smell alcohol on the major's breath.

"Official business, sir. I'm sure you understand."

"Catching that killer, are you?"

"Actually, we're on our way to do just that."

The comment made Hannigan chuckle.

"I bet you are. Where's that Yid captain of yours?"

"Point of fact is, we're on our way to save him, too."

This brought delighted laughter from the major. He slapped his thigh, blew spit on Perlmann, and turned to his MP. "Damn, I like this boy. Got a sense of humor."

Then to Perlmann. "You wouldn't be carrying any contraband, would you?"

Beck spoke for the bewildered detective: "Just some silk stockings. You see, our killer's a lady."

Which brought another round of spit-blowing laughter from Hannigan. Finally recovered, he slapped a meaty palm on their hood.

"Let 'em go through, Lieutenant. Got to get them stockings on the lady. Poke her one for me, Kraut."

Beck nodded at Perlmann, who put the car in gear and pulled out around the other stopped vehicles and resumed their way into the Altstadt.

Past the checkpoint, Perlmann glanced at Beck.

"Don't ask," he said. "The man's a barbarian."

"Maybe we could use their help."

"Not that kind," Beck replied.

He regained consciousness and squinted into the light playing in his eyes.

"Welcome back, Captain Morgan."

He could not see the person holding the light in his eyes. Then he felt a nudge and looked to his right. The movement was too fast; it brought stars to his eyes and made his head throb. But he could now see that he was sitting on the stone floor next to Kate who tried to communicate with him through her gag. Then he realized that he, too, was bound and gagged.

"It is a pleasure to have you both join me here. But I am forgetting my manners."

She turned the light onto herself. She had shed the cloak and now stood in full regalia of the green uniform of an Abwehr officer, the medal of the Knight's Cross and Oak Leaves worn at the throat. The woman's hair was pulled back severely in a bun; her eyes looked translucent. She was on a mission. Morgan recognized the look; he'd seen it enough during the way years with agents sent out for what the Soviets called "wet jobs."

"Baroness Elisabeth von Prandtauer, at your service."

He knew the name. Everybody's decent German. The Abwehr general who died in the failed 1944 plot against Hitler. She had to be the widow. Then further connections: the villa where the last victim had been staying. Beck telling him that he'd run into Kate Wallace there.

Morgan turned to Kate quickly. She nodded as if understanding his silent question.

"And I am sure you are wondering why I brought you here." She smiled; it appeared like a rictus of pain on her face.

"Quite simple, really. While you and your friends hold your trial at the Palace of Justice, doling out your victor's justice, I thought it appropriate to hold my own little proceedings at a higher court."

The final words sent a chill down his back. If he had needed further confirmation of his suspicions, he had them now. *I serve a higher court*. Baroness von Prandtauer was his killer.

"Ah, Captain Morgan, I can almost hear the wheels working in that puny mind of yours. Yes, you are right. It is I, your multiple murderer. I prefer the word *avenger*, however. *Vigilante*, even, dispensing justice as it should be."

He wanted to confront her, to throw her obvious insanity into her face, to arouse her. Anything to take her out of her own script. But he was powerless: no voice nor movement allowed.

"And you thought I was a mere deranged prostitute. A common whore."

Morgan twisted to Kate again, and this time he understood the sadness in her eyes. She had not published the story, but she had obviously told the baroness. He shook his head at her to let her know it did not matter. Nothing mattered now but finding a way out of this. He had brought this on them: He'd wanted to prod the killer, to anger her into unplanned action.

He had, unfortunately, succeeded.

"Such a touching scene, the two young lovers. Their deaths carried out at the scene of their first kiss. Like something out of Lessing, or Schiller perhaps."

Morgan touched his shoulder against Kate. *Courage*, he wanted to tell her. *Have courage. I love you.*

"But I digress. We were talking about our little *Prozess* here, our own little Nuremberg trial. You see, they have the wrong men in the dock at the Palace of Justice. The wrong ones altogether. Tonight, I should like to perform an act of true justice. Tell me, if you can, if the date means anything to you at all— what occurred on the sixth and ninth of last August."

She waited, smiling her death's head smile. "No idea? Dear me, how impoverished the *Ami*'s are in the intellectual department. No sense of history at all, even of events a mere three months ago."

Morgan knew where this was going. If he could only get her to take his gag out, he could play for time, argue the morality of the use of atomic weapons on Hiroshima and Nagasaki, balance the civilian dead in those two cities against the far larger number that would have been killed with an Allied invasion of Japan.

But he could only sit and make unintelligible grunting noises.

Kate had a plan. If only the baroness would come and undo their gags so they could defend themselves, to make this charade of a trial more interesting for herself. She shook her head violently to get the woman's attention. The movement opened some of the wounds at her face where the rats had bitten her, but she was beyond caring.

Morgan at her side seemed to understand, and he, too, began shaking his head and making imploring sounds through his gag.

"You want to defend yourselves, is that it? Yes, I am sure you do, just as our brave soldiers in the dock at the Palace of Justice do. But do they really have a chance to do so? No. Your judges tell Field Marshal Göring to remain silent, to let his lawyer speak for him. Is that justice? To try a man for a crime that you have only now made a crime? I am no legal scholar, my American friends, but there is such a thing as *ex post facto* justice, is there not?"

The baroness seemed so pleased with herself at this pronouncement that Kate wanted to scratch her eyes out.

"But let us proceed. On those two nights in question, American bombers dropped atomic bombs on two defenseless cities, killing a quarter of a million people and unleashing a terrible weapon upon the world. I accuse," she said, her voice shrill and piercing. "I accuse."

They parked behind another jeep. Beck knew instinctively that it was Morgan's. He leaped out and began running up Königstrasse toward Sankt Anna, Perlmann in back of him. Passing a side street, Perlmann stopped for a moment.

"Inspector," he called.

Beck turned and saw the Mercedes parked there. He went to it quickly, breaking the glass on the locked driver's side door. He was amazed that the rubble kids had not already stripped it. He reached through the shattered glass and unlocked the door. He found registration in the glove compartment. General Ignaz von Prandtauer.

"She's there," Beck said. "They're all there."

They raced to the church.

The baroness reached down, picking up the black cloak from the floor, wrapping it about her and placing a hood over her head.

"And now it is time to pronounce judgment. For your crimes against humanity, you two Americans shall die. To atone for the deeds of other Americans, I take these two lives."

From one of the pockets of the Abwehr tunic, she pulled out a pile of velvet and slowly unwrapped it to reveal a strip of metal that glistened in the light cast by the flashlight. She held it up with her right hand, playing the beam of light on it with the other.

Morgan and Kate could both see the scalpel held aloft like a ceremonial blade.

The baroness put the blade to her lips, and then stepped toward them, head held high and humming some strange melody.

The church was empty. Beck played the light in every nook and corner.

"The catacombs," Perlmann said.

They dashed to the altar, found the metal trapdoor, and lifted it open.

Below, they all heard the grate of metal against stone at the same time. The baroness stopped in mid-stride on her way to slit their throats and quickly took up position behind a stack of bones to the side of the stairs, setting an ambush for anyone who came down.

A beam of light showed from above. A first tentative footstep.

At his side, Morgan felt Kate begin to rock back and forth wildly. She had an imploring expression on her face as she rocked, knocking against the poorly balanced stack of bones in back of them. Then he understood and began rocking in unison with her, knocking harder and harder against the stack of bones until it finally tumbled in a pile over them, burying them in the femurs, tibias, and humeri of ages.

Beck instinctively pulled Perlmann back at the avalanching sound from below. A shot rang out, and he heard Perlmann let out a cry of agony. He pulled the detective back up the stairs, but there was no time to care for him now. They were down there and so was the baroness.

"It's no use, Baroness," he shouted down the stairs. "The church is surrounded. Come out now and we can get you the help you need."

Another shot rang out, whistling by his head.

He played his light below and saw a pile of bones. There was a movement in the pile, and he almost shot at it. But another shot rang out from the right, ricocheting off the cut stone of the opening, and he realized that whatever or whoever was under the pile was not the baroness. He turned off the light so as not to give her a target.

He lay next to the opening, hearing Perlmann's groans and tried to think of a plan. Quickly or there would be more deaths.

"I know about Gerhard," he called down to her. "Your artist brother. How he abused you."

He waited. Silence.

"How he hurt you. How he cut your genitals."

Two shots rang out, widely missing. He nodded to himself.

"Liar!"

It was the sound of a wounded animal.

"I was at his studio today. I saw the paintings of what he did to you."

"Pig." Another shot that went wide.

"Is he the one who taught you to sign your notes with a W for Winnetou? Are you the good, strong Indian, Baroness? Don't fool yourself. You're a deeply disturbed person. But it's not your fault. Understand?"

"Shut your filthy mouth."

"It's over, Baroness. Falk is tied up like a Christmas goose. I am sure he'll be happy enough to tell us what he has seen of your crimes. Do you want to completely ruin the name of—"

He paused, about to say her husband, but thought better of it. "Of your father. Or of the great artist Gerhard Thalweg—"

He heard a flurry of movement from below and quickly turned on his beam of light, catching the baroness as she moved toward the pile of bones, gun in one hand, scalpel in the other.

"Stop," he shouted, but she moved in a crouch like one of Karl May's Indians, oblivious to his command.

He sighted down the barrel, squeezed off a round slowly. The crack of the pistol shout echoed through the church. The baroness crumpled to the ground. He scurried down the steps, the flashlight playing on her as he moved. He could see motion. Before he could reach her, she had picked up the Luger once more.

"No," he called from the stairs.

He thought she was going to turn the weapon against herself. Instead, she aimed it at the movement below the bones.

Beck fired off five quick rounds. Three of them found their target.

Baroness von Prandtauer lay still, her blood seeping onto the filthy stone floor.

Later, once they had used the walkie-talkie in Morgan's jeep to call in an ambulance for Perlmann and heard the medic pronounce the wound not life-threatening, and after Morgan and Kate had thrown down two glasses of schnapps from the bottle Perlmann kept in the jeep, they stood under the suspended airplane like the last guests at a wedding.

Another ambulance team struggled the lifeless body of Baroness von Prandtauer up the steps from the catacombs and out to their waiting vehicle. The three of them watched the procession.

"Sorry," Kate began, but Morgan put a grimy forefinger to her lips.

"Later," he said. "None of it matters. That's what I was trying to tell you below."

They embraced.

"It's me who should be sorry," Morgan said.

Beck felt like the best man at the wedding; time for him to go. However, Morgan grabbed his arm.

"What you were telling the baroness, was that just to get under her skin?"

Beck shook his head. "No. But we can go over that tomorrow . . . or another day."

"Another day," Morgan said. "Tomorrow, we bury your mother."

Beck looked at him quizzically.

"I had them cancel the ceremony," Morgan said. "Wasn't going to let them plant her without you there to say a few words."

Beck placed his hand on Morgan's shoulder. "Thank you. Sincerely."

"You're the one who should get the thanks," Kate said. "How did you figure out what she was up to?"

Beck sighed. "Long story," he said.

"Another day?" Kate grinned.

"But you finally get your scoop," Beck said. " 'Widow of General von Prandtauer, the Nuremberg Winnetou.' I can see the headlines now."

She held Morgan's hand and squeezed it.

"I don't think so," she said. "This is one story from Nuremberg that is never going to be published. Our government is going to need all the 'good Germans' they can get in the coming years. They're not going to want to ruin the name of General von Prandtauer."

Morgan looked at her. "Cynical?"

She shook her head. "Realistic."

"That's why I love you. Because you are so damn smart."

Beck left them at the church. He had a trussed Christmas goose to take care of. And instinct told him that this particular goose, the servant Falk, might very well be able to place Manhof at the Villa von Prandtauer on multiple occasions.

He looked back for a moment, about to tell Morgan of his hunch.

But the captain was otherwise engaged.

Acknowledgments

Thanks first go to Otto Penzler of Mysterious Press, whose interest in and enthusiasm for this project were manifested by spot-on editorial suggestions for rewrites. Otto is a publishing legend, and I feel honored he took such time and care with *Ruin Value*. Thanks also to Otto's able assistant, Alex Hess, and to Rob Hart at Mysterious Press for making things easier for me.

Folks at Open Road have also earned my gratitude. Lauren Chomiuk, Associate Managing Editor, and copyeditor Joan Giurdanella have both made this a much better novel by catching inconsistencies, tracking down and eradicating historical faux pas on my part, and generally making the narrative read more smoothly. A big *Danke* to this fine group of professionals.

Thanks also go to my agent, John Talbot, for his early encouragement of the manuscript and for seeing this project through to publication. And, finally, thanks go to my family, my *sine qua non*. Love you guys.

MYSTERIOUSPRESS.COM

Otto Penzler, owner of the Mysterious Bookshop in Manhattan, founded the Mysterious Press in 1975. Penzler quickly became known for his outstanding selection of mystery, crime, and suspense books, both from his imprint and in his store. The imprint was devoted to printing the best books in these genres, using fine paper and top dust-jacket artists, as well as offering many limited, signed editions.

Now the Mysterious Press has gone digital, publishing ebooks through **MysteriousPress.com.**

MysteriousPress.com offers readers essential noir and suspense fiction, hard-boiled crime novels, and the latest thrillers from both debut authors and mystery masters. Discover classics and new voices, all from one legendary source.

FIND OUT MORE AT

WWW.MYSTERIOUSPRESS.COM

FOLLOW US:

@emysteries and Facebook.com/MysteriousPressCom

MysteriousPress.com is one of a select group of publishing partners of Open Road Integrated Media, Inc.

OPEN ROAD

INTEGRATED MEDIA

Open Road Integrated Media is a digital publisher and multimedia content company. Open Road creates connections between authors and their audiences by marketing its ebooks through a new proprietary online platform, which uses premium video content and social media.

Videos, Archival Documents, and New Releases

Sign up for the Open Road Media newsletter and get news delivered straight to your inbox.

Sign up now at
www.openroadmedia.com/newsletters

FIND OUT MORE AT
WWW.OPENROADMEDIA.COM

FOLLOW US:
@openroadmedia and
Facebook.com/OpenRoadMedia

CPSIA information can be obtained at www.ICGtesting.com
Printed in the USA
BVOW08s0130161013

333851BV00002B/7/P